HER
BURIED
LIVES

HER BURIED LIVES

KATLYN L. DUNCAN

Library of Congress Control Number: 2022912956

Printed in the United States of America

ISBN: 978-1-954559-06-6

www.KatlynDuncan.com

Book cover by Design for Writers

For Julie

HER
BURIED
LIVES

1

JENNY

The highway stretches before us, winding through the oncoming mountains like a trail leading to a new life. At least that's what I expect.

I glance at my mother gnawing at her lower lip, her hands gripping the steering wheel as if the harder she digs, the slower we'll get to our destination. But with each passing second, we're nearing her childhood home and all the secrets it entails.

A navy sedan to our right veers into our lane. The tires travel closer to us over the white dotted lines of the highway.

A breath lodges in my throat. No, not now.

I should have driven. The lack of control will only make me spiral even more.

I grip the door handle, tunneling my fingernails into the hard surface.

The edges of my vision blur. My heart races, and I attempt to call for her, but my voice catches in my throat.

She doesn't see the car.

A horn blares. I'm not sure whose. The sound echoes in my

head, but she still carries us over the concrete at sixty miles per hour.

The vision veils reality, and there's nothing I can do to stop it. Twenty-five years of these morbid intrusive thoughts force me to fall into an impassive routine when they show up.

"Mom." The word finally comes out in a low moan.

Her head tilts to the side, too slowly for my reaction. The thick strands of dirty-blonde hair slide across her shoulders. I try to focus on her instead of the inevitable crunch of metal breaking through the squeal of tires. I fling my arm out, as if the parental gesture she used on me as a child will stop what's about to happen.

I'm always too late.

I need to close my eyes and breathe. But I can't. Everything moves quickly now, as if on fast-forward. My eyes remain glued open. My mind needs me to see what I've done to my mother.

The car bumps against ours. I imagine the gray metal molding to the shape of the other vehicle.

Her mouth falls open in a silent scream as she lifts her foot to slam on the brakes. It's too late.

The sedan grinds to a halt. We fly forward. The seat belt snaps back, cutting against my chest. The windshield caves in on itself. Fragments of glass pepper the dashboard and our bodies before pelting the floor.

I'm paralyzed with fear, but all my energy focuses on closing my eyes. This will all go away. I just need to breathe through it.

A large chunk of glass cuts my mother's neck. Thick burgundy liquid pools from the gash. The violence isn't new, and it's not the first time I've watched her die. I grit my teeth and inhale a sharp breath before closing my eyes.

The image of her impending death disappears.

Five.

The number blinks in my vision, replacing the wretched curse haunting me.

Four.

My breathing howls in my head, removing the sounds of the accident and my mother's wailing.

Three.

Another breath. The air filling my lungs burns, but it's a welcome relief.

Two.

The hum of the tires on the highway returns, and a dull ache settles into my fingers. I peel them from the handle.

One.

I open my eyes. We're still barreling down the highway. The navy sedan is no longer careening into our car. Granted, it never was. Other than for that split second before the driver must have noticed and veered back into his lane. But I manifested a scenario far less innocent. A second. Yet my visions live in minutes, the worst minutes of anyone's life.

The other driver clicks his right blinker and heads toward the exit ramp.

My heart hammers in my chest as if I've been sprinting.

"Jenny, are you okay?" my mother asks.

"Yeah," I croak and look at her. Turning my head is much harder than it should be. I expect the worst. Glass cutting her face, the explosion of blood across her chest.

There's nothing to worry about. It's all in my head. It's always in my head. The movies—visions—of a future that doesn't exist feel as real as the concrete road under us.

"You look pale."

I hold back a groan. She's noticed.

"I skipped breakfast." It's not a lie but also not the reason for my pallor.

"If you can wait, there's food off our exit. It's another half hour."

"That's fine." I try to keep my voice even. Burdening her with my tendencies only makes her worry. As far as she knows, I grew out of my visions years ago. My coping mechanisms don't always hide them well, but they work to prevent those around me from misinterpreting what goes on in my head. Otherwise, she'll ask incessant questions and may demand I see Dr. Abel again. While I didn't mind seeing the therapist on a weekly or monthly basis, it was an expense we didn't need and couldn't afford. Over the years, I've learned to hide it. Lately, it hasn't been easy. Not since finding out about my mother's childhood home.

The visions, which I could normally hold off for days at a time, have been recurring multiple instances a day, harder to ignore or go unnoticed.

I face the window, turning my body away from her. The tendrils of the vision remain. I draw in another breath before letting it out slowly. At least I have time to gather myself. As a nervous driver, she doesn't see much other than the road in front of her. She's tugged at the edges of her sleeves dozens of times throughout the ride. Though, I imagine part of her nervousness stems from going back to her hometown, a place she rarely discusses. When it has come up in the past, she's always diverted the conversation.

Somehow, even in the August heat, she's still cold. She tugs at her sleeves, stretching them over her knuckles. I've never seen her without long sleeves on, even in the middle of summer. Her petite frame never gives away the amount of food she actually eats. The stressful years of our one-parent family is still evident even though I'm capable of making my own way. Living together is a matter of convenience. I pay more than my fair share of rent and essentials. We like Ridgefield. The small town gives us enough of a community but also privacy when we need it. Who am I kidding? When I need it.

The thought of food makes my stomach groan. I didn't eat before we left because I'm too anxious and have no idea what to expect. The mental and physical strain of impending visions drains me.

My mother dares a quick glance in my direction before turning her attention to the road. "You look tired."

I shake my head. "I'm okay."

"You didn't have to come."

I wouldn't have missed this for anything. "I know this is a lot for you."

She presses her lips together until they disappear. "We won't be there long. Then we can get our real vacation started."

It was the compromise she gave me for going with her. We would spend three days in Orhaven, Pennsylvania, population 1,138, then stay in the heart of Philadelphia for the rest of the week. I don't remember the last time we were out of Ridgefield.

I've never been to Philadelphia, even though we had our fair share of moving around the country since before I could remember. But it seems to be the perfect excuse to take me along with her to Orhaven. Years ago, I gave up the possibility of ever knowing the full story of where and how she grew up. The first time I heard the name of the town was a week ago, after receiving a letter from a lawyer about the inheritance of her childhood home. She rarely speaks about her past, but I know enough about the traumatic history of her family that three days in Orhaven is more than enough.

This is the only opportunity I will ever have to discover what her life looked like before I knew her. In family homes, there are boxes of memories. Pictures of childhoods. Hers. Filling in the gaps might help ease the questions in my mind about her forgotten family.

After opening the letter, she didn't speak for several hours. Granted, we both had work. Her as an at-home care nurse for an older couple in town, and me at the restaurant. Even with the bustle of serving the lunch and dinner crowds, I checked my phone for any kind of response from her. Between orders, I researched Orhaven. It's a three-hour drive from Ridgefield. We lived three hours away from the town for the last five years, and I had no idea.

There's no family left to meet, but I'm sure there are clues of the past in that house. In a town of a little over a thousand, at least one person has to know more about my mother.

That night, my mission came as clear to me as a vision. Thinking of the violence in my head made me want to go even more.

For twenty-five years, I rarely asked about her family or my father. Even as a somewhat rebellious teenager who went online to research my family, I couldn't find much based on our last name, Miller. It's common enough that I never found any concrete records. Even with the first name of Nora. Without my father's name, I gave up after a time, knowing that we were all we needed in life.

When the opportunity presented itself, those years of holding back my need to understand more turned into a burning desire.

If I want to find out anything about my relatives, it's in that house. While there are years I want to catch up with, I have a bigger purpose.

The near crash on the highway solidified that. The visions that send me spiraling into another dimension where the world insists on maiming and killing everyone around me. If I could find a family member who suffered from them, the loneliness within me might not seem so bad. A hint of information would be more than I had a week ago. With that, I hope to find a clue about how to live with them and if I'll ever have a normal life. I want a family, but I can't inflict these visions on innocent people or pass them to another generation without understanding their genesis.

The need is as visceral as my visions.

The jerking movement of my mother switching lanes brings me out of my head. My breathing has returned to normal, and my stomach growls loud enough to make my mother grin.

She eases the car into the first place we see. We pass the golden arches into the drive-through line.

"Fill up now. I'd like to go straight to the house before going into town for food and whatever else we need."

She orders at the drive-through speaker, her tone quick and almost snippy. Her shoulders creep toward her ears—a nervous gesture I know as well as my own visions.

Between ordering and the window to pay, I ask her, "Are you okay?"

She drops her bony shoulders and curls her fingers around the hem of her shirt. "I'm fine, honey. It's a lot of driving. You know how that stresses me out."

"I can take over."

She plasters a smile on her face. "It's okay."

Whenever stressed, she's the type to distract herself with cleaning or some organizational project. Right now, that's driving, and I leave it alone.

After we get our order, I sort the hamburgers, chicken nuggets, and french fries between us. Warmth spreads through my stomach before I've even taken a bite.

My mother snatches three fries and shoves them in her mouth. Her eyes never leave the road as she pulls back onto it.

"What was it like growing up in Orhaven?" I ask.

She heaves a sigh and raises a burger to her mouth. Her

thumb dimples the bun, but she doesn't take a bite. "It was a normal childhood, I guess."

"What did you do for fun?" I steer her away from thinking of her family, even though it's all I want to talk about. Did anyone else freak out at various moments of the day, imagining worst-case scenarios? Did they live with it, or end up in an asylum? I shiver at the thought.

The crease of her lip tightens. "There wasn't much other than the main road with places to browse. A small movie theater. A malt shop."

"Did you say malt shop?" I smirk. "With milkshakes and servers on skates?"

She cuts a look my way. "No skates, but yes, milkshakes."

"What else?"

She shrugs. "That was about it."

"No school clubs or sports?" I've barely chiseled my way into her cracked facade, and the space closes with each passing second. I need to keep her talking.

She bites into the burger, evading my questions. "I liked the drama club in middle school."

I remain silent, desperate for her to go on.

"There wasn't much time for clubs after that. I worked at the grocery store in high school to help pay the bills. Why the sudden interest?"

Sudden interest? It's years in the making. Though it's my fault for keeping the questions bottled within me. She's opened that door, and I struggle to keep myself in the space before it slams closed. "It's where we're going. It's your past, and mine. Why wouldn't I want to know everything?"

We roll to a stop at a red light. "Jenny, we're just going to get the paperwork to sell the house, clean out whatever is left. That's all. I'd rather leave this part of me behind. You shouldn't give it a second thought." She shoves more fries into her mouth.

My stomach churns as the grease-filled air consumes me. I press my finger against the tab for the window. Stale heat fills the space until we lurch forward. There are so many things I want to say, but she's already closed the conversation. Spending every moment together outside of classes and work has created an almost psychic ability between us. It backfires on me.

My mother turns the knob for the air conditioning. Her momentary distraction from the road brings back a ghost of the vision from the highway. Within seconds, her attention is in front of us again. "Better?"

"Yeah."

The silence between us allows questions to fill my mind. I don't ask them. Creating an argument will only cause her to shut down.

"Have you and Dennis set another date?" she asks.

I stop chewing and flip through the excuses I've come up with for this scenario. Since I imagine many different lives, I always feel well prepared for most of them. "There won't be any more dates."

"Really? He seemed to be smitten with you when we met."

I hate lying to her, but she's spent my life giving me everything I wanted. To tell her that my affliction prevents me from living my life would disappoint her and reveal that it hasn't faded. "He's only here until he gets his master's." A master's in psychology. There's no way we would have worked out. The face I put on for him while flirting at work, eventually turning into a night out, wouldn't last forever. None of my relationships do.

"You and Abbie have survived a friendship over the internet. A romantic one is possible."

It's the only friendship I'm capable of. Abbie and I met playing *Counterstrike* when we were in high school. We moved on to other first-person shooter games. She enjoyed the quick wins and adrenaline, while I found it to be a strange and perfect mask for any violence in my head. She's the only other constant in my life other than my mother. Some might say twenty-five is "too old" for gaming, but those are people who wouldn't understand the reasons it offers a mental reprieve from my life.

"It was one date."

"But at the movies. The perfect opportunity to share popcorn, hold hands . . ."

"Sounds like you would have preferred to go," I mutter.

She rolls her eyes. "I'm not going to be around forever."

"You're not that old."

"While I appreciate that, it would give me a little peace of mind to see you with someone."

"That someone doesn't have to be Dennis." Or anyone, for that matter.

"Okay. I'll let it go."

I finish my meal and collect the wrappers and small boxes while my mind wanders to the date. Staying late after his shifts for a week, Dennis finally asked me out. His damn dimples and charming smile did me in. He left it up to me what to do on our date, and I chose the movies. At least there, he wouldn't notice when I had a vision. It's also why I suggested a romantic comedy over the latest thriller. There aren't many triggers when people are falling in love.

Except for me.

The movie was sugary sweet, and by the time it was over, my cheeks were warm and sore from smiling.

Walking out of the theater, I pictured a future like the couple on the screen for me and Dennis. I wasn't relying on it, but it was a pleasant thought, and it could distract me enough not to ruin the date. For once, I wanted to live in a good moment.

But my will wasn't strong enough, which is why when he

started talking about his plans for moving after graduation, the familiar twisting in my gut returned with a vengeance.

We were on the sidewalk by then. The distance from the movie theater had grown while I sank into the depths of my mind. "What are your plans?"

"For what?"

"The future. You're not going to stay here forever, are you?"

I bet to most it would have sounded accusatory, but he had a natural curiosity about him. "I don't know."

"Any thought about going back to college?"

Sitting in a classroom for an hour at a time at the local community college didn't help my visions. I promised myself after a particularly bad vision of my professor launching himself out of the window, I wouldn't do it again. "I've taken some online classes."

"You can do that from anywhere."

"Why are you asking?"

He grinned, and my stomach erupted with butterflies. "I'm curious if you're staying in the area." The hopefulness in his voice struck me. He wanted me to match his desire to travel the world like he planned.

"Yes." The possibilities that opened during the movie slammed closed around me, creating a curtain of impenetrable darkness instead. "This is a great place."

I glanced at the road. Parked cars on either side of the street of the downtown area blocked any danger. A tendril of a vision appeared at my periphery. This was a not-so-gentle reminder of why I couldn't have a normal life. "I should get going."

"I thought we were getting dinner?"

The streetlamps whined above us. The snap of electricity brought the gruesome vision to life. The groan of the nearest electrical pole filled my ears. He didn't see it. Given that it wasn't real. But standing there seeing Dennis's cold, unmoving eyes staring up at me from the ground while the metal pole crushed his insides was too much. There was no time to count down. Instead, I ran.

A dip in the pavement jostles me from the memory.

The car veers from the main road down another canopied by trees. The aftermath with Dennis is all my short-lived relationships ever are. Over the last week, I've closed myself off from him, even though he's more than happy to try again. But I constructed a wall. It's easier this way. Eventually, he gave up. He no longer lingers after his shift, and soon enough he'll move on. Friends, potential boyfriends, they all do eventually. He'll be better off without someone like me.

"Sorry," my mother says, like it was the bump that bothered me instead of the memory of another brief relationship. "I forgot about that part of the road." She shakes her head before continuing. "When I was around seven, my father popped a tire there."

The hairs on my arms tingle, and my attention snaps to her. I wait for her to stop and not share any more information about her family, no matter how trivial. She proves me wrong.

"He was so mad." The words come out like a lead weight, slowly and with the ability to press against my stomach. "It was in the middle of winter, and at night. There weren't any streetlights then. At least not that I recall. The cold was sharp. I remember my feet aching. He left us there to wait for him while he walked off to locate a garage."

"What happened next?" I accept the risk of breaking through her thoughts and ending her recollection, but I need to know more.

"We sat there for what felt like hours. Eventually my mother came into the backseat to warm us up."

"Your sister was there, too?"

"She was." The remnants of memory fade from her eyes.

The shadows of our family sink into the depths of the past. I imagine my aunt's face, an amalgam of my mother's and the grandmother I made up in my head. Possibly the sharp jaw that my mother and I share painted onto a young girl. Did they have the same color hair? Or was it more like mine? Dark and pin-straight? With no photographs of them, I always imagine the women of the family to look the same and my grandfather as a darker figure. My features could also be from my father's side of the family, but I'm more interested in my mother's past than him.

As much as her family hurt her, a man who left a pregnant woman alone is on my list of people I don't waste my already crowded brain space on.

"I don't know what we will find at the house, but I've forgotten this place long ago. I've worked to create a better life for you. I hope you know that. No matter what this place tells you."

"Okay."

She unwraps the last hamburger. The crinkling wrapper barely conceals a sigh. She has a consistent habit of holding her breath during tough conversations.

There's more to discover, but it will come in time.

A ping from my phone draws my attention. I pick it up. A message from Abbie fills the screen.

Are you there yet?

Almost.

Send pictures! And let me know about the internet situation.

Outside the car, the trees clear as we pull toward a sign for

Orhaven. The painted letters resemble the darkness of the wood. The letters are barely there, but they're burned into my vision as we drive past.

I doubt I'll be able to log on while I'm here.

I get it. But I'm here if you need a distraction.

I can always count on Abbie. She doesn't need to be physically present in my life for me to have someone to confide in. It's better for our relationship anyway.

Thanks.

Dense forest creeps toward the road on either side for several miles, narrowing our view of the town. It's different from the back roads leading into the more populated towns around Ridgefield. At least there are houses there occasionally. There aren't any here for at least five miles. The odometer behind the steering wheel ticks the distance toward an old life for my mother and a new one for me. Images of the house where my mother grew up flit through my mind. In the same way I imagine the faces of my family, the blurry vision of the house is just out of reach.

A small sound escapes from my mother's throat. If I show I've noticed, she'll put on her facade, so I ignore it.

Silently, I count down from five and slightly tilt my chin toward her. Her long fingers grip the steering wheel as if it's the only thing keeping her heart pumping. The thin skin above her knuckles pales. Her nostrils flare, yet no audible air escapes. Her pale blue eyes bore into the road.

The hum of the car beneath us drones on, and I realize we didn't turn the music back on after we ordered lunch. I reach for the dial and turn it as slowly as possible. She doesn't seem to notice my movements, and I won't be the one to wake her from her trance. The metallic twang of a banjo filters from the speakers, accompanied by a crackling of static.

Ahead, the road dips and the trees continue as far as I can see. Even inside a car on a two-lane road, the world shrinks. There's no going back now. The road pitches downward on a steep slope, and instead of the hopelessness of never-ending trees, they seem to take a step back and welcome us with sharp, splintery arms.

As we approach the town, the claustrophobic tightness in my stomach subsides as we navigate the roads. The downtown area reminds me of Ridgefield. From the crowds of people walking the sidewalks, it seems more like a town-wide event. There aren't more than a dozen cars driving on either side of the street, and several are parked against the curb in front of the hardware store, a diner, smaller shops, and the movie theater. I strain to find the malt shop she mentioned, pulling her younger essence from it. One that I yearn to connect to even more than I already do.

Houses spread apart in a familiar pattern, reminding me of our current home. Children run through sprinklers. Men with baseball caps and beer bellies mow the lawns. Sunday summer activities pepper the town.

A fluttering sensation within me adds a skip to my racing heart. I'm unsure why Orhaven feels different from anywhere else. In my mind, I've kept this place cradled in my hands like a cherished snow globe. It holds all the answers for me.

Now, I just have to find them.

2

JENNY

My mother hasn't uttered a word since we left the downtown area, and I'm unsure how to start a conversation as I take in everything around me. The landscape leaves much to be desired. Ridgefield summers are filled with lush, manicured yards. Here, most of the properties further from town are in various stages of neglect or overgrowth. The tans and browns force a swirling, bleak pool of dread into my stomach.

As we rocket toward the house, I recoil at the thought of there being nothing but dusty heirlooms with no answers. I put too much stock into finding the truth of my mind when there's a better possibility of nothing. "Shouldn't we have stopped at the store first in case we might need something?"

"I need a break from driving."

The car lurches forward, pushing us toward an uncertain future, and like my visions, there's no delaying the inevitable.

My mother veers right, and we dip onto another road. The trees creep toward the concrete. A quickening in my stomach halts all thought processes. The road is just big enough for two cars to pass each other.

She tenses. We must be almost there.

It takes five more minutes before the trees retreat from the road, thinning out into an expansive field of yellowing grass on either side.

The white beacon ahead of us is the only dwelling among the sprawling landscape.

Our car jerks again, but this time it slows as the road twists closer. The sharpness of the circular tower at one corner of the house reaches upward to the cloudless blue sky.

My mother presses her chest against the steering wheel, peering closer, as if we aren't heading toward the only likely destination. "It's in better shape than I thought."

The confirmation is all I need. There's no going back. The image of what I thought of the house molds into the reality of what it is.

The Victorian-style structure holds firm to the land, claiming it as its own. From my limited knowledge of houses from the 1800s, I expected it to be smaller. The forest obscures the house on two sides, while the rolling landscape continues toward the horizon.

As we get closer, the years press upon the chipped paint and the orange-tinged rust against the gutters. The painted green shutters appear to be the only part of the exterior not ripe with age. They remind me of the leaves from the trees, watching us from a careful distance.

We crawl up the semi-paved driveway against the side of the house. It leads farther up toward the back, but we roll to a stop two car lengths away from the wraparound porch.

The car idles, and she doesn't put the gear into park. It's as if she's preparing a retreat, even though we just arrived.

I won't let her. "Should we go inside?"

She blinks twice before releasing a breath. "Yes."

After she parks the car, and the keys are out of the ignition, I open the door. She'd never drive away without me, but she's the only way I can open this part of my life. It needs to be on her terms.

My mother shuffles to the house, giving it a wide berth as she makes her way around it. I follow close behind, determined not to miss a moment of experiencing this place. She reminds me of a doe standing in the middle of the road, deliberating the danger on either side. The stiffness in her steps matches the tightness in her expression as she inspects the exterior.

While I'm able to conjure the most vivid and horrifying images in my head, I don't think they're any worse than what she's seeing in her own mind. She twists the edges of her sleeves, pressing them together until I can't tell where her hands begin.

Our feet crunch over the dehydrated grass as we move at a snail's pace around the structure. The disrepair is clear but also gives it a sense of life. It has weathered storms and still stands proudly. If this house can do it, surely, she can. My promise to find out more for myself shifts to include her. I will help her leave this house behind and the memories within. Once I discover them for myself.

Cracks run through the stone front steps, but like the foundation, they hold strong. The planks stretching across the patio have held up over the years with barely any chips.

I crash into her, not realizing she's stopped. "Sorry."

"I didn't expect it to look this put together."

"You said someone was looking after it."

She mashes her lips together. When she speaks, her voice is low and controlled. "I suppose that will help it sell faster." She kneels. The worn welcome mat only shows the remnants of the letters. Underneath is a faded gold key. She digs it into the lock below the handle. The door opens, and she pushes through into the house.

With the blazing sun outside, my mother seems to disappear into a void. The house swallows her as I step through the doorway. The stale air rushes out as if it's desperate for the fresh scents outside. I expect a pinch of mold in the air, but as I take in the stairs leading to the second floor, it seems we're trespassing into a life currently lived.

She stands in the foyer. The dust on the window frame filters the sunlight, leaving a hazy mist around the room. The beams outline her stiff body. She stares into the living space.

I approach her while taking in as many details as possible. This place feels like a calmer vision that will disappear at a moment's notice. The floorboards creak under my weight. Are these sounds familiar to her? Or do they drudge up a past she'd rather forget?

My mother sighs as if the house has reminded her to breathe. She scans the room with narrowed eyes.

I have the urge to run through the rooms, absorbing every morsel of the space.

Instead, I follow her. She moves with precision, not too close to the short wooden table between two floral-patterned couches. They look like they were purchased from an antique store. Most of the furniture does. It lives in another time entirely. The area rug dampens the sound of our footfalls, but the wood groans, letting us know we're not entering this house unnoticed.

I expect to find framed photographs of our family on the mantel over the stone fireplace, but it's empty other than the light coating of dust. I'm unable to get closer before my mother wanders into the next room nestled at the back of the house.

Out of the two rooms, the kitchen looks as if it has time-traveled further, but at least we'll be able to make decent meals during our visit. If the appliances work.

The hum of the refrigerator grounds me in the space. A

carved table sits in the center of the room, surrounded by four chairs. A reminder of the family who once lived here.

I spot a door with a key hanging from a nail next to it. I assume it's a basement. One of the bits of information my mother never shied away from was her fear of them. She didn't explain why, but I don't need to guess that it came from this place.

I round the table and look inside the refrigerator. It's empty, yet immaculate.

"We should make a list of what we need," she says.

"Let me figure that out." Ever since I started working full-time, I chose restaurants. The fast pace of the kitchen always keeps my visions at bay. Working double shifts through high school and whenever possible, it's been my only savior from the violence. In that time, I've become the main cook in the family, as I've learned from seasoned chefs.

I open the oven, flicking on the light. Like the refrigerator, it's clean.

"We have to meet with the lawyer soon."

With her gone, I'm free to explore the house on my own. "I can stay here."

"I want you with me."

The vision of my exploration disintegrates from my mind. I can't refuse her, not while we're here and she's dealing with the memories of her past. Besides, there will be time to look around. "Okay."

Her cell phone trills from her pocket. She silences it. "It's work."

I wave a hand at her. "I'll look through the cabinets and see if there's anything not expired." She makes a modest living as a home care aid, but we never let food go to waste in our house. I have a list of pantry recipes that could fill a cookbook.

She rocks on her heels and glances around the room. Then

her attention lands on me before she picks up the phone. "Hey. Yeah, we just got here. Hold on—I can't hear you that well." She rushes out the back exit, and the screen door slaps against the frame as she disappears from the house. Through the window, I see her round the corner toward the driveway.

I take in the space's silence, breathing it in. The hairs on my arms shimmer awake. I'm alone in this house. I have a few minutes to do anything I want. Exploring the second floor is out of the question, as I wouldn't be able to get back in time without answering questions about why I ventured on without her.

My phone pings, and Abbie's face appears on the screen.

You there yet?

I raise my phone to snap a picture, but my finger hovers over the screen. I want some time to get comfortable before opening this place to anyone else. Instead, I text back.

Yeah, just got here.

Is there any chance there's wi-fi? You know your phone sucks.

I smirk at the message. As a tech nerd, Abbie always has the newest devices. Unlike me. I keep what isn't broken.

Give me a few.

Through an archway from the kitchen there's a dining room. The dust haze is stronger since only sheer curtains frame the windows. In the corner, the turret reveals a cushioned seating space with built-in bookshelves.

My mother is always reading at least three books at a time. I wonder if she's always done that. I imagine her as a child curled up on the cushions, experiencing other worlds outside of this isolated one. Her muffled voice emerges. She's standing in the front, her hand curled on her hip. I back away from the window, checking the space for any modern electronics. She stops within view, digging the toe of her shoe into the dirt.

I leave the room through a second doorway closer to the front door. The stairs to the second floor call to me, but so does the kitchen. Mostly the basement.

The door is locked, and I rip the key from the nail and shove it in the knob. My hands tremble slightly. Why would there need to be a key to a basement door?

The first two steps lead downward into an abyss. I lean closer, looking for a switch.

In all my life, I've never lived in a place with a basement. My mother preferred apartment buildings without them. Anywhere we rented either had laundry inside the apartment or we frequented laundromats. We didn't have enough possessions to warrant storage either.

The musty scent I expected from entering the house wafts toward me, invading my nose. I turn on the flashlight on my phone and test the first step. With the creaking of the floorboards since we arrived, I don't trust these.

It holds my weight, and I try the next one. The small light from my phone illuminates the wooden slabs on either side as they transition to craggy stone. There's no switch, and I wonder how my mother, as a child, would travel into the basement. It has to be why she fears them. My visions create more visceral nightmares than any dark location. This seems like a place plucked out of a horror movie.

With that thought, a swirling pool of heaviness sinks in my stomach.

As I descend, I shake the sensation away. The walls open around me, revealing the space beyond the railings on either side. Grit rolls under my sneaker as I grip the string hanging limply from the ceiling. It's thin and slightly damp. I tug, and nothing happens. I tug again, and the bulb flickers to life with a charged whine. The quick scent of burning fills my nose.

The bulb doesn't light up the entire room, but it's enough. A washer and dryer sit nestled in the corner, along with several damp cardboard boxes melting into the concrete floor.

I turn in a full circle, taking in the muted silence. The walls seem to swallow the sound of my breathing.

Other than the layer of dirt across the floor, the basement is tidy in a way I didn't imagine. Several feet away, another string hangs from the ceiling. A wooden divider cuts off the laundry area. The breadcrumb forces me forward. My hand reaches out before I'm even close enough to pinch the string.

This time, the light is brighter, revealing a hidden nook.

Against the wall is a twin-size mattress made up with a thin quilt and a pillow tucked under one side with a clean precision I've only seen at hotels. A stack of books sits on a small wooden table next to it, a leather-bound one on top. I trace the gold embossed title. *Frankenstein*. Under that are several more classic novels with curled edges and titles I don't recognize.

A *slap* echoes into the basement, and I jolt forward, knocking into the table.

The light closer to the stairs flickers uncontrollably with my mother's footfalls, making the stairs disappear three times before it settles. The dark corners of the room thicken with possibilities of a vision, and I clamp a hand over my mouth in case one of them sneaks up on me. She'll never leave me in this house alone if I freak out the moment I'm left without her.

"Jenny?" My mother's voice is muted, yet the strain pulls at the edges of my name.

"Down here."

"What are you doing?"

"I was looking for food." The excuse disintegrates on my lips, as I realize I hadn't even checked the cabinets.

"Please come up here. I don't want to be late."

"Okay." I straighten the books into their tower once more before checking the table. It slammed against the wall, and I'll never forgive myself if I broke a cherished item within an hour of arriving at the house.

The table doesn't show any damage, but small gray chunks from the wall splay across the surface. A hole gapes like a silent scream. I didn't hit it that hard, did I? I stroke the edge of the hole, and more of the wall falls onto the table and floor. The edges of my periphery shimmer.

"Jenny?"

My stomach plummets, and the shimmering crawls back to where it came from.

"Coming!" I swipe the flecks off the table and adjust the stack of books to cover the damage before heading toward her pleas.

I thunder up the stairs, and the moment both feet hit the linoleum floor, the door swings toward me and slams shut.

3
THEN

The light through the living room window flickers to life. The game of hide-and-seek has started.

A breath releases from my body as I turn to the road, waiting for you.

The high whine of the cicadas slices through the otherwise silent space. I never appreciated our isolation more than I do now.

Your face fills my vision, and a lifetime of memories spring forward. Heat swells in my eyes, yet the tears anyone else would shed don't appear. I will remain sharp.

I told you you'd regret your decision to leave. This isn't my fault. What I have to do is necessary for you. For her. For us. If you can finally see how you need me and I need you, you'd never think about going anywhere else.

With a sniff and a swipe against my cheeks, the emotion subsides. I only get this way for you. No one else has infiltrated this side of me. The human side.

I check the gold watch on my wrist. The oversized face ticks down the seconds until your arrival. My fingers twine around the thick rope wrapped around my other hand. This is the only way to make you listen. It's how Father taught me. Once you realize I'm not the enemy, you'll stay.

The shriek of excitement escapes the open window. I yearn to go inside and scoop her little body into my arms, knowing both of you will stay.

You did this to yourself.

Separating a mother from her child was never part of the plan.

You pushed me.

But after you learn your lesson, we'll be stronger, together.

Two circles of light cut through the distance, and I adjust my grip on the rope while clenching the weapon in my other hand. I never enter a situation without options. We're an unpredictable lot. On my left, you come quietly. On my right, you come resistant.

Both plans flit through my mind as the beams turn into larger circles as they near. I time each bump of the road from the cautious way you navigate in the dark.

I admire the way you explore your surroundings with calculated risk. It's one way we're similar. But the way you trust people and expect the good divides us. I suppose it's not a terrible trait. It leads you down paths you never expect. I like to know all angles. Your reaction, for instance. I've calculated your actions from the moment you see me. The most likely outcome is your flight instinct. It's a mystery to me why someone wouldn't fight for what was most precious to them. That's what I'm here for. That's why leaving makes little sense. It's what I intend to prove to you. Once you know the depths of my love—as much as I'm able to love any one person—and how I will make up where you lack with protective instincts, you'll never leave.

Closing my eyes, I revel in the after. They open a second

later. No time for the future. The now is what will bring me to the end goal.

Us. Together. A trio unlike any other. It's what we've always dreamed, and neither you nor anyone else will take that away.

Once you park, the car idles for a moment.

I step closer. I've calculated the risk on where to approach. The back driver's side corner wins. It gets me as close as possible before you know I'm there. Then I have seconds before your instincts kick in. They're one skill that will help you survive this. It's the only way you will come out the other side with the ability to see your child again.

Whether that takes hours or days is up to you.

The rear lights are still lit. I hesitate on the periphery. I need you out of the car before you see me.

My racing heart slows to a normal rhythm. This is where I thrive while most wouldn't. I've never been a part of any "most." Which is why I'm able to take tough love to a new level.

The engine cuts off, and your door opens. I plant my heel into the ground before rocking forward onto my toes. The crunch of the dirt under my feet won't give up my position.

Your head appears before you duck again. Two paper bags sit on the passenger seat. As you reach for them, I round the car, walking up behind you. The false sense of safety you've always known in my presence allows me to do this to you. You'll realize I'm the one person in your life who can give it and take it away.

The second before you spot me, heat spreads throughout my body. The scent of coppery blood fills my nose. It's a faraway memory, but enough to ready myself for what I must do.

Our eyes meet, and the flash of fear melts into confusion when you take in what I'm holding.

I say nothing. There will be plenty to say when you're ready to listen.

The frayed edges of the rope scrape against my skin.

You dare to drop your gaze down to my hands. A mistake for you.

The car door bumps against your back.

A spike of adrenaline runs through me as I imagine you shoving out your arms and fighting for yourself.

There isn't enough time for that scenario. The moment you turn away from me, plan B takes effect. I raise my right hand and bring it down against the fleshy part of your beautiful neck. The carotid is the sweet spot that won't cause too much permanent damage.

You fall like a brick. I have honed my skills over the years, but it doesn't make what I'm doing any easier. Any other time, it's been for the beast inside of me and to protect our family.

The grocery bags lean gently against your body. This won't do.

I rip one of them in half, and the brightly colored cereal box falls out. I flip you on your side as two oranges bump against my hand, then roll under the car. My hands move deftly, wrapping the rope around your wrists. Over and under. That's the easy part.

Then comes the blindfold and gag. In a perfect world, you'll stay unconscious until we arrive at our next destination, but one can never be too careful.

Once you are fully subdued, I stage the scene. The appearance of a struggle is necessary. The police can't believe that you knew your attacker. No one, including you, will ever find out it was me.

4
JENNY

The reverberation of the door echoes in my mind. I piece together what happened, staring at my mother. She cradles the basement key in her hand. Her shoulders hunch forward, and her chin trembles. "I don't want you down there."

"Why?" I lean toward her, ready for her to reveal some hidden part of her past. She's going to tell me that someone locked her in the basement, which is why she hates this house and the memories within the walls. We'll talk through it and then leave this town closer than ever, and I'll have the answers I need to determine if a normal life is waiting for me or not.

She squeezes her eyes closed. It's how I imagine I look when I want a vision to go away. There's no mistaking the anguish, and a twist in my gut tells me I screwed up. "Did you make a list?" she asks.

I graze my temple with a fingertip. Working as a server and a cook, there's not a lot of room for a short memory. "I don't need to."

"Did you at least check the cabinets?"

"You were outside for like three minutes." Even though time

seemed to stop in the basement, she wasn't outside long enough for me to make a list, regardless.

She stretches for the nearest cabinet. Inside are two unopened boxes of generic-brand cereal. The cartoon cat peers at me with a Cheshire grin. It probably knows more about this house than I do.

She checks the dates. "Still good."

I watch her. She eases into her normal, cautious self after that reaction to the basement. The key rests on the countertop, and I wonder when I'll have another chance to go down there.

I reach for the cabinet closest to the back door. Dusty glasses and mugs stacked together create a warped reflection in their surfaces. The next cabinet has plates and bowls, all with a thin layer of dust. Without a dishwasher, we'll have to clean them by hand.

None of the cabinets I search have food, so I move closer to her. She's cataloging what she finds, pulling items and leaving others. I find soup cans. I review the expiration dates, and they are still good. A question hovers on my tongue. I'm no expert on food storage, but these couldn't have been purchased when she had left all those years ago. So who was in the house more recently? She said there weren't renters, but maybe whoever was caring for the place took breaks inside the house, knowing it was empty?

With each new intrusion into this life, more questions arise, and that need to know grows within me. I imagine different questions I can ask her to open the conversation again. But from the way she smashes the cabinet doors closed, not even a sliver of that window opens.

"We should go." She's already across the room, heading for the front door.

As we leave the house, I silently promise to not force her feelings to the surface like that again. I'll do what she asks and help get the house in a salable condition, but I will get my answers in a different way.

The ride back to town appears to take less time than when we drove to the house.

With the house behind us, my mother melts into her seat, releasing the tension which had tightened every muscle in her body.

"What did Carl want?" I ask.

"Hm?" She furrows her brow before shaking her head. "Oh, he forgot where he put the combination for the medicine cabinet. I wrote it on the instructions. It makes me regret any type of break I take from that house. He doesn't think of the details." She goes on about the issues at work, I suspect to divert my attention from the house, and I allow it. After her panic with me in the basement, we both need a break.

Once we reach the downtown area, she slows toward a parking spot in front of a hardware store. The window displays several lawn mowers and bug zappers through the streaked window.

She unbuckles and turns to me. "I'll meet with the lawyer first. Then we can get some food and settle into the house for the night." She pushes the door open, and the conversation is over.

I slip out of the car and drop my sunglasses over my eyes. The sun strikes down on the concrete, and I swear it's ten degrees hotter here than at the house.

An older couple waddles toward us, linked arm in arm, and I move closer to the curb to allow enough space for them to pass.

My mother spots them and freezes, standing at the front of the car, her gaze darting toward me, then the other side of the street. The older man isn't paying attention, but the woman spots my mother and stares. She opens her mouth, but my mother's words come quicker.

"Mr. and Mrs. Peters, it's good to see you."

Mr. Peters bobs his head, while the older woman holds her eyes. "Never thought I'd see you again, Nora." The porcelain skin under her chin wobbles with her words.

My mother clears her throat. "We're here to sell the house, and then we'll leave." Her tone is sharp, yet her eyes don't meet the woman's. She's grown, yet she's acting as if Mrs. Peters is about to scold her.

Mr. Peters watches them with disinterest. The brown-brimmed hat on the gray smattering of hair shades his eyes, but I assume he doesn't remember her.

"Good riddance." Mrs. Peters curls her lip and tugs her husband along. Her hunched posture doesn't allow a quicker escape, but her jerky movements hint that she'd sprint if she could.

My mother stares after them. Her jaw tightens.

"What a warm reunion," I say.

She lets out a small laugh. "They never were the nicest people. We always avoided their house on Halloween."

"You had trick-or-treating here?"

"Orhaven isn't so different from other places."

I recall the drive through the town. "Did you have to hop in a car to get from house to house?"

"There are some neighborhoods with houses closer together." She walks toward the building, and I follow.

An image of a younger version of her in a princess costume skipping down a street with other kids fills my thoughts. Did her sister go with her, or were they the type of siblings who weren't that close?

She releases her hair from the elastic, and the shaggy mess covers the sides of her face. In a small town like Orhaven, I doubt the Peters' are the last awkward encounter we'll have. We lived in smaller towns before, and most of the time, gossip ran like wildfire. In a place like this, memory is longer than most.

Possibilities open for me. If I can't get everything I need from the house or my mother, then I can talk to people in town.

I test my theory. "I can run to the store while you're with the lawyer." If given the opportunity, I can act like I've lost my way and reveal who my mother is. I imagine receiving fragments of information from the past and collecting them like precious jewels.

"I want you with me." She checks her phone for the address.

I trail behind her, peering through windows of the businesses. With the beating sun overhead, the reflection of myself and the street blocks most of my view inside the buildings.

The law offices of Walter Wallace are on the second floor above a florist. The mingling scents from the flowers bombard the narrow staircase separating the two. It doesn't help that there's no outlet for the air. The weight of it presses over me as if I'm living inside a perfume bottle.

My steps are sluggish, while hers glide upward with purpose and determination.

Through a door at the top of the staircase, the air is crisper, and the coolness clings to my heated forehead and cheeks. Inside a small waiting area, there are six identical wooden chairs paired against each wall. The variation in the color and style of the cushions gives the room a homey feel.

The room spills into a slim hallway, but my mother sits in the closest chair to the door as if she's debating an escape.

"Should we tell them we're here?" I ask.

"They know we have an appointment."

As if our voices echoed, footfalls carry from the hallway. A woman appears, trekking toward us on chunky wedge heels. Her full red lips part into a brilliant smile. Her deep brown eyes hold kindness, which eases my mind about this place. At least not everyone in town is as cranky as the Peters'.

"I'm Holly Wallace. It's nice to see you." She tilts her head slightly in our direction, clasping her hands in front of her. A rosiness shimmers against her dark brown cheeks. She looks to be around my mother's age. I wonder if she has any stories from her youth. "You can follow me through here, Ms. Miller."

I start forward, but my mother holds up a hand. "Stay here."

"You said you wanted me with you."

"Here, in the office."

There's no one here for me to question, or any opportunities for exploration of the past. "I can go to the store now. Kill two birds?"

"Jenny," she says, glancing at Holly. "Please. I won't be long. Stay here." She hurries after Holly, and I'm left alone.

My cheeks bloom with heat, but I sit by the window, obedient. After exploring the basement, I suspect she doesn't want me too far from her sight. Have I already given away my hand in my personal investigation?

Outside, life resumes in Orhaven. But when I'm not in the fray, meeting the people and getting a better picture of my mother's secret life, it doesn't seem as interesting.

I turn to my phone, scrolling through the messages from Abbie. Throughout the day, we send each other funny memes and videos, but she's been silent. She always has an inclination of how I'm feeling, and I doubt she wants to interrupt this homecoming. Guilt presses against my chest like a heavy weight. I hadn't been completely honest with her about the trip. How could I? She has no idea I experience morbid visions. Separating that side of me is the only way I can preserve both of my closest relationships.

"Can I get you anything?" Holly's smooth voice chimes. "Water or iced tea? I made some cookies, too."

"I'll have tea and a cookie. Thank you."

She smiles again. I imagine her at home, singing in the kitchen while making them. She seems like the type to always have a positive attitude. It's foreign to me, but welcome.

"Why don't you come with me? Stretch your legs a little. Nora told me you had quite a ride today."

I push out of the chair. "Thanks."

Holly leads me through the hallway. My mother's voice sounds behind the second door on the right side, accompanied by a booming and jovial male voice. I assume Walter's.

"Mr. Wallace is your husband?"

Holly veers into the room across the hall. "For twenty-three years."

"Wow."

A rattling window air-conditioning unit greets us. A desk sits in the center, just large enough to hold a computer and a printer. A neat stack of folders and paperwork rests on top of the scanner.

In a lawyer's office, she has to know information about my family, even if she doesn't know my mother personally. "Are you from here?"

Holly moves to the table behind the door, supporting a pitcher filled with mostly melted ice and tea, a coffee maker, and a plastic-covered paper plate with a heaping mountain of chocolate chip cookies. "No. Walt and I met during our college years."

"Why did you move to Orhaven?"

"We did the city life for a while. But when Walt's grandmother fell ill, we moved up north to help. Then a job for a local lawyer came up a week after she passed, and we never left. This place might be slow-moving and small, but it's become home."

"Do you have any kids?"

"No, we weren't blessed. But I have ten nieces and nephews to spoil."

"That's a big family."

The urge to talk to her about life growing up with a single mother comes as swiftly as it goes. I don't want anyone to feel bad for me. I want answers.

As much as Holly's kindness draws me in like a warm hug, my mind wanders across the hall toward Walter's office. If only I could listen to what they want to hide from me.

My attention moves to the door to its right. "Do you have a bathroom?"

Holly plucks two cookies from the plate and wraps them in a napkin. "Right there across the hall. I'll bring your tea in a moment."

"Thanks." I leave the room, slowing my steps as I approach Walter's office. I strain to hear any decipherable words. I'm inches from the door when it swings open, revealing a massive man.

The glass of his thin-wired spectacles reflects my terror as I stumble away from him.

His kind eyes and smile match Holly's. He reaches out to shake my hand. "I'm sorry to startle you." He straightens his tie before his hands drop to his sides.

"It's okay." I peer around him. His office is a stark contrast to Holly's. It's cluttered with pictures and degrees hanging from the walls. The sun can't quite pierce the thick white blinds covering the window. My mother sits in a chair next to the desk, her head bowed over a manila folder filled with a stack of paper. One of her hands covers her mouth as if she's yawning or surprised. Her head lifts slightly, and I angle my body behind Walter's. "I'm just looking for the bathroom."

"Right next door."

"Thanks." I scoot in there before my mother sees me. The

bathroom is the size of a closet. I shimmy past the toilet to close the door. A small window set higher on the wall gives enough light in the room to highlight the chipped floor tiles and the subtle dark ring tattooed in the porcelain sink.

I lean against the wall between the office and the bathroom. Walter's voice appears again. Then my mother's. I strain to hear them, but their voices mingle together in a muffle. So much for that plan. I flush the toilet and run the water in the sink before leaving the room.

Defeated, I head out, and their voices become clearer. Walter must have forgotten to close the door after walking back into his office.

Holly is still busy with the tea. I freeze in my spot, not daring to move and shatter this opportunity to find out what my mother didn't want me to hear.

"It's all rather straightforward, Ms. Miller." Walter's voice is softer and more serious than when I spoke with him.

"Nora, please." She sighs. "Is there any way to change it?"

"It's her wishes."

"Screw her wishes," my mother says under her breath. "This is ridiculous."

"It's how you can get the house."

"What if I don't want it?"

There's a long pause before Walter clears his throat. "It's my job to carry out these requests. We've already priced out the value, and you will leave with all the profit."

"At what cost to me?"

"Jenny?" Holly's voice crashes over me. She holds the glass and napkin-wrapped cookies in her hands. She glances into Walter's office. "I told you I'd bring this out."

"Oh, I—uh—I wanted to stretch my legs. As you said."

Holly purses her lips. She doesn't believe me. But as quickly as the doubt scratches at my skin, she smiles again. "I understand." She lifts her chin toward the waiting room, and I peel myself from my spot and follow her. "I sit a lot at work, so I have to set a timer to make sure I get up at least once an hour."

In the waiting room, Holly places the glass on the table next to the chair I sat in before. She hands me the cookies. "Let me know if you need anything else."

I glance down the hallway at the office as more questions flood my mind. Selling the house isn't as cut and dry as my mother had let on. But from the surprise and annoyance in her voice, I doubt she lied on purpose. She expected this to be easy.

Over the years, I didn't push to find out the whole truth about the most important parts of me. Now, I'm not sure if she'll ever open up. Once she gives the house over to a realtor, the last bit of her hidden past will be gone. Pushing her about it when I'd been complacent my entire life won't get us anywhere but into a fight. While eating the cookies and sipping from the tea, I run through scenarios of how to approach her about the fragments I already know, with the goal of opening her up.

Thirty minutes later, my mother walks out of Walter's office.

I leap up from the chair, my nerves bursting with anticipation for news. "How was it?"

"Fine." The flatness of her smile offers the truth.

I wait for her to mention that she heard me eavesdropping, but she doesn't. At least that will give me some time to figure out how to approach the topic.

"Ready to go?" she asks.

Holly peeks out from the hallway. "Have a great day."

"You too," my mother and I chorus.

I open the office door, and the stuffy stairwell greets us with its stale, floral breath. She doesn't show that she wants to talk about what happened in the office. I can't tell her I overheard the conversation between her and Walter, so the only sound between us is our shoes on the steps.

Her shoulders rise and lower slightly, as if she's trying to work the stress out of them.

Outside, she exhales loudly and drops her sunglasses over her eyes. I do the same. The azure sky shows no sign of fluffy clouds blocking the rays.

"The grocery store isn't in walking distance, so we'll have to drive."

"Do you want me to?"

"I'm good." I sense she needs the distraction from whatever Walter said to upset her.

A tinkling bell sounds to our left, and my mom stops so quickly that I barely miss crashing into her. I grab onto her bony shoulders and am about to ask her why when I locate the object of her attention. A man walks out of the store, cradling his cell phone against his ear.

"I'm sure she'll be back later, sweetheart. If you need anything, call me back." He glances at my mother and stops as abruptly as she did. He sputters my mother's name. "N-Nora?"

"Hi, Mike." She breathes out his name as if it's going to be her last, and if it were, she seems entirely okay with it. They walk closer to each other, their hands rising to meet in an awkward mix of a handshake and hug.

Even though the temperature outside is oppressing, a shiver rolls down my spine as if someone has poured ice down my back. The way their gazes lock is intimate enough that I turn away from them.

He blinks and looks to me. "Jenny?"

My attention snaps to his. I've never met this man in my life, yet he's close enough with my mother to touch her after all these years, and he knows my name.

That shiver halts before spreading itself throughout my entire body, settling in my gut.

Her smile falters. "This is Mike Allen. We went to school together."

Mike cackles and smooths his hand up her arm to cup her elbow. "We were more friendly than that."

She's smiling. Smiling! At this stranger. No, not a stranger. They've made that clear.

The word *friendly* takes on a whole new meaning with this man. He's nice-looking, with kind eyes. His tanned, leathery skin gives away that he works outside. His hair is gray around his temples and thinning, but his boyish looks probably caught more than my mother's eye when they were younger.

My mother turns to him. "It's been a while. What have you been up to?"

Mike swaps the small plastic bag between his hands. "I'm working with my son, Scott."

"You're married?" My mother glances at his left hand.

"I was. My wife died."

"I'm sorry."

Mike lifts a shoulder. "We were separated, but Scott stuck around after I'd adopted him. Can't say I don't love working with him, but he's not cut out for small-town life."

She moves her hair away from her face. "He's still young, right?"

Mike tilts his head in my direction. "He's about the same age as Jenny. You're lucky that you two stuck together. I have a feeling he doesn't want to stay here forever."

His presence creates that shimmer around the world as my visions do. It's uncomfortable, yet familiar. It doesn't progress though.

A pregnant pause bloats between us. My mother steps away from Mike. I sense a tightening rubber band between them that's either about to snap or draw them closer. "We should head out."

Mike tips the brim of his hat at her, then at me. "I hope you won't be a stranger while you're here. You both should come by for dinner to catch up."

I wait for her response.

"Thanks, Mike." She adjusts her sunglasses. "We won't be in town much longer."

He chuckles ruefully. "Well, if you change your mind, my number is the same."

She smiles and glances at me before heading to the car.

"Good to see you, Jenny," he says.

"Nice to meet you."

His chin lifts and his eyes narrow. A shadow of something—regret or confusion—rises to the surface.

Even when we're inside the car and pulling away from the curb, Mike doesn't move from his spot. He's like an opposing magnet, pulled in by us. By her.

Only when he disappears from view am I able to break through the strange bubble which consumed us since we met.

I have asked for little in the short time we have been in Orhaven, but I have to know. The question bubbles out of me before I can stop it. "How does Mike know about me?"

5

JENNY

My mother stares at the road, her lips pursed as if she's daring me to pry them open. If she won't talk, I will.

"Did you keep in touch with him after leaving here?" Why would she keep that a secret? A question I haven't thought about in some time shoots to the surface of my mind. The thought that he could be my father.

She sighs and continues to stare at the road. "After leaving here, I kept in touch with one of my friends. She must have told him. Small towns, you know?"

"What friend?"

"It doesn't matter." She waves her hand at me. The warning to stop prying is clear, but she has to give me something.

"He spoke to me like he knew more than what a friend told him." My hands ball into fists, and my fingernails pinch my skin.

"Mike thinks he can be in anyone's business. I grew up here. Of course there are people in this town who know about you."

I chew that over for a moment before coming out with it. "Is he my father?"

"Oh, gosh, no." The corner of her mouth lifts.

"You seemed very familiar."

"We have a lot of history is all."

History she never told me until I witnessed it for myself. But I know enough about her that I need to pry open layers or else she'll clam up. "You had to know I'd ask, eventually."

She doesn't speak for a few seconds, but I wait. Now that we're stuck together in this town, I will get answers before leaving Orhaven. "Everything I've said about your father is true. Once he found out I was pregnant, he left town without a good-bye. It's not the easiest situation for me to relive. But I suppose it's time you knew the truth and could do with it what you want."

I blink hard, and she glances at me before turning to the road. "Go ahead."

The opening is all I need. "What is my father's name?"

"Calvin Cavanaugh."

I let the name rest in the air between us. Growing up with a mother as strong as mine, I never wanted for another parent, especially because of what he did. With a name, the urge to know more blossoms within me.

"Did you love him?"

"I did."

We pull into the parking lot for the grocery store. It's half the size of the supermarket in Ridgefield. She parks us in the farthest spot from the entrance before turning to me.

"I'll answer any questions you want about him, but the reason I haven't before is that I didn't want you to look for him and feel disappointed with what you found. But you're grown now." She trails her fingers down a chunk of my hair before flicking it over my shoulder. It's a familiar gesture, and it centers me.

"It's nice to have a name though," I say.

She nods. "I hope you don't hate me for not bringing it up."

Her eyes become glossy, and I know I've hit a vein of her trauma. A name is all I need to do my own digging. I don't need to pester her unless I can't find something on my own.

"I could never hate you," I say, pushing out of the car.

We walk toward the store, and I allow the idea of Calvin—my father—to accompany me. Like how I want to find out more about my family's past, I appreciate the challenge of finding what we need for food, and answers to fill my mind.

The cicadas' shrill whine choruses outside the window under the moon's light. The rays reflect off the leaves in the trees, casting an eerie glow around the forest. I shift onto my other side. The springs of the bed press against my body at various pressure points. My pillow is the only thing in this room which smells familiar. I inhale deeply and peel myself off the bed. The sheets aren't as soft as I would like and too thick for the middle of summer. I'm in the least amount of clothes possible, to keep the heat at bay. The tank top and shorts still feel restricting.

Before bed, my mother insisted I use the window fan, but I refused. The rebellious teenager who never bothered her mother about who her father was, never mind if he was alive and well, clawed to the surface. The need for sleep overpowers that part of me. I lift the window higher before placing the fan on the sill. At some point, the plastic was white, but small dark spots pepper most of the surface now. Mold. I cringe.

Outside, the periphery of the lawn shimmers in darkness. My skin prickles. The lack of streetlights illuminating dark corners unnerves me.

I reach for the lamp by the twin-size bed and turn the switch. It comes to life, and a breath whooshes out of me. A laugh bubbles to the surface after I glance at all the previously sinister corners of the room.

I've never been the type to fear the dark, but in a house like this and a mysterious history—at least to me—I can't imagine anyone feeling wholly comfortable without answers. Especially when there's a makeshift bedroom in the basement.

My mother's silence about her past is even more deafening while we're here. The evidence is before us, yet she ignores it like it doesn't exist.

After meeting Mike and returning home, she carried herself through the rooms, as if needing to settle her soul into this place. She spent a lot of time on her phone, clinging to her present in Ridgefield while I waited for answers to come to me. I allowed her to explore without the push to dig through all the hidden crevices of the room myself. But she mentioned that all the family heirlooms were in the attic. I guessed some were in the basement as well, but that would take more convincing on my part to get her to go down there after her outburst.

I plug in the fan, and it crackles to life. I sit on the side of the bed, my skin absorbing the movement of air. It's not cold, but the effect cools me down significantly. I shove the thick quilt to the foot of the bed and lie across the sheet. I reach to grab my phone from the side table and unplug it from the wall. There's no one other than Abbie who'll call me while I'm here, but I can't shake the habit of keeping a fully charged phone. Without Wi-Fi, my data plan drained quickly, and without my mother's prompting, I wasn't sure what I was going to do to occupy my time.

The weather app proves disappointing, as each of the days we're in Orhaven, the highs reach the mid-nineties while the nighttime lows hover in the seventies. Of course, we'd travel to a place without air conditioning during a heat wave.

I scroll through my texts and social media, hovering on the edge of sleep. I don't succumb. The sound of the fan's blades keeps me conscious, and the questions from the day roll through my mind.

My mother doesn't have any photographs from her childhood, but I create a childlike version of her and imagine her walking down the steps to the basement, straining to reach the strings for the lights to illuminate the path to her bed.

I shiver at the thought, and the peripherals of the room shimmer.

A vision overtakes me before I can stop it. I've avoided them all day, as I was fully present with her, waiting for any morsel of information. But they've had their rest and rush back with a vengeance. The room darkens around me, and I hesitate to count down from five. It's going to be bad, but here in this house, the spike of adrenaline doesn't panic me like usual. A single light bulb dangles in the distance. I float closer to it. A foul odor stings my nose. A sniffling sound appears behind me. I'm unable to turn around to see who it is. The sniffling turns into light sobs before the wail of a child roars in my ears. My legs and arms persist, but I can't turn to her. Instead, I reach toward the string, wrapping the thin cord around my fingers. I snap my wrist, and the light blinks out.

Then it fills my eyes like I'm staring at the sun. I sit up and shield my eyes from the light burning all around me.

"Jenny." My mother stands beside the bed. Brilliant sunlight beams through the windows. I fell asleep at some point. That's never happened during one of my visions. Perhaps that's why I felt so calm. It wasn't a normal one, it was birthed from exhaustion.

"You're sweating," she says.

I lie back and untangle the sheets from around my legs. "It's hot in here."

Concern wrinkles her brow. She sits next to me, and her fingers brush over my forehead. Her normally chilly hands are just as sticky and hot as every inch of my skin. "I need to go to town this morning."

"Okay."

She checks her phone. "I wanted to let you sleep, but I should go soon."

"Do you want me to come?" The racking sobs of the child from my vision fill me with sadness and rage. I can't pretend to ignore it minutes after. I need alone time.

She sighs. "You look tired."

I settle and curl my legs to my chest. "I didn't get to bed until late." It's not a lie, but not telling her the entire truth creates a sharp twist in my gut. I stare at the window, wishing she'd leave without too much of a fight. Occasionally, I try to use my visions to predict a better version of the actual future instead of one leaving me or my mother maimed or close to death. Sometimes it works. Sometimes not.

I yawn and close my eyes, feeding into the half-truth that I'm tired. Maybe I'll be able to explore the house without her hovering over me.

Moments later, her weight lifts from the bed. A whisper of the sheets moves up my body and rests around me. It takes all the strength I have not to fling my eyes open, but I need to play this right.

For as long as I've known her, her slightness gives her the ability to slip in and out of rooms with little notice. Here, the floors announce her departure. The closing of the front door rattles the bones of the house.

Then the roar of the car engine is the catalyst I need to sit up. The bedroom window looks out over the long, winding driveway. As soon as the vehicle disappears into the woods, I bolt from the bed and head for the hallway, needing to get to the room my mother slept in with the short amount of time I have.

I pause outside the door and shoot a quick text to Abbie.

Can you research the name Calvin Cavanaugh?

I love the alliteration. Do you have anything else on him?

Not yet.

On it.

I grab the knob, and it turns easily. A haze of dust and light settles over the furniture. A twin bed sits in the center of the space with end tables on both sides. This room is a mirror version of mine, other than her suitcase set by the door. The top is open slightly. One tug of the zipper and she's ready to go. She already has one foot out the door, while I'm desperate to linger.

The walls are bare, yet there are small dings in the paint, showing this room once had a personality. With such a small bed, it had to belong to either my mother or aunt.

The dresser drawers are first. All empty, as I suspected. The closet is smaller than the one in my room, but not by much. The space gives no hint of life. The shelf holds no secret box of mementos.

I close the closet door. She can't know I snooped. I move to the center of the room and spin in a small circle. If there was anything to hide, where would it be?

Staring at the bed for a few seconds, a thought emerges. I kneel and press my body to the floor, flourishing the quilt out of the way. The wooden planks continue under the space, revealing nothing.

I press my cheek against the wood. "What are you doing?"

If this place was that horrible, then my mother would never have let me come. She's taken care to protect me from her past my entire life. Why would this place be any different?

I push upward before a shimmer stops me. At first, it seems

like an oncoming vision, which I'm not prepared for. Silently, I count backward from five.

The vision fades, but the hammering of my heart continues. I center my breathing and shove away from my spot. Somehow, it's the correct angle. Light glints off the metal ring under the center of the bed. The bed frame presses against my face as my fingers stretch to reach the ring. It's too far away, so I stuff myself under as much as I can fit.

A rumbling engine cuts through the otherwise silence of the house.

I shoot away from the bed and push the quilt back into place. As I race to the window, an unfamiliar truck ambles toward the house. It parks just out of sight.

I leave the room, closing the door behind me.

My mother wouldn't have left me here if she knew someone was coming. I fly down the stairs and press my face against the living room window. A baseball cap shields a man's face from view as he unfolds from the truck. He's tall, and his work boots give him an unnecessary lift. He rounds the corner, out of sight once more.

I grip my phone in my hand. My first thought is to call the police, but then I wonder if he's the guy who's been taking care of the property. My mother left with the car, so he probably has no clue anyone is here.

I scurry to the door and flip the lock. My mother must have left it open, knowing no one was around for miles. The only other entrance is the back door through the kitchen. I slip down the hallway toward it.

If he's here to mow the lawn, I doubt he'll want me to bother him. Though, he might know my mother. If he does, then I'll have more of an opportunity to question him without her around. With an alternative plan in mind, I step over the threshold into the kitchen.

I grab a bottle of water and head for the door. The moment I reach out for the handle, his hulking body blots out the light.

The door handle jiggles from his side, and I leap back so he can't see me. The sheer curtain covering the window might conceal me, but I can't be too sure.

"Who's in there?" his voice blares. He pounds on the door.

I'm frozen in my spot, yet the plastic bottle crackles like fireworks under my grip.

"I'm giving you two seconds before I'm coming in. I have a gun." He mutters something to himself. A key slides into the metal lock. The knob slowly turns.

I'm frozen in place as the door whips open, revealing the stranger raising the barrel of a gun, directing it at my face. I wince as I hear the gunshot crashing through the air.

6

THEN

The woods come alive the moment you wake. Your screams start muffled in your underground prison and rise like a body from the earth. I inhale. The sharpness of pipe smoke stings my nose. Memories of when he did this to me flood my mind. It helps hold me in place, understanding this is the best way to get you to stay. His method grounded me. It will work for you.

Darkness creeps into my vision. My wrists aren't bound like yours, but the feeling of the scratchy rope pricking my skin never goes away. There are times I wake in the middle of the night, convinced I'm back there. It's the safest place I've ever known. When you see that, you'll understand, and the living nightmare between us will be over.

I tug the black mask over my face. The moment you know it's me, the harder it will be to convince you to stay. I hit you hard enough that the memory of your captor will blur in your mind. That spark of recognition when you saw me by the car is already in the back of your mind as instinct takes over. Survival is all you need to think about. It's the only way for you to get home.

At least that's what you think.

The mask presses against my nose, the only physical reminder of Father that I see every day in the mirror. His mark lives through me and the child.

My hands clench into fists; the leather gloves strain with the pressure. With only the thin veil of moonlight, my hands appear slick and clean. But the stain of blood from my victims forever tattoos my skin.

The image of your blood shakes me to my core. Enough to halt my breath. It won't come to that. It's the only excuse I hold tight to my chest. The one that makes me human. If I don't hurt you, the humanity stays. Not like his. He didn't have such boundaries, but I work doubly hard on it by the hour when you're around.

A high-pitched wail cuts through the night.

I can't help the smile curling my lips. It's why I chose this place. You can scream until your throat is raw, but no one will hear you except for me.

I clear my throat, grumbling under my breath. If you've removed your gag, then I assume the same for the blindfold. I have to keep you away from the answer you already know.

My past is the only crux of this plan. You are the only one who can break it and me.

Leaves crunch under my boots. The heat from the day is no match for the coolness of night which clings to the edges of the flora. Father chose this place for the seclusion. I chose it for the safety. Nothing can hurt you out here.

I hold the only time I'd served in the confining prison in my mind until I could face it again. There's no public record of this place. I checked.

No one would find it unless they were looking. It's what I intend for you. When I finally free you, you won't be able to lead the police here. If you do, I'll be watching. But after you learn the lesson I intend for you, there will be no reason to return.

I move around the back of the structure. The ground dips into a small trench. My boots sink into the moist soil.

The door swings inward, so I'm careful opening it so it doesn't bump into you. The space is just big enough for four people huddling together, but that's not the secret of this place. It's what lies beyond the surface of the structure which holds the true heart.

Your screaming continues. Now that I'm closer, it pinches at my chest. It's the only consistent feeling—a lightness in my body, which keeps the darkness at bay for short bursts. It's why you can never leave me. Left to my own devices, those permanent bloodstains will overflow.

The moment I open the door, I know I'm in no danger from you. I lift the flashlight from my belt and press the switch. The beam slices through the void, finding your face. Your scream stops, and your eyes squeeze closed.

Your breathing is hard, but otherwise you're okay. The short chain I attached to the wall smooths over the concrete floor. The ropes around your wrists hold strong, but I need to work on the blindfold and gag.

I lower my voice, channeling Father. He's the only one who ever scared me, and I need him to help me scare you, too. Scare you into staying until you hear my message. "Don't scream."

I don't expect you to listen, but you can't blame me for hoping.

Your eyes stay closed since I don't take the light away from your face. Tears pulse across your cheeks and soak into the ground.

"No one can hear you."

You stop. Your chest heaves as you struggle to catch your breath. "What do you want from me?"

I wait for my name to caress your lips, but it doesn't. At least that part of the plan is working.

"I have a child." You strain to meet my eyes.

"You can't carry on how you do without consequences."

"You have the wrong person. Please, I won't tell anyone, I promise. This is all a mistake. I just want to go home."

The excuses flow from your mouth. I try not to feel disappointed in you, but these things take time. You're not ready yet, and that's okay.

I can't be away from the house too long. Each step of the plan requires full cooperation.

I step through the doorway, into the night.

"Where are you going?" You scoot as far as you can toward me before the binds catch. "Wait. Don't leave me here. I don't want to die."

I press my lips together, tempted to spill everything within me, opening what I have of a heart to you and giving you all the answers. But I can't. Search for them within yourself first. You have to want to stay and prove to me you understand how important your life with me truly is.

I silence your screams with the door. You're smart. You won't use it for too long before it leaves you entirely. As if you have a hold on my thoughts, you stop. Sobs rack your body, and I want to comfort you. But I won't see anything friendly in your eyes until you're not chained up anymore.

I prepared for a week, but we both want this over sooner.

Each step away from you claws at me. I haven't been without you for a night in as long as I can remember. You're safe, and there's another who can fill that space for now. Our girl.

7
JENNY

"Hey, are you okay?" The guy's voice sounds far away as I remove myself from the vision of him murdering me in cold blood.

He lifts his chin, enough of a movement to see directly into his eyes. There was never a gun. Only a hefty set of keys fills his palm. His gaze flits from anger to curiosity. "I'm sorry. I thought you were—sometimes local kids try to break into this place. I hope I didn't scare you," he says. "I'm Scott, by the way."

Even though they look nothing alike, I put two and two together. "Mike Allen is your father?"

"Yeah." He places the keys on the counter, a gesture for someone who is comfortable being in this space.

"We spoke with him yesterday. Apparently, he and my mom were friends growing up?"

Scott inclines his head; his gaze shifts from mine. "They were."

"I'm Jenny."

He grins, and one dimple presses into his cheek. Up close and without the threat of my imagination, I take him in. The sinister veil lifts away from him. He raises the brim of his hat, revealing a set of dark eyes against his tanned skin. He's younger than I thought.

I want to know more about him, but the tendrils of the vision tickle at the base of my neck. "You said you had a gun."

He wipes a hand over his forehead. "I mean, I have one. Not with me, though. My family enjoys hunting. The threat usually makes the kids scared enough not to come back."

Being in the house with a family member of a man my mother was close with eases the tension in my body. "Don't let me interrupt whatever you were doing."

Scott massages the back of his neck. "I planned to mow the lawn. I can show you where all the equipment is, if you need tools or whatever while you're here."

I chew that over. My mother will return soon, and my exploration of the house will end. But if Mike knows more about my family's history in this place, then the possibility of more information from Scott would be better than her empty room. At least for a little while. "It's not like I have anything else to do."

Scott smirks. His front teeth are crooked, and I can't help smiling back. There's a charm about him that immediately draws me nearer. Maybe it's the thought of finding out more about my family, but when he turns toward the door, I follow as if connected to him by an invisible string.

When he first walked through the door, I didn't realize his height. If he stood on his toes, he would bump his head on the frame.

He opens the door and moves to the side to let me out first.

I'm aware that I'm still dressed in my pajamas. I cross my arms over my chest and scoot by him, careful not to breathe too hard in his direction. The awareness that I haven't brushed my teeth yet fills my mouth with an uncomfortable heat.

I scoot by him, through the space barely big enough for the

two of us. His body warmth gives off a woodsy scent, as if he washes his clothes in a pile of leaves.

Outside, the same scent fills me. There's some shade surrounding the house from the few trees, but the light from the sun stretches across the grass.

"So, you work with your dad?" I ask to end the silence between us.

"He owns a carpentry business, but around here, we do a bit of everything."

"It must be nice to work with family."

"Sometimes." He rubs the back of his neck. "Do you know when the house is up for sale? I'm wondering if I'm needed anymore."

"Oh, I think before we leave?"

"Well, it will be good for you to know where everything is. And if you need help along the way, I can give you my phone number." He eyes my cell phone in my hand.

"Sure. That would be great." I unlock it and give it to him. My hand aches from the grip I had on it.

"We fixed a lot of the issues with the aesthetics of the house. It needs a new coat of paint on the exterior, and the well system is old as hell, but somehow it still works."

He hands the phone back, and we start toward the barn shed again. "I don't think we're going to do much. I think my mother wants the house sold as soon as possible."

Scott nods.

I'm unsure how to proceed with asking about my mother's past in Orhaven, but I can't miss this opportunity. "Did Mike talk to you about my family?"

"Not lately." He approaches the barn door and grabs the metal combination lock, bringing himself closer.

Up close, the barn is even more run-down than I originally thought. The door hangs off the structure as if it's held on by a splinter. "I need to fix the hinges on the door. I can get to that this week. It's been on my list of things to do around here."

Once my mother signs all the paperwork and we pack up whatever is left in the house, it's not our problem anymore. Though, the better shape the house, the more money we'll get for it.

He removes the lock from the door using a combination. "It's 11-22-32. In case you need it." He leaves the lock hanging on the hasp and slips inside the darkness. It swallows him until all I hear is his shuffling shoes on the floor.

I step inside. Something brushes against my arm, and I jerk forward, hearing the crack of the door behind me as we're engulfed in total darkness.

A wave of shivers rolls up my arms, and I'm slammed into the memory of the bed in the basement. A thick scent washes over me. I can't identify it, but it leaves a coppery taste on my tongue.

A flash of light appears, illuminating half of Scott's face. The corners of his mouth tug down with concern. "Sorry about that. There's a brick by the door, to prop it open."

I shove the door and squint against the sudden bright light.

"It's next to the hinge. I was waiting for the part to come in. They don't make 'em that big at the hardware store."

I lift the brick with two hands and place it against the door. Dirt clings to my skin, and I rub my hands together to get it off.

"You're not used to the dirty work, huh?" His airy tone is teasing, but I need him to know that I can carry my own.

"We've always lived in apartments. If you need a dishwasher fixed, I'm your gal."

He chuckles, a low and hearty sound. "That's good to know. I find it difficult to squeeze into the smaller spaces."

"I can imagine."

He scoots behind an older-style truck, which takes up the left side of the shed.

It's rusted in the wheel wells, and cobwebs fill the inside of the cab. "Does this still work?"

Scott wipes a hand over his mouth. "Doubt it. It's been here for years. I don't even know where the key is." Behind the truck, Scott checks the gas on the riding lawn mower.

I walk further inside, inspecting the hints of my family's past. Various tools hang from nails and hooks attached to the wall. As I move closer, I imagine my grandfather working here, repairing furniture, possibly the kitchen table, which looks handcrafted. I drag my fingers over the surface. The tools have seen better days, but nothing that a damp cloth can't clean. With my mother's relationship with my grandfather, I wonder if she will want any of this stuff. At the very least, we could ask Scott if he wants the tools for his father's business. It's the least we could do after he cared for the property for all these years.

As I trail Scott toward the back of the barn, I spot a bicycle, which seems to have made its debut appearance in *The Wizard of Oz*, from right under Ms. Gulch.

More dangerous and sharper equipment hangs from the back wall. I don't know what any of it is used for—outside of creating shimmering hints of a vision where Scott or I are impaled. I whip away from them and count down. My pulse spikes, and I yearn to flee from the space. But what would Scott think?

The sound of metal against metal forces my eyes to snap open. Scott sits on the mower as it roars to life. He turns toward me and beckons me closer with one hand.

He shouts over the sound of the motor. "Do you want me to show you how it works?"

The vision persists. I need to leave. I shake my head and attempt to share a friendly smile before leaving the barn.

The further I get from the shed, the more I can breathe. The sound from the mower dims, yet the vision persists. The echo of bone against metal creates a tightening in my throat. I attempt to ground myself in the present, thinking of the abrupt conversation with Scott about my family.

The moment I reach the kitchen, I fall into a chair and lean on my thighs, breathing hard. I shouldn't have gone out there with him. The urge to know more overpowered my fear of visions, and I'm paying for it now.

Scott steers the roaring mower across the lawn, as I stave off the impending images. I take a few more breaths for good measure and stand. He won't be able to distract me, and I need to get to work.

I double-check the driveway, and Scott's truck is the only vehicle. I glance at my phone. It's only been fifteen minutes since we met.

Fifteen minutes I lost when I could have been exploring the house.

The basement door beckons me, like finding a hidden present. The opportunity to sneak in where I'm not supposed to elicits another shiver that rolls over my shoulders. My mother made it clear that she doesn't want me down there, but that's the reason I need to be. Something happened to her there, and I must know what it was.

I grab the handle and twist, but it doesn't budge. I try again. It won't open.

My fingers glide over the knob and down to the lock. The nail next to the door sits naked and lonely. The thought that anyone needs to lock a basement door sinks my stomach. I try to recall where my mother might have put the key. I open all the drawers and cabinets. None of them reveal a hiding place.

The realization dawns on me. It's how she was comfortable

allowing me to stay in the house. She knows her daughter too well.

My phone buzzes from my pocket. A text from Abbie fills the screen.

Nothing yet. You alive?

I'm checking out the house before my mom gets home.
Will call later.

Heat burns my cheeks. I imagine Scott's first impression of me, and it brings with it the reminder of the vision of him shooting me.

The lawn mower growls toward the front of the house, and I move in that direction. A layer of dust clings to the dining room table. A dutiful daughter would help clean the room for our imminent departure. But the secrets call to me more. I don't open the curtains to get more light into the room. If Scott sees, then he may think I'm spying on him. Even though following him around the house is basically the same thing.

In the basement, the books called to me. If my mother escaped in them, I wonder if there are any clues in the nook filled with them up here. The windows expose my location, but with the porch overhang, I have a feeling Scott would have to be much closer to see me.

I sit on the cushioned bench tucked into the alcove, and particles of dust dance in the air. The bookshelves stretch from floor to ceiling. I read the titles. The spines show worn lines cutting down the length of them.

While the past remains with the older, leather-bound books, I'm drawn to the paperbacks at eye level, closest to the entrance into the dining room. On top of one stack is an open book, resting on its spine, inviting me to look at it. I pull it from the shelf. There's no bookmark or dog-eared corners, but the book is heavy enough that it rests open without effort.

The cover is mildly dusty but otherwise in good condition. The backs of a woman and man holding hands stare up at me. I don't recognize the author, but this isn't a book that would appear in a library of a house where no one lived for years. Someone penciled in the number one in the corner of the inside cover. I flip to the copyright page, needing to confirm my suspicion. I release a slow breath as I locate the date. This book was published four years ago.

I sit again, holding the book in my lap. The mower drones on as I attempt to reconcile the thoughts bouncing around in my head.

Scott mentioned that kids had tried to break into the house previously. I close my eyes and imagine the scenario. A house secluded from the town. With the small-town gossip, they had to know it was vacant. Even with Scott caring for the property, it wasn't as if he was living here.

I flip the book over in my hands, pressing my finger against the page, securing the place of whoever had left it. It seems unlikely that a teen would break into a house and read a romance novel at her or his leisure. The publication date scratches at my mind. My mother left this house before I was born, and she thought it was vacant for all these years. So how did the book get here?

Removing my hands from the pages, the pristine paper reveals the leftover dirt from the door stop at the barn. I scrub at it with the side of my hand, but it doesn't come off.

For once, I can't imagine a scenario. The most logical conclusion is that someone lived or visited here within the last four years. Either with or without my mother's knowledge.

After shoving the book back where I found it, I head into the kitchen to wash my hands. My mind whirs with the possibilities of this place.

A reasonable explanation comes to mind. Is it possible that someone rented this house? I can't imagine my mother leaving for as long as she did, and it looks the way it does without more dust and disrepair.

It makes sense that if someone stayed here, they would bring newer books with them. If this weren't my family's home, I could see it as a private getaway. Maybe a creative person who needed space for their next project?

The moan of the mower halts, and in its place, a low hum fills my ears.

I peer out the window. Scott leaves the barn, holding a shovel and a duffel bag bursting at the seams.

I turn on the sink, and discolored water flows out of it. The same thing happened in the bathtub last night. My hands jerk back, and I wait until the water runs clear. The brownish liquid from the initial pull of water swirls in the white sink before disappearing down the drain.

We picked up two bottles of hand soap from the grocery store the day before, so I allow the water to run while I pick at the plastic around the edge of the pump. I can't locate the perforated edge, so I flick the light switch next to the sink, and a terrible grinding sound fills the air. Water droplets escape from the sink drain in tiny explosions.

I press the switch down, and the grinding slows and finally stops.

My trembling hands grip the countertop. There are two switches on the wall next to the window. I reach over and turn on the one for the light instead of the garbage disposal.

Brightness washes over the sink. A glint reflects off whatever is inside the drain. My head blocks the light, and I try several angles to figure out what caused that awful sound.

I lift my hand and bring it closer to the drain. My fingers hover over it. I glance at the switch for the disposal.

"It's off. It's off." I repeat the words as an impending vision crackles around my periphery. Whatever is inside the disposal needs to come out. Wrecking the only modern appliance in this place won't be what I leave behind.

"Reach in and grab it, then it will be over."

I inhale and shove my hand down the drain. My fingers brush against the blade first before dragging against the bottom. The shiny object moves slightly. I try again, yet it evades my touch.

I lean closer, shoving even more of my hand down. The shimmering in my vision intensifies, and I stare at the switch.

The darker side of me beckons for me to flick it.

I don't, but a searing pain races up my arm anyway as the blades come to life. A scream rises in my chest as blood erupts from the drain.

8

JENNY

The back door opens as I recoil from the sink, taking my whole and nonmutilated hand with me. The echo of the sound of torn flesh from the bone fades, mocking and cackling all the way back to the depths of my mind.

"Are you okay?" Scott glances between the sink and me.

My hand presses against my chest. The thrumming of my heart slams back at it. It's whole and I'm alive.

"I'm fine. I think there's something stuck down there. I was just checking it out."

Scott's brow furrows. "You screamed . . ." He must think I'm nuts.

I force out a laugh, stepping away from the sink. "You startled me."

Scott stares at me for a few seconds before he checks the sink. If he realizes I screamed before he came into the room, he doesn't say it. He peers down the drain, and I can't help leaning toward him. The memory of the blood appears and disappears each time I blink. This vision sticks longer than usual.

A swooping heat sears my skin, and I shuffle to the refrigerator to get away from the blood. My heartbeat throbs in my chest.

"Do you want water?" I ask. I open the door and breathe in the cool air wafting from the pristine space filled with neat rows of water and just enough food to last a few days.

"Sure. I'm sorry I scared you. I understand how you might feel. This place always gives me the creeps."

I remove a bottle from the refrigerator. "Really? Why?" Maybe he can fill me in on a memory of this house.

Scott massages the back of his neck. His eyes scrutinize me as if he's assessing whether to trust me. "Because of what happened here."

"What happened here?"

His eyes narrow slightly as if gauging my question. A ghost of an uncomfortable grimace touches his lips.

"Your grandfather died in this house?"

"Oh."

He rubs his neck again and clears his throat. "You didn't know?"

I shake my head. I know he passed when my mother was young, but in this house? Then she had to grow up here on top of it? No wonder she hates it here.

"I shouldn't have said anything."

"No, it's fine." Scott probably already thinks I'm crazy. I have to make light of this situation or else it might get back to my mother that I'm scared to be here alone. "You don't believe in ghosts, do you?"

He reaches for the bottle, and his hand covers mine. "I don't believe in ghosts per se, but souls leave an imprint on this world. Some more than others."

"That's an interesting way of looking at it."

He opens the water and takes a pull.

I peer at the garbage disposal switch once more before leaving that horrific vision behind.

When he's done, he screws the cap onto the top. "I need to get going."

"Of course." Exploring more of the house creates a popping excitement in my stomach. The aftereffects of a vision always change, but this time, it's energizing.

"I'll come by later this week to check out the disposal. Just don't use it until then, okay?"

"Okay."

"See you later, Jenny." The water bottle crackles under his firm grip as he turns away to leave the kitchen.

I follow him, making sure the back door is closed before hurrying into the living room to watch him depart. With him gone, the energy seems to drain from the house.

Without his presence to distract me, the remnants of the vision weigh against my chest. My hands prickle, and the numbness will settle in soon. I debate lying in bed and embracing it to distract me, but my mother will be back at any time.

I take the stairs two at a time and burst into her bedroom. I sift through the front of her bag. The bottle filled with alprazolam is in the outside pocket of her bag, and I fish it out and take one, letting it sit under my tongue for a moment before biting down on it. The chalky taste floods my mouth, and I nearly gag. For once, I'm glad she thought ahead. My prescription is no longer refillable, but she's made a habit of bringing them anytime we travel. I don't need them often. Besides, it's only one to take the edge off. It usually needs ten minutes to work, but the act of taking it calms me slightly.

I push into the hallway to the door across from hers, into the one bedroom I haven't explored yet. With a new countdown until her return, there's no hesitation as I turn the handle. My forehead nearly smacks into the wood when the door doesn't open. I apply more force to the knob, but nothing.

The physical representation of her distrust strikes me, even though it's always been there. She never explicitly told me not to go into the rooms, but she locked me out of them, including the basement.

My mother and I know each other's moves most of the time before the other thinks about it. There are more than a few occasions where we can finish each other's sentences. Was this her anticipating what I'd do while she's gone?

I check all the doors, anyway. When they don't open, I go back into her room and search her bag. It's a useless task. If she locked me out, then she definitely would have the keys with her.

I lower myself to the bed and sigh. I lift my phone and scroll my finger across the screen, unlocking it to text Abbie. There are several messages from her, but it's the last one which gives me pause.

About to jump online. Talk later

A familiar itch pinches at my skin. One that I could easily quell at home with gaming. Even with my laptop, it won't do much without internet. It was a long shot to bring it with me, but I hoped there would be a time where I could get at least some distraction.

A wave of euphoria weighs my shoulders down as the pill's effects kick in. I want to sink into the bed and fully immerse myself into this house. I lie down and close my eyes for a moment before they snap open.

I almost forgot about the metal piece under my mother's bed. The distance I put between it while I was downstairs and outside with Scott gave my subconscious enough space to realize what it is. It's not a forgotten piece of hardware, but one attached to a secret. At least that's the hope.

I reach under the bed until the tips of my fingers brush over the ring. I strain to grip it enough to lift it an inch before it slaps back into place. I try two more times with the same result.

It can't be that heavy, and I need more room to open whatever lies underneath. I shove off the floor and position myself at the foot of the bed.

The effects of the pill continue to wash over me in waves, and I almost regret taking it. I grip the corner of the bed and lift it slightly, pivoting it out of position. A grinding sound makes me wince. A scratch blemishes the floor at the other end of the bed. It's about six inches long and wasn't there when we arrived.

If she asks me about it, I won't lie, but I have a more important task.

The edge of a hatch appears, along with several dust bunnies rolling from their hiding spots like tumbleweeds. After moving the bed, I lower it to the floor and crawl over to the ring. I trace my fingers around deep cuts in the wood.

My heart thrums in my chest, but more from excitement than fear. It's like the sensation of locating the living space in the basement. The unraveling of decades of secrets fills my mind with possibilities.

I open the hatch and ease it to the ground. Dust clings to my nose and throat, and I cough into my fist as I inspect the opening. Beams separate sections of the space, and my heart deflates as I find nothing inside. I rest on my knees, staring at the hole. There has to be a reason for it.

I scan the room. My mother hadn't mentioned whose we were staying in. Was this one cleared out after everyone died, including this space?

Especially with my mother's traumatic childhood, I can't

imagine her wanting to sleep where she grew up. Did that mean she stuck me in my aunt's room? Were the others locked to keep her memories away and to continue to keep me from her past?

I grab my phone and turn the flashlight on. The beam barely cuts through the brightness of the room but illuminates the void under the floor. I drop the phone inside the hole, scanning the space with precise motions as not to miss anything.

Floating remnants of cobwebs stick to my skin.

With each swipe of the space, my heart sinks even more into my chest. This was a waste of time. My mother won't overlook the scratch on the floor, and she'll know I dug for information in her absence.

My skin prickles, and I tug at the fabric of my tank top, desperate for cooler air. I should shower while she's gone so at least she won't think I was a complete snoop.

The phone tumbles from my hand. A plume of dust billows out, and I suck in a breath and a mouthful of particles. I cough as I reach after it. It fell closer to the edge of the hole, down a pocket just big enough to fit the slim phone. The beam of light is the only indicator of its position as it blends into the dark wood. I squeeze my hand in, feeling around for the edge. I let out a breath, and another dust cloud rushes from the hiding spot.

A thin shadow scurries across the bottom of the hatch, and I jump back. The centipede continues on its way while a wash of goosebumps coats my entire body. I wait a few seconds, expecting more where that came from.

I count to ten before I grab the phone. The beam illuminates the space under the floor. I turn off the flashlight and glance at the hatch one more time. I stare at it, unable to take my eyes away from what my clumsiness revealed. Where my phone had hit the wood, and the movement of the dust, created a sliver of newness in the depths below.

I reach in and remove a thin piece of cardboard. It's almost the same shade as the wood underneath, but the debris gave the illusion that there's nothing inside. That's a lie though. There's something in there.

The familiar hum of an engine fills my ears.

My time is up. I jump to my feet and head for the window. The car speeds up the driveway as if she knows what I've done. I have less than five minutes until she discovers what I've been up to.

I grab the small book from the hiding space. It's thin with a soft but cracked leather cover. I place it on the floor, away from the bed, and close the hatch. My breathing slows as I move the bed back where it belongs. The time I take now will hopefully prevent her from knowing that I found a secret under her bed. I spot the scratch. It's hidden under the shadow of the quilt and the side table. Maybe she won't notice.

The car door slams outside, and I check the room one more time, making sure everything is in its place. Then I close the door behind me.

I rush into the bathroom and turn on the shower. Guilt adds to the weight of the book, but I don't have time to read it now. I shove it in the corner and toss my clothes on top of it. I'm halfway into the tub when three knocks strike the door.

"Yeah?" I call a little too loudly.

The door opens a crack, and I cover my naked body with the curtain. "Jenny, I'm home. I didn't want to startle you."

"Oh, okay."

"I'm going to make some lunch."

The door closes, and I ease under the spray of water. It's not warm yet, but it's enough to cover what I've done. I recall how I left the room, referencing the last look. I doubt she went in there first, yet visions of her bursting into the bathroom, uncovering the secret book, and staring at me with disapproving, cold eyes crowd my mind. A vision of her burning it in the fireplace pulses through me. I charge across the room as the pages curl into each other, blackening with each passing second, keeping their secrets. The epic argument between us is worse than any of the few ones in real life. I scream at her about keeping me away from our past. She tugs at her sleeves, crying and desperate for me to stop.

It feels like hours. The rippling effects from the one thing I've found here wash over me. The despair and loss of any explanation of my past drains me.

When I finally snap out of it, I choke on cool water. I turn the shower off, and my teeth chatter as I reach for a towel.

Sometimes even the visions without physical violence strike me more than the bloody ones. I dry off, trying to shove away the imagined fight and quell the shivers racking my body.

I scoop up my clothes with the book concealed between them, then leave the bathroom, depositing everything in my room. I don't have time to look through what I've found, and the weight of uncovering a secret nearly kills me.

When I enter the kitchen, I spot two ham and cheese sandwiches next to each other on the table. My mother's back is to me as she opens a bag of chips. I steel myself and shake off the guilt of sneaking around on her.

I sit at the chair closest to the door and try to control the waver in my voice. "How was the meeting?"

She drops the bag of chips between us before sitting. She lets out a sigh. "It wasn't the news I expected."

"What do you mean?"

She rubs a hand over her face. "I have to make a trip to get some old paperwork at a different lawyer's office a few towns over. It's how we can get all of this over with."

The thought of getting more time alone in the house creates a flurry in my gut. It's short-lived as I realize she won't allow me to stay here by myself again.

"Are you okay being here without me?" she asks.

I hold back any surprise. "When do you have to go?"

"Tomorrow."

A full day alone. I try to appear as if I'm not doing backflips on the inside. "I can come with you." I drop my hands to my lap, crossing my fingers.

She licks her lips, pulling them together until they disappear. "I was hoping you could finish sorting through some boxes from the attic. I just want to be done with this."

"What boxes?" The locked rooms upstairs apparently hold more than I thought.

"That's our task this afternoon, to bring down those boxes and clear them out. I've already hired Mike's son to bring them out of here the day after tomorrow."

"Scott." I bite into my sandwich. "He stopped by here earlier and mowed the lawn. Did you know they were taking care of this place?"

"I had a feeling, even though Mike wasn't explicit about it."

If she wasn't in contact with him, what made them work here? "Do we need to pay them?"

"The estate covers it. Walter is paid through a trust." She waves a dismissive hand. "It's complicated but covered."

Even without her taking a massive bite of her sandwich, it's obvious she's getting to a breaking point with the conversation.

I change the subject. "There's something stuck in the garbage disposal."

She twists in her chair to look at it. "Why were you using it?"

"It was an accident. I turned on the wrong switch. Scott said he was going to fix it."

"That was nice of him." She turns back to her food.

We fall into a lull, and I'm satisfied enough with her allowing me to explore what's left in the house. Maybe she's not holding all the secrets I thought.

9
THEN

The way children play and imagine displays how we're born innocent. It's only the sins and influence of our caregivers that spin us in the wrong direction. My mind wanders, as it does, while she lies on her stomach staring at the corner of the room. Nothing is there, at least not physically. Her eyes dart from side to side as her imagination reveals a movie. Maybe she sees an imaginary friend.

With her distracted, I fall into the memory of my experience in the woods. The overwhelming silence of the hidden shelter. The claustrophobic pressure. An all-consuming worry that you'll die there. Everything seems different when you think you're going to die. You learn to understand the important things in life.

Good things can come out of the bad, too. Out there, there are no distractions to impede the thinking process. By the end of this, you'll know what you have to do to give us a good life. To give her a good life.

I fall into your role, going through the bedtime routine. Slipping into your mindset is easy. I've been doing it for years. I remind her I'm as important as you, and leaving this place isn't an option. I'm rooted in her life as much as you are.

We sing the "Toothbrush Song." Her smile and laugh fuel my soul. There's no chance I would allow either of you to exit my life. Staring into her eyes, I renew my mission.

After I finish not one but two stories and sing her a fractured version of your lullaby, I kiss her forehead the way you do. Then I sweep my fingers across her skin, moving the soft strands off her face. Her heavy eyes peer up at me before a yawn overcomes her.

She asks for you.

The same sensation when I left you earlier hovers over me. I don't feel like others do. Both of you know that and still accept me.

I reassure her you're away for a few days with friends. "Mommies need a break sometimes."

She believes it, but she misses you.

I miss you.

As I leave the room, she rolls over, and I wait for the hand to come up and wiggle her fingers. It's a bedtime move that she's done since she could consciously move her hands on her own.

The signal propels me from the room.

The babysitter left the house a mess, claiming her only job was to watch her.

I don't mind cleaning. It's one way I process my day. My mind flips on autopilot as I move through the space, tidying the living room before moving on to the kitchen.

The sitter mentioned they baked cookies. The scent of them enveloped me when I returned home, but the scars of the mess cut across every surface of the kitchen.

While washing the dishes, I glance out the window. My warped reflection glares back at me. The shapes meld together until I see you. You're not home. But our shared experiences give me insight into your thoughts. You'll come out the other side of this a more committed member of this family and never regret staying here.

I'm the one who will keep the secret of your commitment. That weight will carry the same way it did for Father. He was physically stronger than me. But I won't treat you the way he did me.

I shiver at the thought. There are times I don't think of others' thought processes in the way I should. I blame Father, but unlike him, I'm always trying to improve. I make a mental note to reassure you I won't harm you. That fear won't allow the process to benefit me.

The urge to study the human mind forces my hand to move faster over the counter. I've done enough thinking. I need to study you. My methods have worked well over the years, on top of mimicking you. It's a trick I learned on my own, a survival mechanism.

When the kitchen is clean, I lock all the doors, even though the crime rate in this town has been nonexistent for years.

At least since the last time I protected our family.

10

JENNY

After lunch, I clean up our plates while my mother rummages around in her purse. She pulls out a key ring, and she proves my theory correct. The small key for the basement dangles from it. I store the information for later.

Upstairs, the room at the end of the hallway reveals a creaky staircase leading into a space with vaulted ceilings. The steps groan under our weight as if waking up for the first time in years. Sunlight filters through the cracks in the eaves. Stacks of more than a dozen boxes form long shadows, reaching toward the staircase as if they are plotting their escape.

The cardboard boxes are without labels, leaving the possibilities open for more information that my mother has locked away in her own mind and past.

She hands over the first box. "Let's bring them to the living room. We can spread out." She inhales and her nostrils flare. The stale air tickles at my nose. "Most of this will end up going anyway, and it will be easier to get them outside." Her diplomatic tone suggests that she's preparing herself to leave most of it behind.

I don't linger in the living room long, not wanting to give away my excitement at delving into the past. As a dutiful worker, I retrieve and stack the boxes until there's only one left. I drop the box next to the stacks I've placed against the wall by the larger windows facing the front lawn. In a neat row, out of the attic, the boxes aren't as intimidating. The lives of those who lived here are concentrated into one sad space.

My mother walks past me and into the kitchen, rubbing her dusty hands together. There isn't much privacy for me to look at the boxes alone with her one room away. I debate it, though, only for a moment until a tickle in my throat propels me toward the kitchen. I need a drink.

The water isn't running, but she stands by the sink, her back facing me. Most of her arm is inside the porcelain basin. Her body twists at an unnatural angle.

The echo of the garbage disposal sound fills my ears. My chest clenches, hard enough that I can't breathe. The onslaught of images from yesterday melds into new ones with her. I rush over, cradle her into my arms as blood and ragged skin drip and hang from her bones.

"Jenny? Jenny, are you okay?"

Her voice doesn't match her lips.

I know what I need to do, but I can't. The sorrow overcomes me.

"Close your eyes, honey."

I do. The images disappear, and the scent of blood retreats from my nose.

"There you go. Five . . . four . . ."

"Three, two, one," I rush.

"Breathe," she reminds me.

Tears cut down my face. She holds me tighter.

"This is my fault," she says.

I open my eyes to find her frowning. "No, it's not."

"I should have done this on my own."

"It's not that," I say, even though I'm not sure that's entirely true. I can't put this guilt on her. "It's been happening a lot more lately." That part is the truth, and I'm not sure why I say it. I know where it's going to go.

"Why didn't you tell me?"

"I can handle it."

"I know you can, but it's okay to ask for help."

I untangle myself from her and stand. Her arms hover next to me, ready to catch me if I fall. I wipe away the tears, and my cheeks heat up.

"We should look in the boxes," I say, needing to get out of this room.

"Are you sure?"

"I'm fine. Promise."

Her eyes narrow, but I go into the other room, hoping she will follow without any more questions.

"Why don't you sit for a minute?" she says.

"I said I'm fine."

"Okay." She flips one of the boxes open and peers inside. "This can get donated."

"What's in it?" I ask as she opens another.

Her body blocks the upturned lid. "China." She pulls out a plate, the blue edges intricately designed. "We never used it. You can go through those boxes if you want to take anything."

"Really?" I ask.

"Sure."

A smile crosses my lips, and I flip open the nearest one. A wooden chest takes up most of the box. I open its top, and a thick gold band catches my eye. I bring it closer for inspection. The round clock face stares up at me with an accusing eye. It's a man's watch. The only man in my mother's past in this house was her father.

I hold it out to her. "You don't want to keep this?"

"I don't want any memories of him."

In the way I don't want her to pry into my visions, I don't pry into her memories. I leave the echo of her words between us and move on to the next.

Sifting through the boxes takes most of the day. Some, she spends longer on, while others immediately go into the donate pile. She insists that we cook an early dinner together, and not too long after, while we're on the couches relaxing, her eyes rest closed and the corners of her mouth tug downward. Her chest lifts and falls slowly.

The boxes beckon to me, but their contents can wait until tomorrow. She freely allowed me to look through them, knowing there's nothing incriminating within them. The hidden book on the other hand might tell me something.

Each step across the room sounds like I'm rattling the house awake. I can't risk her hearing me. But when I'm midway up the stairs and she hasn't budged, I hurry up the rest.

It's warmer upstairs, but I don't turn the fan on just yet. If she wakes up, I need to hear her coming. She can't see me with what I've found. Losing her trust won't help me understand her past.

I close the door, leaving it cracked to alert me of her presence.

The heat is oppressive in the room, so I quickly change into a different tank top and shorts before removing the small book from its hiding place. The bed creaks as I settle on it, and I listen for my mother's footfalls in the hallway. If she does come up, at least I can pretend I went to bed.

After a few moments of silence, I smooth my fingertips over the cover, memorizing each crack in the leather.

I open it, skimming the first few pages before I realize it's a journal of sorts. Excitement courses through me, but then my chest sinks at the thought of putting so much pressure on what it could contain. What if I don't find anything, or what if I find what I'm looking for?

The edges of my vision shimmer. Now isn't the time for a vision.

I close my eyes, count down from five as slowly as I'm able. The forced switch from guilt and nervousness from hiding something from my mother to excitement and anticipation keeps them at bay. When I open them, the world is clear and sharp around me.

I focus on the first entry. I expect pages full of words, detailing the life of the author.

Instead of words, a pencil sketch fills the page.

A young girl stares at me. Her eyes are slightly off center from each other as if the artist chose a particular style, but the open-mouthed silent scream elicits a deeper emotion.

I trace my finger over the curve of her face. Her eyes are wide with surprise.

Or terror.

Her hands are tucked behind her back, and a shadow looms to her right. The second shape towers over her.

My skin prickles at the fear in her eyes, but I move to the next page.

Whoever drew in this journal didn't waste paper. The back of the first page has the same child depicted in the center of an otherwise entirely black surface. Whoever drew this must have pushed the pencil to its limit, allowing no white space. In this one, the shadow seems to have overcome her entire world. But she's not screaming. Only thick tears slash her face.

The following pages proceed in the same way. A lump lodges in my throat as I flip through, the journal depicting more horrible scenarios in greater detail and skilled precision. They fill my mind, like my own visions.

The child's crying fills my ears, and I can almost taste the salty tears. A vision prickles in my mind, and for once, I allow it to overcome me. The drawn images turn into an actual child standing in a dark room while an unseen hand reaches from the darkness to bruise and cut her face and hands.

Tears spring to my eyes. Not because whatever was in this person's mind is horrible, but it's what I see every day in mine.

I come back to reality, needing to understand. Whose journal was this? Could it be my mother's? It was under her bed.

If it was, I could show it to her and get answers. But if it belonged to any other family member, then there's no chance for me to speak with them about what they illustrated. The images in the journal are horrific, but they are a link to this family, showing no doubt that I belong in some twisted way.

"Jenny?" My mother's concerned voice floats down the hallway toward my room.

I shove the book under my pillow and replace it with my phone, seconds before she appears. "I'm here."

She stands in the doorway, bleary-eyed. "You didn't wake me."

"You looked comfortable." The rapid thudding of my heart drowns out my voice.

"Thanks. But the lumps in the cushions are not the best. I'm going into my room. Good night."

"Night."

She hovers in the doorway, a question on her lips. But she shakes her head before asking it. "I love you."

"Love you."

"I hope you're able to find what you're looking for while we're here."

I twist around to face her. "What do you mean?"

She picks at her nails but holds my eyes. "I know I'm not forthcoming with my life in this house, but I have my reasons. Maybe we'll find something good in the boxes tomorrow."

Before I can answer, she sighs and backs away from the doorway. The bathroom door closes a few seconds later.

I turn on the screen of my phone to check the time. I've lost over an hour to the journal, and I'm only halfway through it. The images swallow me whole as my own visions have done to me every single day for as long as I can remember.

I turn the window fan on and flick off the light. Moonlight fills the room as it had the night before. I tuck into the bed and pull the quilt over me. The movement of air from the outside doesn't touch me, but I won't be able to sleep until I've been through the journal at least once. The flashlight from my phone blinds me, and I adjust it to point at the pages. I flip through until I've found where I stopped.

The horror in the images doesn't scare me as much as the thought of someone in my family having the same experiences as me.

As I progress through, the drawings lose the amount of blackness around the edges. The images push through, closer to the surface, but the sketches aren't as precise. It's almost as if someone rushed the artist to get the picture down. When I experience a vision, I'm able to recall it for a short amount of time. If this person was the same way, then they must have wanted to get all the details before they forgot.

The pictures always include the two young girls in various positions of anguish and pain. In one image, they're both decap-itated at the bottom of a staircase. I push past that one quickly.

My view of the artist shifts to my grandmother. My mother had mentioned that hers used to paint when she was much younger. Was the anguish depicted in the drawings hers? There are no words for the weight of the pain, but the pictures give some clue. Back then, I doubt there were the types of psycho-logical help as today, so this was probably her way of processing it. My chest swells, and heat springs behind my eyes.

The hurriedness of the drawings swiftly moves to a different style. Letters cut into the design as if they're meant to be there. It takes a few turns of the journal to realize they spell out a phrase.

DANGER TO SELF.

I flip to the next page, immediately finding a letter in the center. I rotate it again to find another phrase.

OBSESSED.

More phrases link themselves into the drawings.

UNWILLING.

UNTREATABLE.

I'm close to the end of the journal when the illustrations change. They aren't as sharp, almost as if they are rushed. The slates of the structure are warped, like the world in the journal is tilted on its axis. The shape of the cradle is distinct though. Even more so is the emptiness within.

HER.

I shiver. What is the meaning of this image? Even though it's compelling, my stomach twists, and I shove to the next.

The last page of the journal is a half-completed drawing. It's not as detailed, only showing faint lines. I lean closer to the book. It isn't one or both girls, but a man. His twisted body lies in a heap. His eyes are open, staring through me.

One more phrase cuts into me.

STOP HIM.

I slam the journal closed and shove it under my pillow. My breath clings to my arm, but I don't move the quilt. I sink into a vision. The violence and terror living within the artist's mind. A low ringing settles in my ears, and I drop my head to the pillow.

The journal presses against my fingers. I trace the spine. I wanted to know the secrets of this family, and I found a big one. I'm not the only one with this curse. I focus on the feel of the leather under my fingers, keeping myself present even though the images flit through my mind like the soft pages.

Whoever experienced these things has a lot of trauma. I think of my mother. Either she or someone else in this house has been through some horrors, most likely created by the depths in their mind.

I shove the quilt off my face and inhale the swirling air blowing from the fan. It's not exactly cool, but it refreshes my skin enough compared to the heat from my cocoon of nightmares under the covers.

11

JENNY

My dreams swarm with black-and-white sketches from the journal.

I'm used to the nightmares. Sometimes, after a terrible vision, my mind ruminates while I'm sleeping. I'll relive each moment until it sorts itself out. I'm a vessel for these unlived scenarios to live and die.

The moment I arrive at the edge of consciousness, my eyes fling open, desperate to view the mundane. Darkness still consumes the room, but a sliver of light cuts through the horizon.

I move the quilt aside, peeling it off my damp body. I have never needed a shower more.

It's not even six in the morning, but there's no way I'm going back to bed. Other than not wanting to endure the dreams again, I'm no longer tired. The boxes call to me. I don't suspect they will hold the same secrets as a journal hidden under a hatch, but I trust a crumb of information will shake loose.

After guzzling an entire bottle of water in about ten seconds flat, I remove a box from the pile and place it on the table between the couches. A musty smell, like wet socks, wafts from the box and clings to my nose. Moving the top aside, I spot several sets of blank eyes staring at me.

If I hadn't lived in my twisted mind for twenty-five years, I might be the person who would jump away from such a frightening sight. But it's only a box full of dolls.

I lift two of them and inspect the faces. The perfect slight smile and wide eyes hint at a sinister agenda. As a child, I never enjoyed dolls. The frozen faces created a sense of unease within me. There are twenty of them, all girls in varying age ranges. The stiff and coarse clothing scratches against my skin.

"Those were my grandmother's." My mother's voice strikes me.

I grip the doll tighter, pressing my fingers into its soft middle.

She enters the room with a yawn. "I hated those things. My mother insisted on handing them down to me and my sister. I hid them in my closet when I could."

At least I'm not the only one creeped out by them.

She ruffles my hair. "How long have you been up?"

"Not that long. How did you sleep?"

"I feel like I should be the one asking you."

I shrug, understanding that she might not be aware of how tense she's been. One of us should get decent sleep while we're here.

"It's much warmer than I thought." She swipes a chunk of hair away from her face.

"Well, we're not here long."

She clears her throat. "We could have come sooner."

"Really?"

Her sigh fills the space. "I've been putting it off. The letter was the last straw."

Another secret.

She sighs again, as if she's trying to shake the weight of this house from her shoulders.

I don't blame her. The stifling heat in this house and seclusion from town is the opposite of our life in Ridgefield.

"Do you want me to make breakfast for us before I go?" she asks politely while she obviously wants to get this meeting over with.

"I'm not hungry just yet."

"I'm going to shower and then head out. Let me know if you change your mind." She ruffles my hair again and heads upstairs. The movement of water through the pipes sounds above me. We never lived in a building as old as this one, but I admittedly enjoy how this house comes to life whether it's during someone's shower or the creaks in the floor welcoming you into another room.

My phone pings, and an unfamiliar number accompanies the text.

Hey, it's Scott. I have time this morning to fix the sink. Can I come by?

My stomach flip-flops. I hate the way my body betrays me. It's the same feeling I had from Dennis, but Scott is even more temporary.

I'll be here.

While my mother is in the shower, I consume a bowl of fruity cereal. Sticking around the house all day alone isn't appealing, but maybe I can rope Scott into telling me more about what happened here. In small towns like Orhaven, with secluded houses nestled in the woods, surely there are rumors of the last inhabitants of this place.

My mother storms in and out of rooms looking for her keys. When she finds them, she tries to kiss me on the cheek, but her aim is off. Her eyes don't meet mine. I recall the private conversation with Walter in his office and wonder how much more she's not sharing with me. It's most likely why she's leaving me here, alone with boxes she's already checked so I won't find anything she doesn't want me to see.

I shake my head. When did she become the enemy? Looking at her through a new lens, I note the deepening lines at the corners of her eyes and the trembling of her hands. "Are you sure you don't want me to come?" I ask.

She lifts her purse from the side table, slinging it over her shoulder. "I would prefer you go through the boxes. If there's anything you want, put it aside. Otherwise, the rest can go."

I pretend she hadn't already rummaged through them when we brought them down from the attic. "You don't want to look through?"

She blows out a sharp breath through her teeth as if she's holding back a scream or a string of curse words. "I want nothing from this house." With that declaration, she leaves.

I'm unsure what happened to the contented person from last night. She seemed disinterested to look through the boxes, but she wasn't dismissive. Something changed overnight, and I suspect it has to do with where she's going.

With the slam of the door, the house seems to settle, almost letting out its own held breath. I approach the windows, watching our car amble down the path toward whatever step she needs to take to get this place out of her head for good.

Once she's out of sight, I turn to the boxes and inhale. The heavy heat in the room reminds me I woke in a pool of sweat. I need to shower before Scott arrives, and on the way up the stairs, I try to convince myself it's more for my personal hygiene than his lazy, sweet smile and kind eyes.

A knock on the door downstairs propels me from my room. I shove my hands through my hair to air-dry it. My flip-flops smack against my heels as I hustle down the stairs. It's already sweltering in the house, even with the help of my shorts and tank top baring enough skin to keep the heat at bay.

Scott is already at the back door when I arrive. I open it for him, unable to help offering him a smile.

A grin curves his lips. "Good morning."

I glance at the garbage disposal switch, and I swallow hard, reminding myself it was nothing more than a vision.

Scott turns on a thin metal flashlight and aims the beam into the sink hole. "I know you said you saw something, but I don't see it."

I push closer. The scent of mint radiates from him. "It was right there. Maybe it moved to the side?"

Scott puts up a hand. "I'm going to turn it on and see if it still grinds. I hate the idea of sticking my hand down there if I don't have to."

I balk, as if he has any idea what I've seen. "Okay." I inhale sharply, desperate to keep myself from having a total meltdown when that grinding sound fills my ears. It's one thing to experience a vision when my mother is around. I'll rush into another room, and she doesn't blink an eye. But I've witnessed dozens of strangers react to a rogue vision of mine. I don't want Scott to be one of them.

He flips the switch and turns the water on. I expect the blades to catch, but they don't. The water swirls down the drain, but that's it. After a few seconds, he switches it off, biting down on his lip. "Looks fine."

A frown tugs at the corners of my mouth. Was it a vision on top of a vision? It doesn't feel that way. Prickly heat bites at my neck, and I rub the spot with numb fingertips.

"These old houses have a lot of quirks."

I stare at the dark drain. Did I make the whole incident up and waste Scott's time? I examine what I know is true. I saw the item and saw my hand getting stuck, I'm sure of it. Whatever was inside was too large to fit down the drain.

Scott's presence doesn't help me concentrate, but I can't move from my spot. A tingle in the back of my mind awakens as it sifts through my memories.

Then I see her face.

My mother.

Yesterday, she jumped away from the sink when I brought the final box down. I'm unsure that what I see in my visions doesn't match reality. But when I saw her in the kitchen, I wasn't experiencing a vision. She took whatever was inside the disposal out. I'm sure of it. But why? I shouldn't be upset with her, but clearly, she's hiding something from me. And there's no way I'll ever get the answers I want unless I push for them.

Scott moves his tools around in his bag. He's still the only source I have for some truth about this place.

"Sorry to make you come out here."

Scott lifts a worn rag and wipes his hands. "It's not a problem. I want to help where I can." He digs a hand into his hip and glances around the room. "It'll be strange not coming out here anymore after the house sells, but at least I'll have more time for extra side work." He chuckles, and I try to meet his enthusiasm.

The time we have left in Orhaven closes in around me. Scott is here, and he's the only current link to this town. "What do you know about my grandparents?" I blurt out.

Scott's gaze darts to mine. His eyes widen slightly before he shakes his head. "Some."

I attempt to give him a dazzling tell-me-everything smile, but I'm terrible at lying. I go for the truth instead. "My mom is evasive about her past. She doesn't tell me anything, but apparently, my grandfather wasn't a great dad. I'm a bit desperate to find out more about my family. I could really use the help. I won't tell her you said something. I promise."

Scott crosses his arms, leaning against the counter. "Well, what do you know?"

I want to know more about my grandmother and if she was anything like me. I stretch the truth a little. It's not like Scott will tattle to my mother. "I know my grandmother had issues."

Scott's jaw clenches.

I push forward, not wanting to lose him. "My mom's really closed off to this stuff. She just can't talk about it, you know? So, anything you could tell me would really help me out."

"There are always rumors about people in this town. I'd hate to tell you something that's not true. Perhaps your mom is the best person to talk to you about this."

"Please. I'm a little desperate for an outside perspective."

Scott glances around the room as if he'd rather be anywhere else. I back away from him, tuning down my desperation. "I don't want to get in the middle of anything," he says.

He knows something. "In the middle of what?"

Scott gnaws on his lip. "I try to stay out of people's business. And it's been a few years . . ." He glances in the other room as if he's expecting my mother to burst in at any moment.

"Please?" I hate begging. I hate it even more than lying. My mind explodes with scenarios of my family's past that Scott could reveal.

He takes a deep breath. "What do you know about your aunt?"

"I know she died years ago. Did something else happen?"

Scott's forehead glistens with sweat. Is it because the house is warm or because I'm pressuring him too much?

"I know they were close as children," I tell him. "But my mom wanted to leave this place as quickly as she could, so when she graduated high school, she left and made her own life. I don't think they kept in touch after that."

Ruminating over it, I can't believe that's all I know about my mother's sister.

"You should dig deeper." Scott's voice flies into my mind, crashing through a barrage of questions.

"If you know something—"

"It's not my place. But I know where you might find more information."

That stops me from pressing him. "Where?"

The hardness of his eyes softens into pity. I'm not sure which I dislike more. "The library might be a good place to start. Do you want a ride?"

The uninterrupted time with the boxes was all I wanted earlier this morning, but Scott is dangling a lead. Once my mother returns from signing the paperwork, I'm not sure how long we'll have in town. She didn't have a problem leaving me with the boxes, but she never expected me to find a clue on my quest for the truth.

"I'd love a ride. Yes."

The trip to town isn't as quiet and awkward as I expect after grilling Scott for information. Granted, most of our conversation is swallowed by the rattling of tools in the bed of the truck. As we gain distance from the house, my shoulders relax. The last time I was alone with a guy, it didn't end well. Scott has a different presence. There's no pressure between us. I'll probably never see him again after today, so I don't care much about his impression of me. The lack of anxiety keeps the visions at bay.

"What's it like to live here?" I ask.

Scott shrugs. "It can get a little mundane at times, but I like the quiet for the most part. The people here are kind, and my dad is here, so . . ."

"Mike mentioned that you wanted to leave?"

"I haven't mentioned leaving in some time. But Mike rarely forgets anything."

"You two seem close," I say.

"He adopted me after my mom died, and we've been working together since, so I suppose we are."

The town center appears in front of us, and I sit up straighter, anticipating our arrival at the library. I hope it will give me answers even though my gut fills with an unwelcome pressure. Each moment away from my mother is an opportunity to get closer to my family, but it almost seems wrong without her. Though, if she would just tell me things, I wouldn't have to sneak around.

My mother rarely talks about her sister, yet Scott thinks I should divert my efforts away from my grandmother and toward my aunt. I wish he would tell me what he knows.

"Did you have breakfast?" Scott turns the knob for the air conditioning. It's no competition for the air blasting through the open windows, blowing warm air around us.

"A bowl of cereal." He wants to have breakfast with me. His friendly attitude has returned, but now I'm on a mission. I have to know what he knows about my aunt before returning to the house. Once I arm myself with information, I can prove to my mother that I'm worthy of knowing the rest.

"I have to get to work for a bit, but if you want a good late breakfast or lunch, Greta's is the best." He coughs out a laugh.

"Actually, it's the only diner in town, but it's the best in the surrounding counties."

"Sounds good. Thank you."

"Not a problem."

I focus on the road and feel the heat of his eyes on me.

"Family stuff can be hard, but maybe you should keep an open mind," he says.

I have about everything since we arrived in Orhaven. Now, I may have a family member who experiences the same visions as me, and I understand it could be genetic. Peeling open the curtain to the Miller household can't be much worse. "Have you always kept an open mind?"

He smirks, and my gaze drops to his lips. "It took some time. Growing up in a blended family does that, I suppose. But I needed a place or people to feel as if I belong. As long as I'm okay with my own actions, I'm content."

I wonder if I'll ever feel that way. Most likely, Scott knows the intricacies of his past and his family while I don't.

The truck pulls up to a building. The words *Orhaven Library* are cut into the wooden sign.

"Thanks for the ride."

"Anytime." Scott rests his arm on the back of the bench seat. His hand brushes against my shoulder. "If you want to take me up on the offer for a meal, you have my number."

I close the door. The metal groans with the effort. "I do."

Scott's slow grin forces me to turn away. He's like the sun, too bright and warm to look at directly. "I should be in town for a couple of hours. I can bring you back later."

I don't know when my mother is getting back to the house, but at least the promise of a ride won't leave me stranded here. "Yeah, let me know when you're done."

"See you."

"Bye."

I move away from the truck, and he navigates farther into town. He's turning the corner when I whirl around to face the library.

A hard body smashes into my side, knocking the wind out of me. I suck in a breath. "I'm so sorry. Are you all right?"

The girl can't be over thirteen. Her dark eyes well with tears, but not because I hurt her. Fire burns within those depths. She pushes closer to me and points a black-polished finger in my face. I'm too stunned to move. "You!"

"I didn't mean to bump into you. I wasn't paying attention."

She gets in my face. "Where is my mom?"

I step away from her, wondering if I've stumbled into a twisted yet normal version of a vision, or possibly a strange dream. "I'm not from here. I don't know your mom. Are you lost?"

"You came back here. Spawn of that twisted family in the woods. Now, my mother is missing. Where is she? What have you done?"

I blink a few times. There's no one else around. "I don't know what you're talking about. Maybe I can help you look for her?" I glance around at the street.

"Help me?" she shrieks, loud enough for a group of three teen girls to turn and gape at us.

"Whoa. Calm down."

The girls walk away, clearly not wanting to be involved. Almost as much as I don't either.

"Tell me where she is right now!" the girl demands.

"What's going on here, Zelda?" a husky voice calls from behind me.

I tear my eyes away from the girl—Zelda—and come face-to-face with a police officer. Her navy-blue uniform screams authority. Even though I'm not involved with any disappearance, I lift my hands slightly in surrender.

The officer's eyes are hidden behind a set of aviator sunglasses, which she doesn't remove. Her deep umber skin is flawless, but her expression is tight. This woman knows me from nothing and will take the girl's side over mine. I'm going to get arrested today. This is my punishment for leaving the house. I open my mouth to plead my innocence before Zelda interrupts.

"You know it's Zee," Zee snaps at the woman with a familiarity I've never had with a police officer before.

How will I explain myself to this officer when she is on a first-name basis with Zee?

"All right, Zee. I know you want Wren home, but it doesn't do much for you to accuse random people in the streets." The officer tilts her head to me. "You can put your hands down, ma'am. I'm Davina Anderson. Town sheriff. Can I get your name?" She drops her sunglasses, revealing an accusing set of brown eyes.

"Jenny Miller," I say, trying to keep my voice and mind steady.

Zee's hands grip her waist, digging into her jeans as if she's trying to squeeze the life out of them. "They come back, and people go missing. You of all people should think that's fishy." She points another finger at me.

"I understand you're upset, Zee. But we're working on it. I know that's difficult to hear. Don't you have to get to your volunteer job?" Davina has a calm tone with her, mesmerizing even.

"They would understand if I caught the person who did something to my mother."

"That's enough accusing now." Davina stands straighter, angling herself between Zee and me. "I'll stop by after I get my breakfast, and we can speak privately."

"Fine," Zee says with an eye roll and then turns to me. "I'm watching you." She whirls on her heels and races up the stone steps to the front door of the library.

Just my luck.

Davina turns to face me, and I avoid her eyes. But I'm not sure for how long without explaining what the hell that girl was talking about.

12

THEN

Four days is too long for you to be out there. Even though I check on you twice each day—once in the early morning, and at night to conceal as much of my identity as possible—you're not responding to me in the way I want.

I've planned for a week out here before you fully break. There's no way you can stay away from her much longer.

You've been through the steps, each of them ticking a check mark in my mind.

You tell me about your life, your daughter.

You scream at me until your voice is hoarse.

You cry and threaten me.

I remind you that once you've done what I want, you can leave on your own.

You don't believe me. You don't listen. You want out.

It's the one challenge I knew I'd face with this method. You need to realize how important your family is. I want you to cherish us, so when you return home, you'll have a sense of what you need in life, instead of what you think you want. Leaving this place was never an option.

Today feels different. The sun is nearly down across the horizon. I have little time tonight, as she's getting used to me being the caregiver—a position I never thought I would fill, yet I yearn for it. It brings me to a different time.

When you get home, you'll be surprised when you see how close we are.

A calmness surges through me like a cool breeze during this heat wave. Too bad there isn't one. The mask scratches at my face tonight. It's too warm, but my identity needs to remain secure.

Today is the day that you will submit to your life in Orhaven. No more talk of leaving "this place." You say that as if it's a curse. But no other place could handle people like us. We can be who we are in this small town where we've been accepted since childhood.

I try to make enough sound with the leaves and debris under my boots to alert you of my arrival.

I'm typically good at predicting your moods, but in this situation, I anticipate all the versions of you I've seen. Preparation is key to this plan working.

The door is the last announcement that your captor is here. I push it, but it barely moves. I push again, harder.

This is a new test for me, and my heart races at the challenge. You clever woman. At least your fighting spirit hasn't faltered.

My excitement turns to an icy dread when I realize how far you've gone across the room. The rope shouldn't allow you so close to the door. Unless you've somehow freed yourself.

I lift the club from my belt. I haven't used it on you since you've been in the woods, but I won't hesitate. The lesson is more important than your vanity. If I need to subdue you, I will.

I shove my body against the door, hoping to alarm you enough to catch you off guard. The door still resists, and yet you're not there, ready to attempt an escape. It's the most probable reaction, and it's one you haven't tried yet.

The scenarios of your escape flit through my mind. It would make sense for you to wait until I was inside before you use that rope against me. It's the only weapon in your arsenal.

The most significant weapon I have is expecting all your moves. Coupled with the club, you're not getting out of here without my explicit permission.

Movement from the ground forces my foot forward. The heel of my boot connects with your body.

You fall to the ground like a sack of soil. Holding the door open with my foot, I grab the flashlight attached to my belt and shine the beam at you.

A breath lodges in my throat.

Your hair across your face isn't right. I didn't kick your chest.

The scene in my mind shifts to reality. You weren't coming after me. You're coming after no one in that position. My dirty footprint mocks me from the back of your shirt.

"Get up!"

Nothing.

A moan escapes my lips. I rush to the ground and scoop you against my body. I move a chunk of hair from your face. Your mouth parts slightly, and no breath comes out. You're too heavy. Dead weight.

Dead.

I stand on trembling legs and bring you outside. There's enough moonlight for me to examine you and help. If there's anything left to help.

The steps of my process drift through my mind. I did everything right. You shouldn't be dead. You were protected. You're not bleeding . . .

That's where I'm wrong.

As I place you on the forest floor, your head slumps to the side. Blood stains my arms and shirt. Where is it coming from?

I drop the club and flashlight, needing to assess the problem and fix it. You will not die in these woods. The only blood on my hands has been to protect you. Without you, my moral compass will swing back to where it was. Even she can't bring me out of it.

I roll you onto your side. Your wild hair covers your face again. I leave it there. I can't stand to see the stillness in your eyes any longer.

The source of the blood is your wrists. There's nothing inside the shelter you could have cut yourself on. You aren't the suicidal type. You're stronger than me in so many ways. Besides, you have her to think about.

I rip the bottom part of my shirt into two strips. I wrap them around your wrists, tight enough to stop the bleeding.

I need to untie the rope, but my fingers hover over the woven fabric. The bloodstained torn threads barely hold your binds. A heavy darkness spreads through me, and I recoil from your body.

A sharp pain explodes at the side of my head. My eyes close as a whine erupts in my ears, but only for a moment before my instincts snap into place. Father taught me to bounce back from these incidents quickly.

Fingers claw at my neck before the sweet release of air kisses my cheeks. "No!"

You're awake. Somehow, you're here, looking at me with the widest eyes. The surprise morphs into anger. I've gotten used to that expression over the last few weeks, but that was when you didn't know it was me.

I fight the urge to hide my face, understanding that I need to control the situation again. I'll worry about the rest later.

You strike me again with the club. This time, you hit the right spot.

The ground rushes to meet my face. It doesn't compare with the hurt thundering in my head, or the screaming in my mind. Get up! Get up! It's not the voice in my head, but Father's.

For once in my life, my body doesn't do what it needs. Instead, as the edges of my vision peel away into darkness, I watch you run.

If you go to her, you'll never return to me.

I must stop you.

13

JENNY

Davina scrutinizes me. I need to take hold of this conversation or else this woman might think I had something to do with Zee's mother's disappearance. "I'm sorry that I upset her."

We're about the same height, but when Davina lifts her chin, her presence looms over me like one of the massive trees in the woods surrounding the house. "Nora's daughter, right?"

"You know my mother?"

"Yes." Her lips press together slightly, guarding a secret I'm not privy to.

A rush like when I was alone with Scott fills me. This is another person I can question about my mother's past, though I doubt she'll be as forthcoming as him.

"How long are you in town for?" she asks, scoping the people walking by. She offers them a tight-lipped smile and nod. It disappears when she looks at me.

"A couple of days."

Davina takes off her sunglasses, and I almost wish she'd put them back on. Even though she was short with Zee, there was understanding there. Not with me. "I suggest you and your mother keep to yourself in that house while you're here."

"Because of Zee? I told you, I didn't do anything."

She looks away, almost as if she's speaking to someone a few feet behind me. "Orhaven has been a quiet and peaceful town for a long time, and I intend to keep it that way."

"You think we're going to do something?"

Her lips purse together.

I can't help but dig. "What do you have against my mother?"

"Do as I ask." It sounds formal, but she lands the hard consonants of the words, effectively shutting me up for fear of landing myself inside of her car. She lifts her phone from her belt and reviews the screen for a few moments before replacing it. "Do you need a ride? I'll happily escort you."

The accusation from Zee and subsequent evasiveness of the cop makes me want to go in the library even more to question the girl.

"No, I'm fine. I have my car." I gesture at the street, hoping she doesn't call my bluff.

"Well then. Have a nice day." Davina dips her head before slipping by me.

I walk in the opposite direction. This time when I count, it's not to stave off a vision but the possibility of another encounter with Davina. Scott is gone, and I can't call him to take me back to the house this soon after leaving. I have to find out more. Davina said she was coming back to check on Zee, so I have a limited amount of time, and I intend to make every second count. With a deep breath, I peer over my shoulder to make sure Davina is gone before heading back toward the building.

· · ·

Inside, the library lobby's arched doorways lead my gaze upward to the second floor. A railing wraps around the balcony, revealing stacks of books leading farther than I can see.

Across the room, a woman sits behind what I presume is the checkout desk. She stares at a computer screen while I absorb the rest of my surroundings. An open glass door next to the desk reveals a computer lab.

I debate asking the librarian directly about events in the town's history that might involve the Miller family, but I take my chances in the computer lab first. I need a more direct question to ask her other than snooping around like a lost child.

In the room, two rows of four computer stations face each other with a wooden partition between. Three other people sit facing the windows.

I walk around them and claim the station on the end facing the door. I don't need Zee surprising me again, or Davina spotting me when she comes inside to check on the girl.

The mouse buttons are worn, and the letters on the keyboard are barely visible under a rubbery plastic key cover. I grab it and slide over the pad. The worn fabric advertises a local bank. The ball on the bottom catches on the pad and the screen wakes.

The internet browser takes more than a minute to load. I glance at the doorway, wondering if I'll have better luck speaking to someone. I catch the eye of the man sitting closest to me. He immediately lowers his gaze to the screen in front of him.

I check my phone. The service bar goes between one and zero. The computer is my only chance.

I type search terms into the bar: Valerie Miller. Orhaven, Pennsylvania.

I scroll through the results. There have been other Valeries linked to the location, but most of them obituaries. Not one with the Miller last name.

Which is odd since she passed years ago.

I add the word *death* to the search bar.

The next results show a strike through the name Miller. A headline catches my attention:

Local Librarian Murders Beloved Doctor

I hover over the first result. It's from the Orhaven newspaper. The top of the site shows that this is a subscription service, but how many people would be clamoring for news from this town? Though it's probably why I wasn't able to find anything before.

The two-sentence blurb underneath reads, "Valerie Whitford has been charged with the death of Dr. Archibald Bradley. After a town-wide search, local authorities unearthed the body of the doctor, who had served the town of Orhaven for over thirty-five years."

I click the article, and it opens the top banner of the news site. The words don't appear until several agonizing seconds later. My heart counts them down with thundering bumps.

The date of the article is two years ago. The mugshot of the woman slowly reveals itself. My leg bounces with anticipation. I glance at the other computers. All of them look like they're from the nineties.

When it finally pushes through, there's no doubt in my mind that this woman, Valerie Whitford, is my aunt. The slope of her nose and the slight crooked smile match my mother's.

I scroll down.

The article goes into detail about the accusation of my aunt murdering a local doctor. The facts are all there, but my mind takes it a step further, pulling from the violent depths of my visions, plugging in my version of the story between the words. I see the police in a backyard, pulling out an older gentleman's dead body from the earth.

The journal pages return to me. The last picture. The faint sketch of the living room.

The man on the floor.

My gut twists, and the rush of an oncoming vision blurs the computer lab.

"Five," I push through gritted teeth, closing my eyes. A flicker of light from the room peeks through. Refocusing my mind and grounding myself in public rarely works, but I need it to happen now. I've avoided enough public places with my visions, but when they happen, it's not a pretty sight. I can't draw more attention to my family than Zee's already brought to the sheriff.

"Four." I breathe slowly and peer through blurry eyes. No one else in the room notices the world inside my mind falling apart.

"Three." My fingernails dig into my palms.

"Two." I open my eyes and focus on the blurry words on the screen. This is what I came here for. This is what I need to do right now.

I hold at two. The cracking of bones, depicting what may have happened the night of the doctor's death, rolls in a continuous loop in my mind.

"One." I breathe through it, focusing on the words. While I'm experiencing the vision, they don't make sense and are a jumble of letters. But the more I stare at them, the easier the vision fades until I take control of my mind again.

I read the article again, deliberately absorbing each sentence. The body of the doctor was buried in the garden at the house— my mother's house—and found weeks after his death. My skin prickles.

This must be what Scott meant about not wanting to talk to me about my aunt. My mother lied to me about her. She said Valerie had died years ago, and I believed her. I suspect it was one way she could prevent me from researching my family. My mother must have changed our last name at some point, as she never married my father. But Valerie was convicted two years ago.

I understand Zee's outburst now. Somewhat. My aunt murdered a prominent person from this town, but assuming we're involved in her mother's disappearance is a stretch. Though I'm sure my aunt has made quite an impression on the people in this town. Since my mother hasn't been to Orhaven in years, the two events could be more than coincidence for them.

The journal with the horrific images, which I initially pegged as from my grandmother, shifts in my mind. If Valerie committed this crime, she has violence inside her. Unlike me.

My stomach rolls, and I dig my fingers into the shortcut keys to print out the article. The printer in the corner churns out the three pages, and I race over there to grab them before anyone sees the horrific article title and asks questions. I can't imagine the citizens of Orhaven want to relive a time when someone in the community was murdered on the outskirts of town.

When I reach the computer again, I go back to the main search results and plug in a new last name: Valerie Whitford. Orhaven, Pennsylvania.

The articles reveal several mentions of Valerie throughout the years before she murdered the doctor. She'd been a part of local fundraisers, appearing in pictures but never smiling. She had a stand at a local farmers market and even received accolades for her produce.

In that article, the photo is grainy but clearly her. Valerie wears a striped frock, and her hair is tied in a tight bun at the nape of her neck. The article date is almost five years ago, but she's dressed from another time. The billowing dress swallows her frame.

I sit back in the chair, a low buzzing rising in my ears. My mother said my aunt was dead. But here she is, clearly alive and thriving long after my mother left this place. Now, she's a convicted murderer.

I search for the murder with directed keywords.

No other website talks about her murdering anyone. Apparently, this case didn't move outside of Orhaven, even though the conversation with Zee shows the impact of how others in town look at our family.

I recall meeting the older couple and Mrs. Peters' reaction to my mother. At least that's consistent.

I print as many articles as I can find with her name, mostly shorter announcements of town events. The clock says I've been in the library for over thirty minutes. I'm cutting it too close to Davina returning and finding me so close to Zee after her clear warning. Outside, I may have appeared somewhat innocent, but I wouldn't if she caught me here.

I race over to the printer and pull the remaining pages from the tray. With the articles in hand, I roll them up and stuff them into my bag. I have to process this information with no one around. Once I can do that, I'll have enough evidence to confront my mother. She'll have no choice but to talk.

I leave the room, more aware of everyone around me. I wait for someone to point out I'm the niece of the Orhaven murderer. I imagine the modern version of pitchforks coming after me and my mother, accusing us of our involvement with the crime.

Movement from a room the size of a closet calls to me. Zee holds a stack of books and is shelving them. A piece of paper taped to the wall outside reads "Book Sale" in a slanted scrawl.

The massive double doors at the front of the lobby beckon

me as I remember Davina's warning. But with the urge to know more, I ignore it and go to Zee.

Watching Zee without the scowl on her face, she looks younger than she did before. The lines of anger cutting her cheeks are gone. Am I really about to interrogate this girl who's terrified about her mother going missing?

Reality settles on me. This isn't her burden.

I veer to the left, knowing I can't involve her in my family.

"Hey!" Her voice strikes me more than the loud accusation outside. Zee glares at me with narrowed eyes, her fingers curled around the books against her chest.

"I was just leaving," I say.

"Don't." Her eyes dart toward the front door before settling on me. "I need to know where my mother is."

"Like I said, I don't know anything." As I approach her, she shoves the books onto the shelf and crosses her arms.

I'm several feet away before she holds her hands up. "That's far enough. What about your mother?"

"I don't know why you're accusing my mother of having anything to do with yours."

"She was the last person to contact my mom."

I blink a few times. "That's not true."

Zee shakes her head. "I have proof." She lifts a phone from her pocket. The case is pink with a floral pattern across the back. It doesn't seem like her style. "She's attached to this thing more than I am. She goes everywhere with her phone. Read the last texts." She holds out the phone, and I reach for it.

She snatches it away from me. "You can read it from there. I don't need anyone destroying the evidence."

This girl sounds as if she's seen too many crime shows.

We need to meet

This isn't over yet

I can't live like this anymore.

Please.

Our spot.

OK.

The contact of the last text isn't saved in the phone, but I recognize the familiar string of numbers, starting with my area code. I check the time stamp. My mother responded yesterday morning. It was around the time when she woke me to tell me she needed to meet with Walter.

Zee takes her phone back. "You see why I would accuse her?"

I do. "Did you show this to Davina?"

"She brushed me off. Said she was going to talk to your mother about it."

As much as I hate that my mother is lying to me about her whereabouts, she's not a criminal. My aunt is. There are secrets in this family, and I intend to dig up each one. But I can't convince myself that she would ever hurt another person. There has to be an explanation, and I won't allow this girl to accuse my family of more disappearances.

"I've been with her the entire time we've been in Orhaven. The only people we've met so far have been Mike and Scott Allen."

"She's not with you now."

Touché.

"Whatever," she says. "I know my mom met yours somewhere. The texts prove that. We know what your family does to the people in this town." She takes a wide berth around me and walks behind the checkout desk. The librarian's stare remains fixed on me.

I don't want to leave yet. I've opened the secrets of our past, and I want more. Like my visions taking over against my will, this situation drives me toward the truth, no matter how much it's already resembling a nightmare.

To get away from the librarian's incriminating stare, I enter the small room, hoping Zee will return to stack more books. I grab the first one. The bright blue spine is cracked with use. I flip through it and turn it over, pretending to read the description.

I check out four more books before peering at the desk again. The librarian types away on her computer, but Zee hasn't returned. I don't know how long I'll be able to keep up the ruse.

The cover of the tattered romance book in my hands nearly rips. It tears away, starting at the top corner. I struggle to hold it in place until I note familiar handwriting in the corner. It's in pencil, noting the price.

The book in the home library looked the same. Did my aunt buy books from this sale over the years?

A flash of the basement comes to mind. The stack of books next to the bed. At first, I assumed my mother slept down there. But what if it was my aunt? Was that why she locked the basement door and kept the key? Was she trying to lock away any evidence that I might find of my aunt?

With a new lens, the itch to get back to the house overwhelms me. More answers wait for me there, as I'm finally equipped with the twisted questions.

I scoot out of the room and race to the front doors.

Outside, my overwhelming excitement about discovering more in the house deflates as I realize that I can't get back there on my own.

I grab my phone and cradle it in my hands. With my mother thinking I'm at the house, I can't call her. I open two of the ride-sharing apps on my phone and check for nearby vehicles. I'm not surprised when I find none. My insistence on leaving the house was too spontaneous to consider how I would get back.

Scott is the only option.

I found what I needed at the library. I need to get back to the house. Are you around?

While I don't expect him to return my message right away, three typing dots appear almost immediately.

I'm sorry I couldn't tell you about what she did. Didn't feel right. Are you OK?

Scott knowing the full story of my murderous aunt—and still treating me like a normal person—gives me hope that Zee will eventually stop accusing my mother of her mother's disappearance.

I'm fine. Thank you.

I can't get away right now, but Mike is in town. I'll ask him.

I hesitate. Mike and my mother have a past. Surely, he will tell her what happened today. Though, the risk is worth it if I get more alone time with the house.

OK.

The conversation between my mother and me about Mike comes to mind. He was perfectly kind to us and seems to hold good memories with her.

Go to Greta's. He's heading out.

Thanks.

I head toward the diner. It's a few doors down from the library, but I keep my eyes open for Davina or anyone else trailing me. Outside the diner, the windows peer back at me with a blurry version of myself.

A vision creeps its inky tendrils into my peripheral vision. I wobble on my feet until my back bumps against the glass.

No, not here.

"Whoa there, you okay?" Mike's gruff voice resounds.

I widen my eyes, desperate to shove the darkness to the depths of my mind where it belongs. Mike's body and the street behind him ebbs and flows. I fight harder than I have ever before to keep conscious and not experience a vision in front of him.

"Do you need some water?" Mike lifts a bottle from his pocket and twists the cap open, handing it over.

I sip the warm liquid. I wonder how long it's been in his back pocket. "Thank you."

"This summer has been brutal." Mike lifts his gaze to the sky, tipping the brim of his hat. Now that he's not hiding under its shadow, I get a good look at his eyes. They're pale blue and striking as the sun lightens them even more.

"Did Scott get in touch with you?" I'm desperate to move on from the embarrassing situation.

"Yeah, he did," Mike says from the corner of his mouth. "Good thing, too. I was about to head out myself."

"Oh, I don't want to be a bother."

He turns to me, his expression tight. "I never said you were a bother. I only meant it's on my way."

"Great."

His stubby fingers point at a truck parked against the curb. "Your chariot awaits."

14

JENNY

Inside Mike's truck, the scent of cigarette smoke permeates the ripped leather cushions. In some spots, duct tape lines the damage. Searing heat burns the backs of my legs, and I prop my toes to sit them higher.

"Sorry about that." Mike tosses me a towel from the pocket on the door.

I shove it under my legs. "Thanks."

He pulls away from the curb and heads down the road. "Where's Nora today?"

"Picking up paperwork for the house." So she says . . .

Mike adjusts his hat. "Seems like selling the house is more work than she thought."

"Yeah." I sip from the water bottle.

"What were you doing downtown?"

"I wanted to go to the library."

He glances at my bag. "You get what you were looking for?"

"Yeah." I consider mentioning how Scott brought up my aunt, but I don't want to get him into trouble with his dad. But if I don't ask, I'll never get answers. "I wanted to find out more about my aunt."

"Valerie." Her name catches on his tongue as if he's swallowed something foul. "I wondered how much Nora told you."

"She's told me nothing." I can't help the thick scorn in my voice. Mike and Scott brought her up so easily, yet my mother hasn't uttered our true surname in my presence.

"I'm sure she was trying to protect you."

"I think I should know if a family member of mine is a murderer." I'm not sure why the words flow out of me, especially to practically a stranger. But it feels nice to get it off my chest.

Mike clicks his tongue. "She's serving the time."

"Did you know Valerie well?"

He lifts a shoulder, dropping it ever so slightly. "As much as you know anyone in a place like this. Most kids play together since there's only one school. I was more friendly with your mother since we're closer in age."

"How much older is Valerie?"

"Four years, but that doesn't make much of a difference in this town. Your aunt loved your mother from the day she was born. She always protected her so fiercely. Much different to how I grew up."

"How so?"

"I had an older brother, but we couldn't be more opposite."

Had?

As if he heard my internal question, he carries on. "He died before I graduated high school."

I sense the strong period at the end of that sentence, similar to how my mother closes a conversation when she's not interested in talking anymore. "I'm sorry."

"It was a long time ago."

I don't want to be rude, but the trip to the house isn't going to last forever, and I have to get as much new information about Valerie as possible. "Do you know why Valerie killed that doctor?"

He cocks his head to the side. "Only she knows that."

"She confessed though?"

"She did."

"Without an explanation?"

He sighs, reminding me of my mother. The clock counting down her arrival to the house ticks loudly in my ears.

"When she lived here, Valerie enjoyed her solitude. She said what she meant and only answered just enough of a question asked. If you want answers, she's the only one who can give them to you."

"She's in prison."

"It's not a far ride from here."

I watch Mike's expression for any sign of what he'll say next, but he doesn't continue and keeps his focus on the road. Silence gives my mind the opportunity to wander. I have no clue where it will take me.

"Do you know why my mother said Valerie died?" It's a personal question that I'm sure only she can answer, but it's worth a try. Mike knew her when she was a child. If I can get a sense of a full picture of her, it's from him.

The woods creep up, surrounding the road within seconds, and the rest of the world disappears. I sit against the seat, even though the heat sears my bare shoulders.

"They went through a lot in their childhood. It seemed as if Nora wanted a clean break when she left. She didn't even say goodbye to anyone. Not even her sister."

From his tone, it seems like he's still not happy with that. "From what you know, did she ever contact Valerie?"

"That's something you'll have to ask her."

Once again, he brings up talking to Valerie. How is that even possible? My mother would never allow a visit to see the sister she cut off all those years ago. Even as the pieces come together, my mother's story is the only one missing. It will bring the narrative together so we can both move on.

When the house appears up the winding road, I realize I've been quiet for several minutes. Mike hasn't interrupted my internal struggle, and I suspect he knows how much understanding my family means to me. "Thank you for the ride."

"We might seem like country folk, but we are tight knit."

"I can see that." I recall the conversation between Davina and Zee. In two days, I've discovered more secrets and lies in this place than in any other town we've lived in before. Or maybe all towns are like this, and I never paid attention.

Our car isn't in the driveway. At least I still have control over this situation for the time being.

The truck rolls to a stop. I don't open the door right away. Instead, I turn to Mike. "Would you mind keeping my visit downtown between us?"

Mike chuckles. "Of course. But just so you know, some secrets kept are more harmful than if shared."

"I'm going to tell her." Eventually. I shoulder my bag. "Thanks again."

I shove the door open and slide out. Mike waves before driving away.

Alone with the house, I peer up at it. It seems bigger than it did before. I imagine my mother as a teenager, wanting to get out of this place. I don't blame her, but I don't intend on living out of the loop any longer.

Walking inside with more information, the space seems new and unexplored. Every surface has been touched by my aunt. She's the one who lived here two years ago. Scott talking about local troublemakers breaking into this house may be true, but it hasn't been that long since Valerie lived within these walls. He must think I'm dumb or uninterested in my family.

I head for the living room, intent on using whatever time left to go through the boxes. I'll tell my mom what I know, but not until I have a fuller story. Once she realizes what I've done in my search for the truth, there's no way she can refuse to fill in the gaps.

The emptiness of the house coupled with the idea that a murderer lived here creates an unsettling twist in my stomach. I turn on my music app and shove my phone in my back pocket to push as much of myself into the space as possible, keeping Valerie's negative spirit outside my bubble.

I go through the boxes, finding stuffed animals and knock-off Barbie dolls. They're even creepier than the ancient dolls. Some of them barely have hair, and thick red marker mars the surface of the unclothed bodies. The lines dissect the dolls like a surgeon might.

My stomach rolls. I don't need more than one guess to know whose they were.

Small glass cases fill the next two boxes. Collectible coins and decorative spoons remain frozen in time. I inspect the dates on the coins. Some date back to the 1800s. The coins might be worth money, so I put those aside.

Clothes burst from the next box. The scratchy fabric and brown knitted patterns scream the 1970s. A small jewelry box takes up a corner. Inside are necklaces, bracelets, and earrings. I sift through them and find a diamond engagement ring.

I slide it onto my finger, and it fits perfectly. I hold it out. The diamond doesn't shimmer, but it's beautiful regardless. There was a time when my grandparents were so in love that they promised their lives to each other. Whatever happened after is unfortunate, and I remove the ring and drop it back into the box. I add the jewelry box to my "maybe" pile and put the rest on the growing stack across the room to be thrown away.

The other boxes don't reveal Valerie's twisted mind, but the last one holds several photo albums. The spines crack open to plastic pages stuck together. I peel them away from each other, the plastic protectors ripping slightly. The color from the photos faded with time, but they are clear. The images of my grandparents as young parents fill the gaps in my mind. Their faces don't resemble what I originally thought. They're all fair-haired, even my grandfather.

I suppose my father's genes colored my dark locks.

The years go quickly as I progress through the albums, starting when my aunt and mother were born. Each of the images appears staged, and neither of my grandparents show a hint of amusement or happiness.

The memories of this family are as bleak as they are now. Valerie and my mother are the only ones still alive, and one of them is in prison.

I bring the albums to the couch and sit, scrutinizing each season of their lives. There are other people in some pictures who I don't recognize, probably others from town. I'm unaware if we have any other family members, but once again, I now have to question whether what I know is the truth.

The memories span from when my mother was a baby through adolescence. It ends with a birthday party. My mother sits at the kitchen table, her mouth pursed to blow out the candles on the cake in front of her. On the happy occasion, my grandmother sits next to her, poised with an impassive expression across her face. My mother looks closer to Zee's age, and I can't believe all those years of her life took up one album.

I pick up the next one and open it. I expect the pictures to continue, but the page is blank. I flip to the next, and there's one picture in the page's corner, but the rest of it is empty. The pages throughout the album are entirely blank or there are one or two pictures in no order. They continue the timeline of my mother graduating high school, plus birthdays and holidays. Neither my aunt nor my grandparents are present in any of the photographs.

Closer to the end of the book, darker spots hint that someone removed pictures after they were there for a while. I flip through faster, needing to find a connection to why some pictures are there while others are missing.

The last book is newer than the rest. The cover is a pale pink with small silhouettes of rabbits peppered throughout. The inside isn't as worn as the other albums. There are no pictures or any hint they used this in the past.

I put that one aside and look through the second album again. I know I won't have answers until she comes home, but it's nice to see her carefree.

The major difference is her choice in clothing. As a teenager, she wore tank tops and flowing, short-sleeved T-shirts. When did her fashion choices shift to tight, long-sleeved clothing?

A car sounds in the distance, and I stand to go to the window. Our car travels up the driveway. Somehow, my mother's presence doesn't excite me as much as I thought it would.

I put the albums away and drop them into the "maybe" pile. The items from her past barely take up a corner of the room. It's sad that the lives of four people are reduced to a pile of garbage. Once they are taken away, the memories within the items will be forgotten. For her, it seems easy to put aside her family, but my heart aches at the lives that will cease to exist once the house and the contents inside are gone.

With her so near, I wonder if she already knows about my visit to town. Mike said the people in Orhaven are close, and Davina knows everything about everyone. Would they have contacted her before her arrival home? Their loyalty isn't to me, but I hope to be the one to explain to my mother that I have new information and want the truth.

Heat surges under my skin, and prickling anxiety swells within me, building up enough that I'm about to burst when she enters the room.

"Hey," I say a little too loud.

"Hi." Her tone is flat and less enthusiastic than mine.

"Everything go okay?"

She settles on the couch, tilting her chin toward the ceiling. She doesn't want to talk, but it's what I need after being alone for so long. I turn off my music and sit next to her.

"This is a lot more complicated than I realized." She massages her forehead.

Dark circles rest under her eyes. Whether it's the heat or the memories of this place keeping her awake, she's not doing much sleeping.

"What do you need to do?"

She ignores my question and glances at the corner of the room. "You got a lot figured out."

More than she knows. "I left these for you to go through. And the last two boxes are old photo albums. I wasn't sure if you wanted to keep them."

"I don't."

"Not even one?"

"Jenny, I don't think that's a good idea."

"Why not?" What else is she hiding? She was in the attic while I brought the pictures down. She had time to remove what she didn't want me to see.

She sighs. "It's been a tough day."

"Did you take the pictures out?"

"What pictures?"

"Dozens of pictures are missing from the albums."

"I didn't take them out."

"Did Valerie?"

"What are you going on about?"

I won't accept her lies anymore. The need for the truth bubbles inside me. Like the drive of a vision, I push through my tendency to always stay silent. She has to know I'd find something to negate what she's told me over the years. "Why did you lie about our last name?"

Her exhaustion snaps away from her as if she's come out of a trance. "Excuse me?"

"Whitford."

"Where did you hear that?" She's standing now, the hem of her sleeves straining under her rigid fingers.

"It's true, then?"

"Why are you asking when you already know? I want to know who told you."

I take a moment to absorb what she's said. "Everyone here knows, except for me."

"It's for your own good."

"I found it myself." With prompting from Scott's cryptic questioning about knowledge of my family, but getting him into trouble won't help. "I googled it. Why did you hide this from me?"

"I didn't want you to know."

"That your sister is a murderer? Instead, you told me she was dead." I can't help the emotion filling my voice. We never yell at each other, but I can't help it.

"She's dead to me!" She matches my tone, and tears spring to her eyes. "To me, she died a long time ago. Killing that innocent man was the last nail in her coffin." Her face crumples, and she tries to hide it behind her hands.

"I would have understood." I can't stand to see her like this. We've never fought this hard before, and I want to open the conversation, not force her into closing it.

"I never wanted you to understand. I didn't want you to know anything about this place."

"Because she killed someone?"

"It's more than that."

I wait for her to explain, but she turns away from me, crossing her arms over her chest.

"This was a terrible idea. I should have never come back." She speaks so quietly that I barely hear her. I'm unsure if she's speaking to me or herself.

"Then why did you?"

She sucks in a breath. "Believe me when I say I regret it. I thought this would be a way we could both let it go."

"Both of us?"

"I know you wonder about your past. You wouldn't be human if you didn't. But if you saw the house, it might have bought me more time. But now, everything is different."

Her eyes are far away, but I don't break through. It's as if she's living inside one of my visions, detached from the world and living only within the horrors of her mind. She has to realize it herself, and hopefully that will help her open up more.

"Valerie was always different. Scary sometimes. She wasn't well. I left as soon as I could to get away from her, and I've been running ever since."

"She's tried to contact you?"

"I'm done talking about this."

"Is that why we moved so much?"

"Please, that's—"

"No." The gaping holes in the story seem to widen, even with more information. The more Mom tells me, the more questions I have. Ignoring them will only fuel my need to answer them.

"Leave it alone, Jenny. Following Val anywhere only leads to trouble. She's a stain on this family, and I intend to rid myself of her after selling the house."

"If you just tell me, I won't bother you about it anymore."

"That's enough." The sharpness of her words cut through me.

A flame ignites inside of me, and I lean into it. It won't be enough until I find out the truth. If she won't help me, I know one person who knows the other side of the story who might share it.

15
THEN

I'm unsure how long I take to get up from the ground. The moment I close my eyes, the relief tricks me into thinking it's what I want.

Sure, it's what I need after two blows to the head, but if you make it home, there's no way to explain what I've done. I know you. You won't listen to me.

The blocks of the plan shift as I try to force my body to heed my mind. You already know it's me, so how else can I make you stay? An apology? That's what normal people do. Given enough time and the explanation of my plan, you might find it in your heart to forgive me. I can offer to seek help.

Out of everything I know about you, you yearn to create harmony in your life. It's how you will forgive me.

I push up from the ground, and the world tilts. I squeeze my eyes shut and continue to a kneeling position. I let out a breath, then move again, standing and falling.

A pinch cuts into my skin. I peel one eye open, wrapping my hand around the stained rock. One edge is sharp, like a shiv.

You were hard at work during those days, weren't you?

Too bad you weren't working on an attitude shift. Your therapy might need another level, but I have to stop you first.

It takes two tries before I can open my eyes. A blurry version of the world appears. But I'm on my feet, and that's all that matters.

I stumble forward, through the invisible path I've taken so many times I could do it blindfolded. I won't. I need to be clear. No more mistakes.

Before I take off, I pick up the rope, wrapping it around my arm. I put the club and flashlight back on my belt and tuck the mask and rock into my back pocket. I anticipate the worst-case scenario, where I take her, and you go to the police to tell them about the person who captured you. You'll bring them here to try to find evidence of what happened. There will be nothing of me left here, and you'll fall into madness, losing the attention of anyone who has the potential to help you.

Either way, you will be in my life always.

There's no clear path to the shelter. Traveling to it at all hours in different light might confuse a novice, but not me.

I pick up my pace to where I don't feel as if I'm going to pass out. You got me good. A smile curls my lips. Your fury appears in my mind. I had too much faith in you. I should have seen a trick coming.

I push my mind to think the same way you do. I've thought about what I would do, molding this situation into what Father did to me. But what will you do if I don't get to you in time? What's your plan?

You'll want to leave me behind. You've always been able to get over things quickly and move on. I doubt you'll move on entirely, but she'll help you.

Without me.

The radiating pain in my neck surges again. There is no life without you, not a good one.

A low rumbling deep in my bones spreads through my body. Heat pulses. Redness tints my vision.

We will never be the same, but I'm not against creating a new normal with you. It's what I have to do to keep everyone in this town safe. Without you, I can't make any promises. With each victim, you'll hate me more, and you'll never understand that it's what I need to survive.

It's you or them.

A snapping sound fills my ears. It's not the sticks under me but the realization of an alternative plan. Admitting everything is how I'll keep you with me. You can't turn down this damaged person, no matter what I've done.

With an alternative plan, I push harder, and the road appears within a few minutes.

The car remains hidden under the cover of the brush I specifically curated for this venture. Hope swells within me that I can stop you before you get to her. Once you have her in your arms, I might have to resort to using her in a way I never wanted—against you. I'll do what I must.

I pull open the door, and the world shifts again. The light from the inside shows a pale version of my outline. Dirt and debris cover the side of my face. I try to wipe it away, but my hand shoots away from the sharp sting seeping blood from my ear.

There isn't much time. I'll deal with my wounds later. You're my focus.

I'm coming for you.

16

JENNY

The next morning, I break from the depths of sleep with a new sense of purpose. Last night, I allowed my mother to believe that my search for information was over, that I succumbed to her wishes. She's not a stupid woman, and I'm sure she knows I'm going to try again, but I will play along for now.

The lack of service at the house barely allows the internet on my phone to function. But I can't go back to the library. The town already has it out for my family. If Zee and I meet again, I'm sure she'll alert Davina. And if the sheriff thinks I'm stalking a teenager, I'll never get answers before my mother insists we leave.

With the paperwork for selling the house in place, I may have one more day in Orhaven before she whisks me away from the entire truth.

I slip into my clothes, jeans this time, even though they stick to my skin as I tug them onto my legs. They have a purpose. I can't take the car. Abandoning her in this house would be cruel, but I can't sit still. I need to talk over my plan with someone who will help me.

Scott's texts fill my screen as I check the time he agreed to meet. I have forty-five minutes to get downtown. He wanted to pick me up, but that won't help me escape my mother unnoticed. She'll get a note in the kitchen, knowing that I'm safe. I hope she understands my need for space. She won't know what I'm up to until after it's over. I won't ask her forgiveness until after I've already done the task. Only then, I'll have enough information to be done with Orhaven in the same way she has been for years.

I place the note on the kitchen countertop, sneak through the back door, and walk to the shed. Long, gray clouds stretch across the horizon. The air is cooler outside than in the house, and the trees surrounding us come to life with the creak of branches and the chirping birds.

Every few seconds, I glance back. My vision fuzzes. I hear the echo of my cell phone ringing, knowing it's her. The echoes of her screaming at me fill my ears. I grit my teeth, knowing my phone is on silent. I ignore the vision as it plays out, grounding myself in the present, and pick up my pace to the shed.

I open the doors and place the brick against the wood. Without Scott's presence, the dark corners of the space seem to move and form ominous figures. I focus on the ground, ignoring the shadows ripe with the possibility of a vision to form. I clutch the handlebars of the bike, and I burst from the shed. My legs straddle the sides. It wobbles at first, but with an iron grip on the handles and the drive to not face-plant onto the ground, I straighten out and find my pace. I release a breath and race down the rolling lawn toward the road. The driveway isn't an option. The crunch of the tires over the gravel may wake her.

When I reach the road, I'm sticky with sweat. The ride is much smoother, and I pick up my pace. A cool breeze washes over me, clearing my mind and body as I focus on leaving the house behind before she even notices I'm gone.

About halfway to town, my legs ache, and the humidity clings to my skin. I hope the movement of air over me masks the already sticky stench permeating from my body. I need Scott to get on board with my plan without sensing—or smelling—my desperation. He was the one to tell me about Valerie from the start, and he's the only one who has a vehicle to get me there.

After separating into our rooms last night, I pushed my phone to the limit with the painfully slow reception and researched the location of the prison where Valerie resides. It's almost an hour away—too far to bike. I haven't figured out a good excuse to tell my mother, but I also don't care. The freedom of these thoughts blooms within me. As a legal adult living with my mother, I've been trapped in the mentality that she controls my life.

My cheeks puff out with effort and the mounting anger inside of me. Like my visions, I can't quite control the situation with her. I love her more than the world, but her ignoring a chunk of our history frustrates me. Once I find the information, she has no reason to control the narrative any longer. I pedal faster, leaning into the freedom.

When the downtown area appears, the streets aren't as busy as I've seen on other occasions. I pass two cars, and the sidewalks are devoid of people. I spot Scott's truck parked against the curb outside of the diner.

With the conversation so close, I go over what I want to say to him in my mind. The talk will be easy, and he will help me. I have no idea why, but he's helped me each time I've asked. He's kind, and I hate taking advantage, but he's also to blame for giving me all the information I needed my mother to tell me.

The road dips, and the front tire slams into a small pothole. The bike swerves and bumps the curb. My feet plunge to the ground. This isn't a vision, but the scenarios play out anyway.

The bike didn't come with a helmet, and a vision of cracking my skull on the concrete steals my breath.

I recover quickly, knowing the vision was closer to coming true than most. I shove the bike away from me, and it clatters to the sidewalk. My feet stumble over the pavement as I suck in the sweet air around me, tasting more like a cinnamon bun. Did I hit my head? I check myself, and there's no blood coming from any part of my body.

"Are you all right?"

I turn to find Scott in the open doorway. The rush of sweet-smelling air wafts out of the diner behind him. He rushes over to me, the corners of his mouth cutting against his face. Under his cap, his hair is still damp, and his gray shirt is the cleanest I've seen him in so far.

"I'm fine."

He peers down at the bike. "You popped the tire."

He's right. The rubber flops against the concrete.

"Are you sure you're not hurt?" he asks.

"Just my ego."

Scott snorts out a laugh and lifts the bike from the ground, and he places it in the bed of his truck.

"I haven't ridden a bike in years either. Come on, let's go inside." He holds the door, and I scoot through. He's right behind me, enough that I notice the heat of his breath. He's already had a heaping supply of strong coffee, evident from the steaming mug in front of his chair.

Our table is by the window, with a full view of the street. No wonder he rushed out to help me. He had a front-row seat to my disaster arrival. I attempt to ignore the heat rushing into my cheeks.

He sits, facing the window, while I slide into the chair with my back to it. A shimmering sensation within me wants to sit next to him so I can identify each person who walks into the diner. I imagine my mother has a sixth sense and knows where I am. I see her rushing through the door, insisting we leave Orhaven for good.

There are only twelve tables tucked together; the brown-carpeted floor could use an update. I allow my mind to wander, wondering if the children from the photographs in the album came here often. I imagine my mother and my aunt sitting together, playing cards at the table or kicking each other under it. If my mother came here, would she feel nostalgia or regret?

A waiter approaches the table, and I snap to the present. Scott's staring at me, more curious than judgmental of me sitting in my thoughts.

"Want a coffee?" The waiter's gravelly voice touches a deep part of me.

"Yes, please. With cream and sugar."

He pours the coffee into the mug in front of me before sliding a one-page laminated menu my way. My stomach is too tight to eat.

"The house platter is great." Scott presses his finger against the line on the menu. "It's enough food for two, with leftovers. We can split it."

"If you want."

Scott leans back, slinging his arm over his chair. "The usual," he says to the guy.

The guy nods and walks to the table next to us, turning his attention to the older couple.

"You found what you needed?" Scott asks.

"Not everything."

He leans forward, resting his elbows on the table, inviting me to tell him more. At first, I clam up. What part of my family's past is his business? Yet my aunt stained this town with the blood of the doctor. At least if I give Scott the truth, that's one narrative I can control.

"She still isn't opening up to me about what happened with my aunt. She said she was messed up as a kid, but nothing about the murder."

"She might not know the details. Mike mentioned that she left a long time ago. I doubt they kept in touch."

I whirl the mug handle in my direction, and the edges sear my skin. "I want to see her."

Scott chokes out a sound before sipping from his mug. "Do you think that's the best idea?"

"I need to see her."

"How are you going to do that without your mother knowing?"

I stare at his forehead, not quite meeting his eyes. "I was hoping for some help."

He wipes a hand over his face, the same gesture as Mike. "I don't know if it's my place…"

"I just need a ride. I'll pay you for the gas."

He snorts. "I'm not concerned about fuel, Jenny." His tone suggests I'm about to get a lecture.

I stiffen my spine, willing to push to make my case. "She's not going to tell me what I want to know. I need to speak to Valerie face-to-face."

"There are rules for visiting inmates."

"I'll call them. What's the worst that can happen?"

A massive plate with a heaping pile of food appears on the table as I pull out my phone. My stomach growls. A mound of bacon and sausage sits on one end, with eggs propped in the center, glaring at me with accusing yellow eyes. The other side boasts a stack of toast soaked with butter.

"Eat first." Scott lifts his fork and digs into the eggs. The yolk runs free like a slow river toward him. I grab a piece of toast and nibble on the edge.

We eat in silence for a few moments.

Even though he's not saying anything, the sharp movement of his eyes back and forth gives me a hint he's thinking about my proposition. He empties his mug, places it on the table, and crosses his arms. "Say you go."

"I can't do this without you."

He tries to hide the quirk in his lips but fails miserably. He uses the napkin to wipe his attempted poker face. "Is it worth breaking trust with your mother?"

"I wouldn't do this if she was more willing to talk to me."

"Have you given her opportunity to do that?"

I've given her years of my life, and a confrontation the day before. "Finding the information on Valerie opened her up slightly. She didn't want to talk about it after that. If I speak to Valerie about her side of their past, then maybe I can force my mother into it."

Scott's jaw tenses. "What do you want to ask Valerie?"

His questions pry at the insecure part of me. On the surface, I want to know what happened between them to make my mother leave.

"There are two sides to every story. I need to know the truth . . . about a lot of things." I leave it at that, and Scott doesn't press for more.

"Valerie isn't going anywhere," Scott says after scooping up the last of the eggs. "Maybe you should wait."

"We're so close." I can't imagine taking a day trip through here after we leave.

"Is it worth hurting the relationship with your mother? If she had the terrible childhood you described, I'm sure she's fragile now and needs support."

He's right, and I hate that. But I need to do this. The look on my face must tell him I won't back down.

"Just let me know when," he says.

Our server drops the bill on the table, and Scott reaches for it.

"Let's split it," I say.

"I invited you to breakfast yesterday. You can get the next one."

After we finish at the diner, Scott drives me back to the house.

"Looks like rain." Scott peers at the top edge of the windshield.

"Maybe that will help cool this place down."

"I have several extra window units if you need them. There's not much circulation in these older houses. They hold the heat most of the time."

"Thanks, but I think we're okay." I'd hate for him to bring the units when he'd have to take them away again, along with the boxes.

"It's not a problem to help. Anything you need, I'm here."

My neighbors in Ridgefield are kind and helpful, but Scott beats all of them put together.

"I want to thank you for helping me through this," I tell him.

Scott glances at me before turning back to the driveway. The truck slows as if I'm not the only one who doesn't want this moment to end. I don't understand why that is, but I revel in it for as long as I can. It's the closest I've ever been to wanting a relationship with a guy, and it has no future.

"I wish I could be of more service to you. The relationships between the kids in this town are so strong. I was a transplant to this place, so I never experienced it as Mike did, but I feel like I've gotten as close as I can."

It's as if Scott's peeled open my layers and settled into a place where he's able to accept me for everything. He doesn't know about my visions, but he knows about my aunt, and he's only been kind.

The truck idles. I hold my breath, watching my mother rush from the house, screaming at me in a rage for sneaking out. But the movement of the driver's door slamming against the truck shatters the vision. I inhale sharply and push out of my seat.

Scott's next to the bed of the truck, holding the bike.

"I guess this is going to end up in the donate pile." The joke falls flat on my lips.

"It's a quick fix, so whoever gets it will have a real antique on their hands."

"Most of what we pulled from the attic are antiques." The dissected dolls appear in my mind, staring at me with their frozen eyes.

"Text me when you decide you want to go visit Valerie." He pushes the bike toward me, and the flat tire flops over the gravel.

"Thanks again."

While walking the bike to the house, I try not to turn around and let Scott know he's on my mind.

A thick drop of rain smacks against my cheek, and I tilt my chin toward the sky. Scott wasn't kidding about the rain. Thick, dark clouds block out the sun entirely. I inhale the sweet scent of the storm and head for the back shed.

I doubt my mother is still asleep, but if I can get away with bringing the bike back and throwing the note away, it will make the morning more tolerable.

That relief falls away with the sound of grunting as I round the house. Movement from the garden stops me. This vision is unlike the rest. It's not ignited by stress, and it's not violent toward my mother.

She's in the garden, on her knees. She leans forward, and a patch of skin moves upward from the dirt. She's digging. Her body writhes as she collects more of the soil within her grasp. She grunts and lets out a sob.

I blink. This isn't a vision. She's digging in the garden. With her hands. There are tools and shovels in the barn, but this looks primal. I glance toward the driveway, and Scott's truck is gone.

Three more raindrops pepper my face, harder and faster.

"Mom?" My voice cracks. She keeps digging. I call for her again, louder this time.

I'm unable to move, and my hands grip the handlebars much harder than necessary. My fingers curl around the metal in the same way she scoops the dirt.

She stands, shoving her sleeves over her arms. She pats the mound of dirt with her shoe. "We should go inside. It looks like rain." She turns on her heel and stalks into the house.

17
JENNY

The back door slaps against the frame, breaking me from a trance. Rain pelts the ground, propelling me to get inside. I lean the damaged bike against the house and rush after her. The lack of explanation of her frantically digging in the garden strikes the same line of questions I've had about my aunt and grandparents. Along with the odd behavior, I've never seen her so emotional and determined before.

As I pass the place where I found her digging, the richness of the soil marks the ground. I make a mental note of the location.

It appears that I'm not the only one hiding a secret this morning. What the hell was she doing in the garden?

Inside the kitchen, the basement door is slightly cracked open. No doubt in her rush to avoid me, she forgot to lock it. I whip it open. The black hole beckons me to uncover what she was doing down there. The groan of the water pipes above me signals that she's showering and avoiding the conversation. Not for long.

The uncharacteristic manic scene of her digging in the garden fills my mind. I walk down the steps. A flashlight lies on the floor, more evidence of what she's been up to. I pick it up and swing the beam across the concrete floor. This isn't like the first visit down here when the space was new. There can only be one place where she would want to find an item from this family's past to bury.

The bed in the corner seems smaller than I remember. But if I had any doubt of what she wanted down here, the overturned table and books scattered across the floor alert me to her mission. A gaping hole in the wall peers back at me, behind the small table with the stacks of books.

The hole is about the size of two fists. I push the beam into the hole, unsure of what to expect. There's nothing inside of it, but I've been here before. I'm reminded of the journal's hiding place, and shove my hand inside, searching for what's hidden.

The stone foundation cuts against my skin as I drag my hands around the space. Cobwebs wrap around my fingers. I shake them off and go back inside, pushing away any sensation of tiny legs skittering on me.

The groan of the pipes ceases, and I stand up. There haven't been many moments where I've had the upper hand, and now I have a hole and witnessing my mother in the garden like a wild animal burying its kill.

I shudder at the thought. My aunt is a killer. But now, there is a piece of my family hidden in the garden, and I intend to find out what it is, with or without my mother's permission.

After sprinting up the stairs, I whirl around, closing the door behind me. I spot the key on the kitchen table. I pinch the metal in my hand, hesitating. I could replace it on the nail by the door, but that would give her an opportunity to lock me out again.

But if I don't replace it, she'll ask for it. At least that will open the conversation, but I won't allow her to keep me out of her life anymore. The situation is too bizarre to leave alone.

I walk to the sink, rolling the key over in my palm. Outside, it's dark enough to be night instead of morning, and a curtain of rain unfolds across the yard. I open the window, allowing a cool rush of air to enter the room. If I go out there, I may not find what she buried before she stops me.

A new purpose overwhelms me, and I place the key on the table where she left it.

I sink into the memory of my mother's actions as I move throughout the house, opening windows. With each one, a gust of cooler air gives me more clarity.

The closed rooms on the second floor no longer call to me. There are more answers within her mind, and outside of this home, that my tolerance of ignorance about her past dissipates.

I'm in my bedroom when the bathroom door opens, and she steps into the hallway. "Morning." She's fully clothed, with jeans and a worn long-sleeved T-shirt. She appears normal, but nothing about today is. She heads into her room, and I follow. She smooths the sheets over the bed, setting the pillow at the edge.

Is she really pretending I didn't see her out there?

A flash of lightning splits open the sky outside her window.

"What were you doing in the garden?" I ask.

She stands straighter. "I could ask you the same about disappearing while I was sleeping. You can't imagine how I felt when I saw your bed empty this morning."

"I left a note." I already know she's moving the conversation away from her, but I have all day to play this game.

"You did."

She moves around the room, folding her pajamas before stuffing them into her bag.

I give her a minute before I lean into what I saw. "You're not going to tell me what you were doing?"

She sighs, as if I'm inconveniencing her by asking.

The hairs on the back of my neck rise. "You can't lie your way out of it."

"What were you doing in town?"

I want to scream and put my foot down on the issue, but only after I answer her. She may need prompting, but I hold part of my conversation with Scott in my pocket.

"I had breakfast with Scott."

My mother shakes her head.

"He gave me his number, and I wanted to have a hot meal. I'm tired of cereal."

"It's not a good idea for you to be around that boy."

That boy? "Aren't you friends with his father?"

She snorts. "Hardly. I left this place behind years ago. I was just being polite the other day. The less you become entrenched here, the better."

"Is that your way of telling me you won't explain why you were in the garden?"

"Jenny." Her hand moves to her face, and she rubs her palm against her forehead.

I can't help but push harder. "I saw the hole in the basement. What are you hiding from me?"

"I wish you would get over this."

"Get over this? You mean get over the fact that a family member you claimed was dead is not? Also, she killed someone and is in prison?" Zee's face flashes in my mind. The string of texts between our mothers still needs explanation. I want to put her in a corner with her lies, but not hurt her if I can help it.

"I've let it go. You should, too."

"You've only done that because you have the entire story. I can't let something go that I don't understand."

"She's not worth your thoughts. You should be grateful not to know what she's capable of."

I'm anything but grateful.

"She's dangerous and hurts everyone she meets. You're better off not knowing her."

If she won't tell me directly about my aunt, I know I'll be able to move around the subject. "What did you put in the garden?"

"Jenny, enough."

"You know I'm going to push harder on this."

"This has nothing to do with you." She crosses the room and leaves through the door, ending the conversation.

There's nowhere in this house she can go without me following. I keep her pace, even as we both careen down the stairs. "I won't let this go. Why is there a bed in the basement? Who slept down there? What were they hiding?" My voice rises with each new question.

My mother whirls around at me, and I stumble back, nearly crashing into the television. "Why are you pushing me like this? I've worked your entire life to give you everything. Your aunt has done horrible things. More than the people of this town know, and you're focusing on her?"

I inhale sharply. Her glossy eyes tell me I've gone too far. I've never seen her this close to breaking. The need to push her overwhelms me. I strike while she's vulnerable. A sick feeling rolls in my stomach, but it's the only way I'll find out the story without going to Valerie myself.

Shimmering tendrils creep into my peripheral. At first, it appears like another flash of lightning, but it's not a white flash, it's like the inky black of my visions, but tinged with red. A tingling sensation pricks at my skin.

The pages of the journal rush to the front of my mind. The girls. They are Valerie and Nora. The cradle. Valerie experiencing the loss of her sister. The loss turned to grief, then anger, then murder.

I fall into them, as if the world around me disappears. I no longer have an anchor. Numbness washes over me, and I can't feel my limbs. My mother's disembodied voice drones on, but the sounds don't form coherent words.

I wallow in the darkness while snippets of images move forward before disappearing. The girls clutching each other from the journal pages sharpen and come to life. A child cries in the distance, and I need to find her.

The cracking of wood mixed with the sound of panting and digging.

I'm outside now. Rain falls around me, but I'm not soaked. I walk toward the garden. My mother is on the ground throwing dirt around her. I move closer. Her body blocks the hole. I need to know what's inside.

She continues to dig, and my legs feel like they are a thousand pounds each. The effort it takes to move them leaves me breathless.

I reach forward to touch my mother's shoulder, to move her out of the way. But I stop when I realize my hands and arms are covered in sticky red blood.

I fall to the ground, and my mother disappears. A hole is exposed, and even though I wanted to see what was inside, I already know.

The blank stare of the doctor bores through my soul.

A presence appears behind me, and I turn to face my mother.

No, not my mother.

Valerie stands there in the same floral dress as the picture from the article. Now, it's covered in the same blood as me. She throws her head back at an unnatural angle and cackles. It gets stronger and louder until it overcomes the sound of the surrounding rain.

"Stop!" I scream.

She does. The sound cuts off immediately, and she faces me

again. This time, I'm standing in her place, dressed in the frock.

"Jenny!"

I close my eyes, willing the images to disappear.

"Count, honey."

I grit my teeth as the scent of the rain fills my nose.

"Five," she says.

"Five," I croak.

"Four." Her voice cracks, and so does the vision.

My stomach rolls, but I need to push out of it. "Four," I say through my teeth.

I don't know how long it takes to get through the numbers, but reaching the end breaks me out of my vision as if someone had chipped the façade with a sledgehammer.

"Jenny?"

I crack open my eyes. My knees throb under me, and I try to unfold them.

"Stay there," she says, tucking me against her.

"I'm sorry," I say.

"Don't be."

"That was a bad one."

"I can tell. Do you want some water?"

"Please don't move."

"Okay."

I breathe in and out, steadying my racing heart. My skin is damp with sweat, and I swear the stickiness of the doctor's blood clings to me as well.

A sob escapes my mother, snapping me into reality. "I wanted to protect you from her. From this place. If I tell you the truth, you won't see this family the same. But I suspect you won't now anyway."

Her long, thin fingers grip the hem of her right sleeve, curling around the fabric ever so gently before pulling them up.

Thick, twisted scars distort my mother's thin wrist. She reveals the other wrist with the same marks.

As a child, I was never allowed to see my mother naked. I thought she was just private, when in reality she holds a terrible secret.

"This is what Val has done to the people in her life. Ones she's claimed to love. Some have mental scars, while others have these. This isn't love. It's manipulation and a sickness inside of her."

The scars tell a story she's kept secret for so long, even from me. While I should be horrified, a part of me is intrigued. This house calls to a new side of me. One desperate for the truth, no matter how terrible. "Why didn't you show me this before?"

She shoves her sleeves down, concealing her scars. I expect her to keep the secrets within her, but I can't allow it. We've gone too far now.

"Do you think I wanted you to know all of this?" She shoves her hands through her hair several times.

"I would have understood."

"No one should understand this!" Her lips tremble, and tears leak from the corners of her eyes.

My insides lurch, but I wait for her truth. "What did she do?" The lines of her scars burn into my memory. I doubt she will ever wear short sleeves or tank tops in public, but showing me was a step forward. The next might give me more information surrounding her trauma.

She winces. "It's too much."

I take her hands in mine. She pulls away slightly, but I hold tight. "Nothing is too much for my mind. Please, Mom. I need to know. Keeping this to yourself isn't good. I'm here for you. No matter what."

She swallows hard. "Opening this part of the past doesn't involve just me."

"What do you mean?"

She licks her dry lips. "Jenny, this isn't the first time you've been here."

I drop her hands. A fluttering erupts in my stomach, and the room tilts. I grip the arm of the couch to hold myself upright. The comfort I've felt in this house isn't just because I sought the truth. The scars and her admission of my past here come together like the perfect mold of our lives. Yet the cracks in the surface expand, and I have the impulse to fill them. "You told me you left here before you met my father."

"That's not quite everything."

"What is it, then?"

"Calvin is from Orhaven. He never liked it here and always had dreams of moving away when he was old enough. I was so naïve then, I thought I could convince him to stay."

"But he didn't?"

"He left before you were born."

"What does this have to do with your scars and Valerie?"

She blinks as if I've pulled her from a trance. I've never heard her speak about my father for more than a few seconds, but this place seems to have us in its grip, no matter how horrific it is. "Without him, I stayed here with Valerie. She helped me raise you."

I search my mind for any flash of recognition of the woman in the newspaper article.

"When did we leave?"

"You were almost three."

"Why did we leave?" I glance at her covered arms.

"She abducted me."

"What? You lived with her. How could she?"

"I trusted her, too." Her tone is flat, as if there is no emotion attached to the fact that my aunt apparently abducted someone who already lived with her.

Those cracks in the story etch themselves further into the mold.

"One night, she attacked me when I was coming home from the grocery store. She left me in the woods, pretending she was someone else. There's a place out there . . ." A violent shudder moves through her like a human-sized earthquake.

I reach out to help steady her, but she backs away from me, pulling further into her memory. Her shoulders hunch, and her arms curl against her chest as if she's still stuck in the woods. Her trauma is worse than I thought. For most of my life, I focused on my grandparents having something to do with her wanting to hide her past. While they still might have had an influence, I shift my focus to the more direct problem with her family. The woman who killed an innocent doctor and scarred my mother both internally and externally.

"She left me there to die."

"But you didn't."

Another shuddering breath escapes her. "I had to get you away from her. You were the only light that kept me alive, Jenny. She would not snuff you out, too. So I escaped."

My expression urges her to tell me more, the story of her abduction in excruciating detail, even though it will challenge my visions to make it worse.

My mother looks at me with a mixture of fear and determination in her eyes. She opens her mouth and tells me, "And I never looked back."

18

THEN

The road to our home is empty as always, so I press the gas pedal harder. I scan either side of the road for you limping for your life, trying to get away from the person who took you away from your family. I picture finding your slow form, pulling over, and grabbing you. You'll try to fight me, but I'm filled with such purpose, you can't escape again. I'll explain that I did this all for you, for her, for us. I'll beg for your forgiveness. I'll tell you I'll get help. Only if you stay.

I'm practiced enough in emotions that I can bring them on within seconds and turn them off just as quickly. It's one of my more useful talents. You'll believe me. I'll leverage her, too. I'm the only family either of you have left. You know I'll give you whatever you want; money is no object. You also have shelter and protection. I proved the latter by what I've done. You'll know never to cross me again.

When I get to the clearing, away from the forest-covered road, I glance at our house. The lights are on. I slow the car and check the rearview mirror. The time on my watch blurs, and I try to count backward to when I had arrived at the underground shelter. I can't grab onto the time before I went to see you. Before you ruined everything.

A pulsing heartbeat thunders in my ear. The bleeding is not good. But if I stop now, then the entire plan will crumble.

I debate going back to the road, shining my headlights on either side to find you. But my gut tells me to move forward. It's the same feeling I've had each time I took someone away from this earth. All becomes right in the world if I follow it.

So, I do.

The purpose of the gut feeling becomes clear within seconds. The front door to the house opens, but it's not the babysitter. My focus has been on you for so long, I didn't notice that the extra car was no longer parked next to the house.

Too much time has passed. I see that now.

I know what I must do.

Instead of pinching the bruised soft spot on my arm as I normally do, I take advantage of my wound. I don't need a lot of pressure to make the tears spring to my eyes. The weakness pours out of my face as I slow to a stop in front of Father's truck.

You're already inside the cab, but on the passenger side. I don't need to see her to know what you're doing.

This has gone too far.

"Stop!" I call out the moment I'm out of the car.

Your head doesn't pop up in surprise. You know I'm here. I suppose you'd have to be hard of hearing not to. I suspect your senses are sharper now, especially with the adrenaline running through you. Too bad you've never experienced the elation of giving yourself over to the emotions attached to that surge of energy.

The passenger side door closes. I expect her to pop up and watch Aunty cry for the only time in her life. It will be the last time. She'll never see me weak again.

"You come a step closer, I swear I will kill you."

The words coming from your mouth move out of order and echo in my mind. You've never had a violent tendency in your life. They left all that to me.

"Nora, how did you get here?"

"You're not the only one who played in the woods as a kid."

I could have taken a shortcut, but the babysitter needed to see me leaving the house in the car so she wouldn't suspect. My plan unravels more with each passing second. I step toward you with my bloody hands in the air.

"Don't." Moonlight glints off the barrel of Father's pistol. We were both taught not to point a gun unless we meant it.

The rush of the kill swells inside me. It's been too long. "You don't want to do this." Even in the darkness, the dirt and grime from the forest cuts across your face like war paint. This is a battle for you to stay. I have to fight. I shove a sob out of me. "I'm sorry. I wanted you to stay."

"By kidnapping me and leaving me in the woods to rot?"

"I wanted to show you what was important and that I will always protect you. You were never in danger."

You lower the gun, and I take a step forward before it springs up again. You won't be able to hold that position for long.

"I know how twisted you are, but that's not my fault. You're getting worse, and I can't have Jenny exposed to you anymore."

The words don't jumble this time, but I still don't comprehend them. There is no good life for me without you. "You don't understand what I've done for you."

"I have some idea."

I stop sniffling and stand straighter. My ear throbs, but with enough focus, it turns into a dull ache. There's no need to pretend anymore. You made me reach this level. If you would have accepted your place here, I wouldn't have to do this. "You can't leave here. I'll get help."

"You're beyond help. I'm going."

"Please?"

"I won't ever forgive you for this. You need help, but there's no one in this world who can take the darkness from you."

Redness invades the edges of my vision. I never thought my violence would focus on you, but you've given me no choice. My hands curl into fists as I rush you. I'm already ten steps ahead in my mind.

What I don't expect is the blast of sound and light exploding inside of my head. I register the gunshot too late, and the ground thrusts itself against my face. I slam into it, that light erupting behind my eyes again. My breathing is heavy in my ears, but I'm still breathing.

As the light clears, your shoes come into view. They smell of the richness of the deep woods. A sliver of a memory peeks into my mind. Woodsmoke and blood. My skin prickles and tingles, signaling that I'm still conscious. You shot at me.

"Don't come looking for us, or next time, I won't miss." Your feet move toward the truck before they lift into the air and don't return to the ground. The truck roars to life and disappears from view.

I know enough about injuries that I won't be able to catch up to you right now. But that doesn't mean I'll ever stop looking for you both.

19
JENNY

After my mother tells her traumatic story, I'm speechless. The thought that anyone, including her sister, could do those horrible things to someone they claimed they loved doesn't seem real at all. It feels like a vision I've created. A chasm of questions opens in my mind, and only one person can answer them.

My mother sways on her feet, and I grip her wrists to steady her. She jolts, but I squeeze the marred skin. "Sit down."

She follows me to the couch and sinks into the cushions. I peer around the room with a new perspective. Hers. Coming back to this place must have been hard for her, even more difficult than I originally thought.

My throat tightens, and my own words echo in my mind, pushing her to tell me her story before she was ready. Without my insistence, would she ever have told me on her own? "Are you okay?"

She bobs her head. "I worked so hard to block it from my mind. I suppose you had to know someday."

"You've had no contact with her since?"

"No."

"She lived here all these years by herself?"

She looks around the room, wincing as if the air pains her. "It seems that way."

"Did you contact the police after what she did?"

"I couldn't."

I sit back, crossing my arms. "What do you mean?" This supposed traumatic event put my family in danger, and yet she couldn't call anyone?

"You wouldn't understand. Valerie and I experienced a lot together. She's been like this for as long as I've been alive, but she's still my sister."

"She kidnapped you and killed someone."

"I know. She was so good with you, and with me. Until she wasn't." She chokes out the words around a sob. The tears flow faster than they did before. "I took our father's truck that night. Other than what was in my purse, I had nothing else. I sold the truck and worked as hard as I could to pay rent on an apartment the size of a closet. Then I moved us farther away, convinced she'd find me. It was only after a few years that I believed I escaped her. But when I found out about the doctor, what she did to him, I knew what I did was wrong. I should have reported her. That way, the police would know. They could have helped get her treatment. He died because of me."

She can barely get out the last words. Emotion floods my throat. She's the one who needed therapy. More than I did. I guess I'm not the only one hiding my true self.

"She killed him. You didn't," I say. While I have no memory of the time spent living here, I imagine what it would have been like. Are my visions suppressing events that happened, or are they a link to this family and the violence within?

"I didn't stop her."

I stand as a crawling sensation rolls up and down my legs.

It's as if snakes and insects have found a new home inside my body. I stave off a shudder, trying to keep my emotions in check. I have so many questions for her, but for each layer of secrets, she breaks down more. If I pull the rest of them, how far will she fall apart? "Is that why you changed our name?" I'm not sure I'll ever consider myself a Whitford, but it's in my blood.

She sniffs hard, and I pass the tissue box we purchased from the grocery store that first day. She blows her nose before continuing. "She worked as a librarian and had a keen ability to find what she was looking for. Changing our name would keep her away from us, while preventing you from finding any link to my past. I thought it would be best if her reputation didn't stain your life. Before coming here, I asked Walter to not use my true surname. I'm sorry for all the evasion, Jenny, but this was the only way I thought we could get through this week without Val's shadow over everything."

My aunt isn't the only one who's invaded our lives. This town and its people, connect to the house and those who lived inside, no matter what decade.

I think of Zee and how her link to this family still carries on. With the truth spilling from my mother's mouth, I can't hold back what I know anymore. The truth needs to permeate all parts of our lives now, or else how can I ever trust her again?

"I met a girl in town. A teenager. Her mother is missing." With the situation close to my mother's abduction, it seems too much of a coincidence for her to go missing right when we returned to town. But Valerie's in prison, so it can't be the same as before. What else is she hiding?

"What does that have to do with us?"

"The girl's name is Zelda, Zee. She showed me her mother's phone with a text chain between the two of you."

Her lips part slowly. "Wren is missing?"

"Apparently. What do you know about it?" And why did she lie about contacting her?

Her gaze flicks to mine before she pushes off the couch. She crosses the room and then paces toward the front door. For a moment, it appears as if she's going to attempt an escape, but in a rush of movement, she darts for her purse. She lifts her phone out and scrolls over the screen.

I walk to her. "Who is Wren to you?"

"She's an old friend." She presses her lips together as she scrolls.

"And you know nothing about her disappearance?"

She cuts a look my way. "Of course not. I meant to meet up with her yesterday."

"I thought you were going to take care of paperwork for the house?"

A blankness crosses her face. Only for a second, but a second too long. She's lying, again. Even after our conversation. Though, I suppose it's a knee-jerk reaction at this point.

"It's hard to explain."

"Try me."

She sighs. "I left an entire life behind that night, Jenny. I never thought I'd come back, and I don't plan to after we leave. She reached out to me, so I went to meet with her."

"Why didn't you tell me?"

She presses the phone to her ear.

I cross my arms, letting her know I'm not done with this conversation yet.

"Davina." She turns her body as if the movement will block my ears. "I just heard. Yeah. I did." The rain patters on the windows, blocking the silence emanating from my mother. "Okay. I can do that. What time?" I count to twenty before she responds. "I'll see you then."

I don't even give her the chance to hang up. "You have Davina's number?"

"Yes."

"Are you close?"

"There was a time we were." She shakes her head as if trying to erase the memories of that part of her life. "Wren is still missing. It's escalated to a missing person."

"It wasn't before?"

She sighs. "Usually not before forty-eight hours."

"Who is taking care of Zee?"

"I'm sure she's fine."

"How do you know?"

"She has to be with Wren as her mother. Wren can be selfish with her time. She always has been." As she speaks, her gaze goes to another place. The past, probably.

Another layer gone, revealing a new set of questions.

"Why did you lie to me about meeting her?"

"I didn't lie."

"Omission is a lie. You've burned that into my brain."

"I think that's enough for now."

"No—"

"Jenny, a friend of mine has gone missing, and now that you know what I've been through, please have a little patience while I absorb this."

I want to push more. We're at a precipice of information, but it's too much for my mother. The only way I'm resigned to not pulling the truth from her is that there's another way. A plan reshapes in my mind. "Okay," I say through my teeth for fear of the truth spilling out.

"Thank you."

She lifts her purse and walks upstairs. The barrier between us is up again. She can't even trust me to be in the presence of her phone. The only reason I can let her go that easily is because I have another source of information. Valerie Whitford.

My mother and I remain on stable ground the rest of the afternoon and into the evening. She distracts herself with the boxes, and I take over cleaning duties. Even though my wandering mind usually leans toward the morbid visions, with a directed path, I focus on the plan for the next day.

Scott obliges my request to visit with Valerie. He sets up an appointment with the prison around the same time that my mother is meeting with Davina. Once she suspects what I've done, it will be too late. I hope I'll already have all the information I need, and she will have to fill in the gaps with her side.

You're on the visitation list. Under Jenny Miller.

My skin crawls. My mom didn't want Valerie to know our new last name, but she found a way to uncover it. What else does she know of me?

Still want to do this?

I glance at my mother. She's dropped the last box at the door. "I have a headache. Probably from the dust. I'm going to lie down."

"Okay," I say.

She peers around the room, probably making sure there isn't an opportunity for me to bring up her past. Little does she know I already have a plan in place. Then she goes upstairs.

I stare at the phone, considering Scott's question. The visions aren't getting any better. In fact, they're worse since coming here. It might be because of the stress of all the questions and lies, but I can't leave here without knowing. After the house sells, I'll never have a reason to return. If Valerie experiences a sliver of what I do, then she might be able to help. The more I ruminate on what I don't know, the more my visions fill the cracks with utter nightmares. I won't risk not knowing.

Yes.

After showers the next morning, my mother and I exchange pleasantries over instant coffee. Without prompting, she informs me that my aunt never liked coffee so there wasn't a pot in the house. Valerie preferred tea.

She seems pleased with herself that she's given me such an intriguing tidbit about my aunt. I smile at her and accept the olive branch. At least when she gets back to the house later and finds me gone once again, I can look back on this moment to when we were both on even ground. She seems well rested and ready for the day, and I don't disrupt the balance.

"Jenny, while I'm gone, could you put all the boxes on the front porch? I'm going to have Scott come by tomorrow to pick them up. We'll leave shortly after."

"We're leaving already?"

"There's no reason to stick around anymore. The paperwork is with Walter, and he has an agent who'll handle the sale."

"What about Wren?" She buys my concern over someone I've never met, but sharp pricks of anxiety fill my chest.

"I'll give them the information they need, but I'm sure she'll turn up."

The time left in this house presses against my body. What if I hadn't already planned the visit with Valerie? She's trying to get me away from Orhaven and finding out more of the narrative she's concealing.

I have one opportunity to get Valerie's story before it's too late, and the visions trickle in, hinting at what to expect from my murderous aunt.

A few minutes after Mom leaves for town, Scott's truck arrives. I'm already outside when he pulls up to the house.

The sky is overcast, and the grass has already soaked up the rain from the night before. A slight chill clings to the air, cooling my heated skin. With his hat on, I can't see Scott's eyes, but the way his head shifts slightly as I near the truck, he's watching my every move.

I open the door and hop onto the seat. "Hey."

"Morning."

"Did she see you? You must have crossed paths on the main road."

"I wanted to get here on time. There are a few parking spots along the side of the road that hide a car pretty well."

I raise an eyebrow.

"It's mostly for parties and people who hunt in this town. Not me."

A smile sneaks across my face. As long as my mother has no clue what I'm doing, I'll be able to concentrate on what's coming with Valerie.

He accelerates down the driveway. "You seemed pretty over-whelmed yesterday. Do you want to talk about it?"

We have close to an hour's drive, and he is taking the morning off to help me. Talking to him is the least I could do, other than covering his fuel cost for the trip.

"She's hidden so much from me. I don't even know if I've processed that yet."

"You said she was trying to protect you, but I wonder if she's protecting herself."

I mull that over. I came to Orhaven to find out more, but her trauma from the abduction and running away from this place has to feel worse. Though Scott doesn't know that.

He's probably heard terrible tales about my family, and the town lore about the Whitford women is twisted by gossip. But knowing the full story will only worsen our already violent legacy.

"I hope you understand why I have to visit her." With his agreeing to help every step of the way, I don't need to push for him to side with me. I need him to tell me I'm right for doing it.

The side of me which always obeys my mother claws at my insides. Her voice comes to me, telling me I'm wrong and I need to get Scott to turn the truck around and wait for her side of the story, whenever she feels comfortable giving it. It's not too late to go back, and she'll be none the wiser. We can go on our trip, and I can wait patiently until she decides what to tell me and when.

I reel myself back. Jenny Miller may be satisfied with that, but Jenny Whitford wants more. I can't go back to the house, not until I have some clarity. My visions don't just belong to me, and I have the journal to prove it. They're not a curse that makes me a freak. They help me understand the truth. Half of the story belongs to Valerie. It's only fair I get as much of it as possible. After that, I'll never need her again. My mother will understand someday.

"This is the way for you to get what you need right now," he says.

"You don't agree with me lying, though." My fingers twist in my lap.

Scott quirks his lips to the side and narrows his eyes at the road. "If my mother was still alive and I could have another day with her and ask her why she made the choices she did, I wouldn't hesitate."

It's not as if Valerie is dying soon, but his meaning is clear. I let out a breath and press myself against the warm leather. While talking, I sit hunched like my mother did the night before. I roll my shoulders, teasing the tension from them.

"Are you ready to meet her though?"

I sigh. "I don't know if anyone could be ready in a situation like this."

"Do you have a list of questions?"

"A list?"

"If you get nervous or she's not what you're expecting, it's always good to be prepared."

"I don't." I didn't expect him to be more helpful than he already is by taking me to the prison.

"Do you want to talk through some? You're not allowed to have a cell phone in there, so we can practice."

"How do you know so much about visiting people in jail?"

"They went over the list of rules on the phone."

"Are they going to pat me down?" I mean it as a joke, but the way he glances at me answers the question.

"I suppose they could do that, but they have metal detectors. They need to make sure you don't give the inmates anything. But in Valerie's part of the prison, you'll be behind a barrier. They don't allow physical exchanges."

With his description of the prison and its rules, my vision shimmers, revealing a large white room with cubbies for the inmates and their visitors. An old-fashioned telephone hangs from the barrier. A shadowy figure enters from the corner, a faceless woman, thin like my mother but more commanding, glides toward me.

"We can go another time." Scott's voice cuts through the vision, and I inhale sharply.

The concern in Scott's eyes gives me a hint he's noticed how I've disappeared into my mind.

"We're leaving tomorrow. This is the only chance I'll get."

"Then you better not waste it."

I don't plan on it. But I only have the fragmented truth from my mother to go on for the full story of our past. Scott wasn't around when Valerie was young, but he had to be a part of the gossip mill around town after Dr. Bradley's murder.

"Can you tell me what happened in Orhaven after they caught her?"

He sighs. "It was strange. Orhaven itself is peaceful most of the time. But the closeness of our family to yours cut a bit deeper. At least to Mike."

"How so?"

"Mike's brother was close with Valerie when they were our age."

"How close?" Something inside me bristles. I sense his hesitance, but I'm used to pushing now.

"Mike said they had dated at some point. But he died when he was in his early twenties."

"What happened, if you don't mind me asking?"

"A hunting accident."

"I'm so sorry."

He shrugs a shoulder. "Mike rarely mentions him, so I don't pry. I only heard about it after they convicted your aunt. Since your mother was gone for so many years prior, they couldn't focus on family members to make sense of it all. Everyone had their theories. People were looking for 'signs' everywhere."

"Signs of what?"

"Valerie was a librarian, and she rarely went anywhere except for work or community events. Most people in town left her alone, so discovering that she murdered Dr. Bradley was a shock to everyone. They wanted an explanation for why it happened since she never explained why she did it."

"That's wild."

"Don't focus on that though. You should ask her about your family. It might be the last time you see her."

The first and last. This is the one opportunity I'll get to see Valerie. There's no way my mother will trust me again after she figures out how I betrayed her.

20

JENNY

The prison facility looks more like a college campus than a place for criminals. Other than the barbwire-topped fences surrounding several of the buildings, I expect to find students lugging their backpacks between classes. As Scott drives us toward the parking lot, the posted uniformed personnel with weapons attached to their belts disrupts the pleasant collegiate vibe.

My stomach lurches, and my palms dampen. I check my phone for the tenth time in the last five minutes. There's no message or phone calls from my mother. I wonder if she's still at the station or coming home to find me gone once again.

"Do you want me to take your phone in case she calls? Or would you rather leave it in here?" Scott asks.

Either he can read my mind, or the panic swelling within me has taken residence on my face. "I'll give it to you."

He eases the truck into an empty spot. There are several parked cars scattered through the lot, and I wonder how often people visit their loved ones. For Valerie, this might be the first visit since she arrived here. My mother and I are the only family she has left, and I doubt anyone from Orhaven would bother to come out here to visit a murderer.

"Should I be aware of anyone else contacting you while you're in there?" he asks.

I think of Abbie. For years, we've been in touch daily, but she's slipped my mind since I arrived in Orhaven. I know this is her way of letting me explore my past, but I'll catch her up on everything that's about to happen with Valerie. I owe her at least that.

"A boyfriend maybe?" Scott presses.

The last memory of my date with Dennis surges within me. "No boyfriend."

He pretends to wipe sweat from his brow. "At least you'll only have to explain this trip to one person."

"It won't be a good conversation." I try to push away the developing vision of the impending discussion with my mother about sneaking away again.

I hand over my phone and push out of the truck, while counting down silently through gritted teeth.

Scott navigates to the nearest building as if he's been here before. A sign for visitors is clear as day outside the door.

He shoots me a shaky grin. "We have to check in here, and they will take you to the facility."

"Okay."

Scott brushes his fingers over my shoulder. I slow my pace, unable to look him in the eyes. The sun soaks into the pavement, and I swear I can feel it radiating into my shoes, boiling me from the inside out.

His touch captures me, and I realize he's the best person I can be with right now. "Try not to think about why she's here. You're on her list. She wants you here. Just talk to her like you would a family member you haven't seen in years. Ask her whatever you want."

I don't recall my time living in Orhaven when I was a toddler, but from what my mother told me about how she feels about Valerie, there must have been love there at some point. I hold on to Scott's suggestion and take the first step toward the building.

The urge to take charge of the situation coils inside of me like a thick knot. The ends tug, but I sit in the emotion, allowing it to become a companion instead of a hindrance. There's no reason I shouldn't be nervous to see Valerie, so ignoring it will only add to the tension.

Inside, we walk through a set of metal detectors monitored by a burly officer whose stare could melt glass. I focus ahead on the desk with a clear partition between us and three uniformed officers. My gaze drops to the guns attached to their belts.

The officer looks me in the eye. "License, please."

I slide my ID through a thin slot in the partition. She copies it and hands over a form on a clipboard. After I finish the paperwork, Scott allows me to choose where we're sitting. I pick the farthest corner from the door.

I lean close to Scott. "How long is Valerie in here for?"

Scott shakes his head. "Years probably."

From the story my mother told me about Valerie's tendencies toward violence, I can't help the relief that she won't be out of here soon. It's bad enough visiting her, but if she thinks we'll have a relationship once she's released, I doubt my mom will forgive me that easily. Putting our family in danger is the last thing I want.

Though, if she gave me the information I wanted, it wouldn't have come to this.

Scott bumps my arm. I tumble out of my thoughts and hear a brief echo of my name. I don't know why, but I squeeze his hand. Once again, his touch soothes me, and a swirl of courage propels me toward the door.

Two officers, both female, stand in the open doorway.

"Jennifer Miller?" the smaller of the officers asks. Her blonde hair is in a tight bun at the base of her neck. Her heart-shaped face seems kind and welcoming, unlike her partner. It's the same officer from the front desk, and even more menacing without the partition.

"That's me."

I glance at Scott. He gives me two thumbs-up.

The blonde officer is several steps behind me. A fluttering sensation of a vision tickles the corners of my periphery, but I focus hard on the present. I can't go away into my head in front of armed corrections officers. I don't know if they can revoke access to the prison if they think I'm not well. Besides, I don't want to show Valerie that side of me just yet. If she doesn't have visions, she may consider it a weakness.

Once we reach the next building, the first officer looks at the camera attached to the outside wall and moves aside.

"Look directly at the camera, please."

I do as she says.

After what feels like minutes, the door clicks open. The officer holds it open with just enough space for us to fit.

This building is more modern than the visitor one. The white floors are slick, and the sharp scent of cleaner stings my nose. There's a desk to the right. Two officers sit behind the glass.

"Name?" the male asks.

"Jennifer Miller for Valerie Whitford," the blonde officer says before opening the door to get inside the office.

The male officer grunts and types into the computer before eyeing me up and down. "You family?"

"S-She's my aunt." I unclench my fists, needing to steady myself.

Another buzzer brings me and the first officer through a set of doors.

The room is narrow, offering enough space for maybe two people at a time to walk side by side. On the right side of the room are almost a dozen windows peering into a similar space. Wooden partitions and chairs separate each visiting area.

My breathing inverts in my ears as the room shifts slightly. I'm moving, but I don't control my body.

"It's just you, so take whatever chair you want." The officer takes her position at the back of the room, standing with her arms locked behind her back.

I sit one chair away from the door. It's made of hard metal with a thin red fabric lining. I glance at the black telephone connected by a metal wire. It reminds me of an old phone booth, but with zero privacy.

"You have one hour," she says.

On the other side of the glass, a male officer appears. He has an athletic build and is incredibly handsome, like a model strutting down a runway. From the way his chest juts out, he knows it, too. He swaggers to a door in the room's corner and opens it.

Valerie and I are about to meet again for the first time in years, and my mother isn't here to stop me. I inhale a shuddering breath. I have the urge to flee the room. My fingers grip the chair, keeping me in place.

On the other side, the door slams closed. The male officer escorts a woman from the space. Handcuffs swing from her wrists.

There's no doubt this woman is a part of my family. She's an older version of my mother, with several hints of me in the curve of her nose and chin. Unlike my mother, who tries to appear the smallest person or item inside of a room, Valerie glides over to me like she's in a pageant. Even in a tan jumpsuit, she demands attention with the sharpness of her eyes.

I draw in a breath as she sits across from me. Our eyes don't waver, and even though I'm in no danger of falling into a vision, I might as well from the way my mind tunnels the world to include only us. She points at my phone, curling her long fingers around the matching one on her side. I bring mine to my ear, and my breathing fills the receiver.

"You're exactly as I imagined." Valerie's voice is smooth and deep. "Such a radiant woman."

"Am I?" I cringe at the squeak in my voice.

"This must be difficult for you."

I nod.

"I don't get many visitors, so this is a treat for me." The smile remains in her voice, even when it doesn't quite reach her eyes. "But I'm guessing if you're here, your mother has no idea."

Heat licks at my skin. "She doesn't."

Her eyes narrow slightly, but she seems pleased to see me. Too bad my mind has gone entirely blank. Even with Scott's prompting about going over the questions I want to ask, her presence is more overwhelming than I thought. A few days ago, Valerie existed as a ghost of this family. Unearthing her past and what she's done to the town of Orhaven wasn't an expected event.

"How much did she tell you about me?" she asks.

"You were close as kids. Um, but you died."

A spark of amusement lights her eyes. "I don't blame her for leaving that night. But I regret not knowing you. Please don't lie to her about coming here today. Honest communication is important with family."

My mother's lies swirl in my mind, rejuvenating my reason for coming here. I sit straighter. "She told me you—" I glance at the male officer. "The reason she left. Is that true? What you did?"

"Yes. She wanted to leave Orhaven. I had to show her how

dangerous the outside world could be. What loss felt like. Instead, I was the one who lost everything." The truth spilling out so easily surprises me. Maybe because I live with someone who keeps it locked away.

"How did you think that would make her stay?"

Her lips purse for a moment before they smooth out. "She wasn't supposed to know it was me. She wanted to take you away. She thought I couldn't keep you safe, but I wanted nothing more."

Her reaction wasn't the best way of showing it. "Since I've known her, she's never been content. We move around a lot."

Valerie drops her chin slightly, but her expression is unreadable. Does she feel regret that we left, or that my mother unveiled her plan? "That explains why it's been so difficult to get to her."

"You've tried to contact her?"

"I tried to. We forgive family of their actions, especially when they make mistakes. I bought our father's truck back from the dealer she sold it to. I forgive her, but she's yet to do the same for me."

That's the truck in the barn. A few of the pieces click into place, making me desperate to finish the puzzle before I leave her.

If we're supposed to forgive family, what of my father? "What do you know about Calvin?"

Valerie purses her lips, and she relaxes in her chair. "That man was the first person to hurt your mother in the most sensitive time in any woman's life. When she told him about you, he left town without a second glance. I picked up the shattered pieces of Nora's heart for months before you were born." Her eyes light up. "You filled both of us with such joy. It was the only real happiness I've experienced."

Valerie was in her twenties when I was born. She hadn't felt happiness before that? "What were my grandparents like? What happened when you were children? How did they pass? Did they ever hurt my mother or you?" The questions pour out of me like a poorly structured dam.

"I want to answer all the questions Nora hasn't. But I warn you, we didn't have a good childhood in that house. Nothing compared to the love she has undoubtably shown you. I understand her wanting to shield you as a child, but you've grown into an intelligent woman and deserve to know everything. But that's a risk you must agree to. I have no issues bearing the truth on you, but the burden isn't light. Your impression of this family will change. Knowledge can be power, but it also comes with a cost."

Valerie's known me for ten minutes, yet she's burrowed her way into my psyche. Her warnings of knowing the darker side of the family intrigue instead of frighten me. "Okay."

"Let's start at the beginning."

21

NOW

How I wish you could be here with us now, Nora. Our family together, at last. Jenny is unaware of what she's walking into. Her eagerness is a weakness, but with my truth, she will understand that everything I've done for this family wasn't my choice. The need grows even more in this place where I'm unable to satiate it. The calmness of my tone and my calculated movements are the only control I have.

I hesitate to rush into my story, noting how she leans into the phone and against the table as if her body intends to move through the glass to get closer to me. I revel in that for a moment as I recount the traumatic past of the Whitford family.

"Our father was a troubled man. He was introspective, angry, and strong. The combination of those traits didn't make our mother's life easy. Their marriage was one of convenience, and it didn't prove to give her any relief until after he passed. The time of his life where he had two spirited girls to care for tested his weaknesses. I caught on to this before Nora did and took it upon myself to protect her."

The shock across her face doesn't reach the desired effect.

She's holding back. You told her this already. No. She assumed it. She's smarter than you give her credit for. The darkness in this family doesn't end with me. Her interest strikes a match, a scorching flame I haven't felt for years. I shove down the urge to enjoy it in front of her. This is a private moment I will return to while I'm alone in my cell.

"Even now, in this place, that's my aim for our family. I will always be there, even when I'm not wanted."

I pause, awaiting her reaction. Will she accept me because I'm family, or does she need more probing into my life? I suspect she's more like me than you, dear sister. She disobeyed direct orders not to delve into our history, so her rebellion is present just like mine. I was never an unwilling victim. It fed the monster inside of me.

"I distracted him, forced him to pay attention to me during his sober hours. He taught me how to care for the land around us, fix the house, and how to dominate whatever I wanted. I endured his toxic masculinity to prepare for survival after the eventuality of his death. Every birthday, I wished for him to die."

She inhales sharply. But she's not disgusted like you, Nora. The wrongness within me always scared you. But not her. I can't push her too far. I need her to trust me, care for me even, before I reveal every piece of the history.

"My wish came true, eventually. With an unfortunate drunk tumble down the basement stairs, he left our family for good. Mother should have been pleased that she'd never have to experience him again, but she retreated further into herself until she wasn't useful at all for raising children. What I'd taken from Father proved to be essential to our survival. I cared for Mother while Nora made friendships, excelled in school, and had the best life a child could in a place like that. I took over the roles of mother and father, caregiver, and fixer. Mother's broken heart eventually took the last bit of life from her. She'd suffered so much for years after Father's death that it was almost a relief for her to go." She was weaker than the monster. Father beat that into submission years before we were born.

I allow one tear to slip from my eyes. Her gaze follows it until it descends to the table. I shove emotion into my words, needing her to see what is necessary for my plan. She will feel for me—and you—and it will shape her view of this family and yourself.

Jenny and I have the same nature. I've known since the moment she was old enough to use her hands. The way her gaze veered off in the distance before her little fists balled up and her eyes widened. My job is to give her the relief she seeks, but it won't be easy when I'm here instead of on the other side with you.

"I was old enough for the house to carry over to my name, and Nora and I continued our lives together. The deaths of our parents created a sense of lightness in our house. We were free from the chains of our parents and could live the lives we'd always wanted." I sit in that moment, watching her. She's not skilled in keeping her imaginings away from the world yet. They flicker to life under the surface of her eyes. Your eyes.

"I never wanted a life outside of Orhaven, even after the experiences inside the house. Nora wasn't as affected, so I chose not to be. Raising a better family held me in place more than anything else." This time I don't need to position the emotion into my voice, but I do twist it into a more appropriate one. "I had the opportunity when I got pregnant."

Her eyes flash with surprise. I temper the anger from the unnecessary loss. You never told your daughter about her cousin who died too soon. "But miscarriages aren't rare. In fact, after that, I found how common they are. When Nora got pregnant years later, I was cautious around her, desperate to protect you, Jenny. I don't know if it's because I lost my girl, but the expansion of our family gave me hope that the next generation in our house would change our history." I wish she knew how this is more of the truth than the rest of what I'm telling her. I have a duty to her more than to you. I promised her that from the moment I saw what we shared. There was a time I pictured her and her cousin running around the house the way you and I did before Father's overbearing nature shifted my view of life. It was never a possibility after my loss, but it altered the structure of our lives entirely.

She opens her hands between us as if she's inviting me closer. "Why did you abduct her?" The whisper in her voice gives me the slightest hint that she's digging into your side of the story instead of mine.

I'm practiced enough in controlling my emotions that I don't snap even when the audible crack fills my mind. There's so much she doesn't know, but with all my free time, I've plotted it out. She's jumping ahead, and I need to reel her back. I made the mistake of underestimating you once, I won't do the same with her. "I did it to show her what she'd miss if she left."

"If everything was going well with you two—with us—why did you think she was going to leave?"

I should have known she was more like me than I realized. Cunning, intelligent, and too strong for you to handle.

She's calculating, even though those muscles aren't shaped and honed yet. Her face tells me everything going on in her mind. I've lost so many years to your insistence that I wasn't her best protector. You were wrong to take her. Now, she wastes her skills, and each step of the plan clicking into motion moves the cogs forward to the next one. I frown slightly. The muscles twitch uncomfortably, wanting to return to their natural flatness.

"She thought she could be anything she wanted. While you

blessed our house with everything we might ever need, she always wanted more. I thought after your father left, she would see what a deadbeat he was. But she insisted on finding him. Foolish girl. There was only heartache in any discovery of where he went." Along with a truth that threatened our relationship. You can't know what I did to keep you close, and neither will Jenny. There are certain parts of people's minds which have to remain hidden to keep those we love safe.

Disgust cuts lines into her face. I never said this was going to be easy. But I'm here to make it simpler. Once she leans into what she's naturally good at, then she'll get what she desires quicker than denying the inevitable.

"Instead of telling her you didn't want her to go, you locked her away in the woods?"

"It worked for me. I was much younger when my father showed me the underground shelter." And all the secrets it contains. Father and I weren't always at war. He honed my skills from a young age. Showing me everything there was to know about the anatomy of smaller animals, using some of the more intricate trapping mechanisms to keep them alive until we got there to deconstruct them. Your supposed trauma isn't half of what I experienced. But you're not like her. Jenny is special, and soon she'll know that and be mine.

22

JENNY

My mind reels as Valerie answers every question with quickness and ease. It's almost too effortless. The hairs on my arms stiffen. Where my mother has constructed walls around our family's past, Valerie has taken a sledgehammer to them, splintering the metaphorical wood into a heap of shards. Her honesty is what my mother should have given me over all these years. I'd have no reason to visit a prison if my mother had been honest from the start.

My mother's words about Valerie's mental illness echo in my mind, feeding the frenzy of skepticism in my gut. I lean into her caution. Valerie murdered someone and abducted her sister. I can't trust her. Can I?

A tingling sensation prickles the back of my head, tugging at the hairs. It's where I place my visions when they're not torturing the front of my mind.

"I found your journal."

"Huh. I thought I had destroyed them all." Another quick answer, yet she seems unfazed by it.

"It was under a bed."

Valerie licks her lips, considering my response. "That used to be your room."

I stiffen. My mother would choose the room that couldn't haunt her as much as the others. "What are those pictures?"

Valerie's eyes narrow slightly, more with interest than malice. "I have a feeling you already know."

A swell of heat fills my eyes. The one person who understands the torture within my mind is a criminal. What does that say about me?

"You experience these visions like I do?"

Her head tilts to the side before her eyes slowly close, and she nods. "I don't remember a time when they didn't come to me. When I was a teenager, they intensified. It didn't help that when Father locked me away in the woods, I lived with them for days. There was no longer the opportunity for distraction."

"Distraction?"

"Yes. Whenever I would sense an imagining, I diverted the energy."

An imagining. It sounds better than vision, less mystical, more real. Yet grounding them in reality doesn't explain them fully. "How?"

Valerie clicks her tongue as her gaze lifts to the ceiling. The brief reprieve from her eyes makes me yearn for them again. As much as I can't trust her, it's hard not to when she's so like me.

"I might have taken to cutting wood for the fireplace or mending a part of the house. Once I expelled the energy, they would go away a lot quicker. If you're asking, then I assume you're having trouble controlling them?"

"You know how to do that? Have they gone away for you?"

"My dear, they never go away. That would be like losing a limb."

I sink in the chair. If there is a way to carve them out of my brain, sign me up.

"Releasing the buildup of energy satisfies them. The longest they've held off for me is about two years."

My jaw slackens. Two years? I've never been two days without one. "What can I do to keep them away?"

She doesn't answer at first, but she's staring at me as if she's waiting for me to speak. My skin flushes at the scrutiny. "They are a part of you. There's no need to fear them. They give you an opportunity."

Opportunity to experience intense terror and loss? "I don't want them."

Valerie's lips curve into an amused smile, as if I've told a joke instead of expressing my displeasure with the way my brain constantly tortures me. "My grandmother experienced them. My mother did as well, but by the time I took any notice, she was too far gone. This isn't something you can shake, Jenny. Lean into it."

"Is that how you stopped them for two years?"

Valerie doesn't hesitate with her response. "That, my dear, is a question I'll answer at your next visit." She stands, turning away from the booth, but the phone is still firmly against her ear.

"Wait. I can't come back."

"Sure you can."

"We're leaving tomorrow. For good."

"I have already cleared you for another visit. I'll see you then." She hangs up the phone and turns toward the guard.

"Wait!" I call.

Valerie carries on toward the door without a second look in my direction. The guard opens the door, and she walks through. A shadow of another guard in the next hallway leads her away.

I sink against the chair, allowing the conversation to wash over me. Like the revelation from my mother, I'm filled with the warmth of answers, but also the drowning sensation of more questions multiplying in my mind. And there's no way I can get the truth from her.

The walk back to the first building is quicker than before, though I fall behind the officer several times. Enough that she glances over her shoulder every few seconds to check my pace.

We enter the same back door of the building, and she opens the door to the waiting room. Scott sits quietly. He turns from the window.

My knees wobble slightly as the weight of the conversation with Valerie washes over me.

Questions flit across Scott's face, though neither of us speaks until we leave the building.

"How was it?" He matches each of my sluggish steps.

The more distance I put between myself and Valerie, the less I want to leave. The promised hour wasn't over, and according to her, there's more story to tell. There's no chance I can get back out to the prison to fulfill the need within me.

"Do you want to talk about it?" he asks.

"Sorry. It was fine." I glance around us. The number of cars in the lot thinned a bit since we arrived. "She wants me to come back."

Scott reaches for his keys. "Aren't you leaving?"

"I told her that." I arrive at my door but can't force my hand to open it. My tongue feels heavy, as if the weight of questions presses against it. "There's so much more to this family than I realized. She said she'll tell me more next time."

Scott opens the door, moving closer to me. I lean against the bed of the truck, allowing myself to feel something solid behind me. The entire time I was with Valerie, the floors and walls seemed softer, as if at any moment they could swallow me alive. Now, the world is hard and rigid with razor-sharp angles, ready to cut.

His hand finds mine. At first, it's as if he wants to hold it. I reach for him, but instead of his skin against mine, hard plastic rests in my palm. "Your mom called, and you got a few texts from someone named Abbie."

"Did you answer?"

"I didn't."

I wrap my fingers around my phone and slip into the truck. Scott closes the door.

The air is stifling, and the leather sears the backs of my legs. Instead of lifting my toes, I press harder. Sucking in a breath, I absorb the firmness of the present, while my mind locks more of the pieces of the past together.

Scott's presence shakes the truck, and the engine turns over. Hot air blasts from the vents, and he rolls down the window.

I no longer feel the seat against my legs. Yet I'm calmer than I was a moment ago.

The edges of my phone press against my hand, and I wrap my fingers around it. I can't call my mother yet. I can barely form a coherent thought.

Scott is patient with me, and it's not until the prison is behind us that my aunt's story spills from my dry lips.

Unlike how he talked with me through my mother's past, as he had on the way to the prison, Scott stays mostly silent, allowing me to analyze the conversation with Valerie. I leave out the personal bits about my imaginings, instead briefly mentioning that she had issues with her father—which he could easily pin on her being a murderer. There's nothing I can do about her reputation in Orhaven, so I don't try.

We stop at a diner about halfway through our trip. While Scott orders our food to go, I call my mother. I don't want Scott to witness her yelling at me like a petulant child, even though I know I deserve it. The moment I place my trembling hand to my ear, she picks up.

"Jenny, are you okay? Where are you?"

"I'm fine. I'm with Scott."

"Again? Why didn't you tell me? At least last time, you left a note." Her voice breaks, and tears well in my eyes. I'm such an idiot for not leaving a note. I imagine, after the questioning about a missing person, she comes home to a missing daughter.

"Sorry, we had poor service." I hate lying, but I need to ease her into the conversation about visiting Valerie. Without my presence, she'll have time to pack up the car and ready herself for my arrival. Then she'll force me to go. We can't leave. I have to go back to Valerie. It would be better if she comes with me, so we both can close the Valerie chapter in our lives, but she'll never agree over the phone. Today's events will wait until I see her face-to-face.

"What's going on between the two of you?"

"Nothing serious, Mom." Scott's too far away to listen to her side of the conversation, but my cheeks flush regardless.

"Well, what am I supposed to think?"

I need to get out of this conversation. "We'll talk when we get home."

"Don't do that ever again, you hear me? Leave a note or text at least."

I won't promise her anything until I get the full story. "Did they find out more about Wren?"

She sighs. "She's still missing."

"That's awful."

"Love you, honey. I'm sorry, I'm a mess today. This situation is just . . ." She trails off.

"Love you, too. See you soon."

As I hang up, Scott's already on the way to the car, carrying two brown paper bags. They're both darker at the corners, stained from whatever greasy food is inside.

He eyes me. "Everything okay?"

The scent of the food calms me. "It will be."

As if he senses my need to get home, Scott unwraps his burger and eats one-handed as he drives. The juicy burger hits home, and I realize I haven't eaten all day. I devour mine faster than Scott, stuffing massive bites one after another as if I haven't eaten for days. Besides my hunger, I don't want to talk to Scott about Valerie anymore. I have to tell my mother about the visit. There will be a fight. I prepare by leaning into the imaginings that form. My mother slices through the air with her hands, refusing to let me go back to the prison. Then I chase her up the stairs. She's in her room, throwing her belongings into her bags. I plead with her to stay as she gets into the car. Then it starts over. The scenarios repeat themselves, but each time with the same outcome. My breathing intensifies, and heat spreads through me. My stomach protests the food, and I regret eating so quickly.

It's not until the truck stops that I snap out of it. I focus on the house in front of us. In the time I was deep in my thoughts, Scott silently drove me back to the house. I ball up the wrapping for the burger and fries before shoving it into the paper bag. "Thanks for taking me."

Scott bobs his head. "I hope you get everything you're looking for here." A shadow crosses his face, and I can't help the guilt within me at not speaking to him much on the last part of our ride home.

I turn to face the house. The living room curtain shifts. She's waiting for me.

"If you need someone to talk to, I'm here," he says.

"I appreciate that."

My mother steps out to the front porch. Her arms fold over her chest as she stares at the truck.

"I think that's my cue." Scott grins at me.

I set my mind, preparing for a fight. She won't intimidate me into leaving without speaking to Valerie again. "I'll let you know if I find anything else about the doctor. Maybe you could be the first to give the newspaper the scoop."

"Ah, my life's goal."

I can't help laughing, and his broad smile makes my breath catch. "Bye."

"See you."

I get out of the truck with a hollowness in my gut. A part of me lingers on the seat before I pull myself away.

"Did you eat?" my mother calls from the porch. It's a strange introduction after the phone call, but I sense she's easing into it.

"Yes." I round the house, meeting her.

Her hands grip the top of one of the wooden rocking chairs as if she's about to snap it in half.

I lower myself into the one next to her. It creaks under my weight, and I lean forward so it doesn't fracture under me. There's more bare wood visible than the white paint coating it.

"We're not leaving tomorrow." She looks out toward the road, not meeting my eyes.

"Why?" Does she somehow know about where I've been and how Valerie wants me to come back?

"Davina wants me to stick around until they have more information on Wren."

My heart shatters. She has no clue I went to the prison. The conversation about her sister isn't going to be easy. At least I'll have some time to ease into it.

"Why do they need you?" I ask.

"It's complicated, honey. I hope you don't mind."

This entire trip is complicated, but getting another day is going to help my cause. If I can get her on board.

"This was supposed to be easy. In and out." She blows out a breath, big enough that it seems to deflate her lungs entirely. "After what Valerie has done to this town, it's hard to shake that stigma."

"You haven't been here in years."

"Small towns can hold grudges."

"Against you?"

"This family in general. I guess that includes me. Anyway, tell me about your day." She sits on the rocking chair next to mine. "I need a distraction."

As much as I want to lie, I can't expect Scott to bring me to the jail twice. So I give her what I want out of our relationship, the bitter truth. Valerie wasn't afraid of it at all, and as much as she's a murderer, I take a page from her book. "I went to the prison to visit Valerie. That's where I was with Scott."

"What?" She snaps the end of the question like a crack of a whip. "You did what?"

I stand tall, not allowing her to make me feel bad for making my own decisions. "You weren't going to let me visit her. I had to know more about your past that you insist on keeping to yourself."

She shoots out of her chair and crosses to the railing. Her hands tuck against her chest, her fingers curling over the hem of her sleeve. "I can't believe you went behind my back. How did you even get in there?"

"I'm on her list."

She lets out a rueful laugh. "Of course you are. She—" The rest of the words disappear on her tongue.

"She what?"

"Nothing."

I won't let her close the door on our family again. "What was I supposed to do? You have no interest in telling me anything about this place other than a shred of the story."

"Val is dangerous, Jenny. You shouldn't have done that. With her knowing that we're here . . ."

"She's in prison. She can't hurt us anymore."

Another laugh. "How I wish you were right about that."

"Then why don't you tell me?"

She mashes her lips together as if she's fighting an invisible force pressuring her to crack them open and reveal the truth. "Valerie's presence in this family hurts us. As long as she's alive, she's never going to stop. She's like a puppeteer who won't relinquish the strings. After all these years, she still got me back here."

"I thought this was about the house?"

"It is. Walter oversees the estate while Val is in prison. She offered to give me the house to do with it as I please, if I came back here to see her."

She's disappeared twice in two days. "Did you visit her?"

"No."

"Are you still selling the house?"

"I'm trying to find a way around it. But I don't want to decide while we're here. If she wants to keep it, fine. Though we could use the money."

"Come with me tomorrow. She already set it up." Knowing I'll be able to know more drives me to push my mother. She left our conversation at a cliffhanger, knowing I would want to return.

"Absolutely not. Giving in to her only makes it worse."

"She told me about growing up here. About your parents. Your father specifically. I understand how hard it must have been for you."

I wait for another overblown reaction, but she sits down. Her fingers tangle in her lap. "Did you tell her what I told you?"

"She did most of the talking." I hesitate, dropping my gaze to the jagged wood under my shoes. "She spoke about her urges. She said she'll tell me more about our similarities if I go back. I have to go back."

It's my last card, and I hand it over, wanting her to do the same. This family tortured her. Even from a young age, she taught me there were two sides to every story. It still holds true, even when one of them is a murderer.

"She's manipulating you. You are nothing like her. You're kind, and—"

"It has nothing to do with kindness. There's something different about my mind." The thickness in my throat surprises me as my breath catches. "The things I see."

My mother frowns, and I'm sure I made a mistake telling her. She'll do anything for me, and if I can convince her that this next visit is for a reason to do with me instead of her, my plan might work.

"I found a journal of hers. The pictures show danger and terror. It's what I experience."

"Bringing Val into your life isn't going to help you."

"She knows how to stop them."

Her eyes narrow. "Is that what she told you?"

"Yes."

I love my mother more than anyone in my life. When it comes to why I came here and our current standing in this town, she can't stop me from doing what I need. "I'm going."

"Jenny."

"You don't have to help me, but I have to do this. If you never want me to see her again after tomorrow, I'll respect your wishes. I can get Scott to take me." Even though I hope I don't have to.

She swallows, a painful gesture as if she's shoved gravel down her throat. Her eyes close. "He won't take you."

"He will."

"No, he won't. Because I'm going."

23

JENNY

The shift in my mother's attitude surprises me. "You're going to talk to her?"

"I said I'll take you." Her shoulders stiffen, and her fingers pinch the hem of her sleeves.

If she's not going to see her sister with a bulletproof shield between them, then there's no chance she wants to see her again. I can push for her to get closure, but I tread carefully so she doesn't change her mind.

She heaves a sigh. "I'm still unsure."

"You said it's a condition of the sale."

"I know what I said."

"I'll be there with you."

She trails a finger across the railing. "It would be nice to have money in savings. But at what cost? Giving in to her? I'm not sure I can, Jenny. I'm sorry."

"You don't have to decide now."

"I wanted to protect you from all of this, honey."

"I know the story."

She turns away from me, focusing on the sprawling landscape. Is she seeing the ghosts of her past on the property? Knowing my visions, I would.

I twist my fingers together. I've held back what's been inside of me for so long. Valerie's ease in talking about herself strangely inspires me. "Even though she's done terrible things, it's nice to feel connected with someone else. Instead of feeling like the only freak in the family."

"You're not a freak. You're nothing like her. There's so much more . . ." Her voice trails off, and she seems to disappear into her mind.

I watch her, wondering if that's what I look like when I fall into a vision. I want to push more, but she's already agreed to accompany me to visit Valerie. She could take that away at a moment's notice, so I drop it.

"This is it, Jenny. The last thing I'm ever doing for her. You understand? I want to be out of here the moment Davina says I can go."

"I understand." I won't waste the last hour I have with my aunt. Pulling my phone from my pocket, I open the prison's website to check visiting hours. Scott handled it last time, so I'm unsure of the process.

Every second between now and then, she can change her mind. My mother has always kept her promises. Even with this one on shaky ground with her personal trauma, I know it's going to happen.

Visiting hours open at eight in the morning. My time in Orhaven is down to hours, and with each passing moment, the threads holding me here snap as I move toward what I've needed to find in this place.

With the decision about the visit finalized, my mother tasks me with bringing the donation boxes to the porch for Scott to pick up. When I finish, she's in the kitchen, mopping the floor. A set of cleaning chemicals sits on the table, and I bring the wood polish into the dining room.

Her voice floats in from the other room. "What else did she tell you?"

I don't hold back the way I did with Scott. She's the only person who knows about my imaginings, and if Valerie can help me stop them, then my purpose in Orhaven is worth all the arguments and heartache between me and her.

She listens quietly, not inserting any accusations about the truth of the story, so I assume what Valerie told me is accurate. Much of Valerie's story takes place during times my mother claims not to remember. From the way curiosity raises her eyebrows, she can't hide her surprise with every new bit of information. Her confirmation of the facts of this family unfurls a lightness throughout my body, an ease within me that gives me even more confidence that Valerie can help me. Without the visions, I can finally start living my life like a normal person.

I dust the book area, scanning the titles once more with a new lens. Instead of imagining a younger version of my mother sitting in the alcove, I picture a grown Valerie lounging there after a day at work, snuggled up with a romance novel. I'm unsure why it's hard for me to imagine her murdering someone. But I suppose that's why she had such an impact on the town. No one saw it coming.

I move into the kitchen, and my mother is scrubbing the sink.

The basement door is closed, but the key hangs from the nail next to it. The trust between us isn't entirely gone. There's hope for a new normal, and the murkiness of the future clears.

"Who slept down there?"

She glances at me over her shoulder. "Val."

"Why?"

"Our father meant it as a punishment for her. I don't remember when it happened."

I eye the key. How often did my grandfather lock his daughter in the basement? My stomach churns at the impending vision. I force my gaze to the floor as it overtakes me. Young Valerie doesn't fight when the man from the photographs presses the bottom of his beer bottle against her back. With her head down, she willingly travels into the void. He slams the door on her heels and turns the lock before slipping the key into its place. He turns slowly, taking a long pull from the drink before his eyes meet mine.

"The punishment was a one-time thing. She chose to stay down there. She liked it. Or it seemed that way . . ."

I snap into the present, drawing in a breath as slowly as I can so I don't alert her to my vision, though my lungs scream for release.

"She stayed there even after he passed. Until—" She twists around, staring at the floor. Her head shakes slightly. "The day of my mother's funeral, Val moved upstairs to the same bedroom our parents slept in."

"That seems morbid," I say.

She snorts. "Knowing what I now know, I'm not surprised."

She continues removing our mark on this house while my mind wanders to the window. I focus on the spot where she dug around the garden. There's more closure I need on this property. She removed something from the hole in the basement, and it's there for me to discover.

Now isn't the time to ask. We're in a good place, and I need her to take me to the prison. I'll find a better time after I get what I need from Valerie.

. . .

195

Later that evening, we drive to the downtown area for dinner. For most of our visit, she's kept away from public appearances in town, but I have a feeling she's trying to prove that she isn't like her sister. We're not connected to a disappearance like Valerie. As soon as Wren turns up, the town can clear her name. Then we'll be on our way with no more rumors of the Whitford family spilling from the lips of people who don't know us.

We go to the same diner Scott and I went to the other day. The sun setting across the horizon creates a haze moving through the dining area, coating the patrons and reflecting the tables' surfaces.

When we enter the room, a few people glance over. Some give us double takes. My mother's shoulders roll forward, shrinking into herself. She scoots toward the nearest empty table. She dips her head, her hair forming a curtain over her face. The impact of our arrival crosses the expressions of these strangers.

"Do you want to go somewhere else?" I glance out the window, wondering if there is another restaurant in this town.

"They're going to talk no matter where we go. Besides, I won't be my family's reputation anymore. It's small-town gossip, that's all. When we leave, it's gone for good."

I lift the laminated menu from the table. It's one page, much smaller than the double-sided breakfast one from the other day.

She makes a noise in her throat, and she stares across the room.

I peer over my shoulder, finding the person who caught her attention. Mike Allen sits at the corner table. The chair across from him is empty, yet there's a half-eaten burger sitting on a plate in front of it. My stomach swoops at the anticipation of seeing Scott again. It seems like every time I say goodbye to him, it's never our last.

Mike has already spotted my mother, and a smirk crosses his

lips. A door opens toward the back of the room, and it's not Scott who walks toward the table, it's Zee.

"That's Wren's daughter."

"It is?" My mother chokes on the words.

For once, I know something about Orhaven that she doesn't. "Why is she with Mike?"

Mike waves her over. Zee spots us, and her eyes widen. She doesn't sit. Instead, she glances at the door.

"Are you sure it's a good idea to talk to him?"

My mother shrugs. "I didn't do anything."

"Zee was really upset the other day."

"Maybe if she meets me. Or if I explain that I was good friends with Wren." She stands from her chair and lowers her voice. "Besides, we're not criminals."

She seems adamant to speak to Zee and Mike. She walks from the table, and I'm not sure if I should follow. Zee may think we're ganging up on her. But if I stay, does that make us seem more guilty in Wren's disappearance?

I don't have enough time to decide. Zee zips around the other tables, heading in my direction. She shoots a look at my mother before sliding into the chair across from me. She tucks her arms close to her body.

My mother sits next to Mike and glances at Zee before speaking to him. They're too far away to hear their conversation, even though the volume of the other patrons stays at a casual rumble.

Up close, the darkness surrounding Zee's eyes becomes more apparent. "How are you doing?" I ask.

"Terrible."

"I'm sure the police will find her."

"Your mom was no help." She scrubs her wrist under her nose.

"Did you really think my mother had anything to do with it?"

Zee drops her head into her hands and sniffs. "The texts were everything. Now, there's nothing."

I try to hold on to the idea that Zee is young and in an emotional state, and not insinuating my mother would do this. She'd never, after what happened to her. I wish I could tell Zee that, but it's not my place.

She wipes her glossy eyes. "I've been so mean to her lately."

"It happens."

Zee curls into herself. "She's always out late with whoever she's dating. This place isn't huge, and there aren't many great options. She thinks if she's hooking up with men outside the house, then it doesn't affect me. I blew up at her the other day. I called her some nasty names."

"I'm sure she's not upset with you."

"I called her a slut and might have thrown a bitch in there, too."

I can't help wincing.

She lifts her chin to the ceiling. "I won't ever say anything bad to her again. I just want her to come home." Her abrasiveness disappears, and a child sits in front of me. I can't help placing myself in her shoes.

"This is a small town. I'm sure something will turn up."

"Not if she's rotting somewhere." There's no longer any emotion in her voice. It's flat and morbid. I have experience with that, but my heart goes out to this girl. I can't imagine if I was that young and my mother went missing.

I reach out and touch her hand. "Don't say that."

Zee locks eyes with me. "We're going on day four now. This is the longest she's ever been away from me."

"Zee?" Mike's gruff voice appears from behind me. His thick fingers curl against the back of my chair, brushing against my hair. He holds a Styrofoam container in his other hand. "I got your food to go."

Her eyes flick to his. "Coming."

"Do you have anything to say to Ms. Whitford?" he asks.

My mother clears her throat. "It's Miller now."

Mike chuckles. "Old habits die hard, I guess."

My mother shakes her head. "You don't need to say anything to me, Zee. You're going through a rough time, and I can imagine how you're feeling." She moves aside, but Zee stops in front of her.

I've seen her in several states of emotion, and I wonder which one she'll fling at my mother. "I'm sorry I accused you of hurting my mom."

"You did what you thought was right. I'm sure this will all be a misunderstanding when she comes home."

Zee shrugs and scoots around Mike to the door.

Mike touches the brim of his cap. "See you ladies later."

He leaves, and I peer through the window, spotting Mike putting his arm around Zee. She leans into him.

My mother sits across from me and lets out a sigh.

"Are they related?" I ask.

She shakes her head. "Mike and Wren dated a few years ago apparently, but Zelda's staying with him and Scott until this is all resolved."

I recall Scott's unwavering patience; she's in good hands with that family.

"Did he tell you anything else?" I ask.

She flips the menu over. "No."

"That's hard to believe. This town seems to be held together by telephone wires. They have nothing else to go on other than your texts?"

"I guess she's been careful about who she's with lately. Mike seems to think it's because she saw how upset Zelda's been about her dating. Wren has never been one to have anyone hold her back."

"What about Zee's dad?"

Mom glances out the window. "It's a toss-up who he is. From what Wren says, it was a one-night stand. Everyone took her word on that."

"Do you believe that?"

"Wren might like to have fun, but she's not stupid. She probably sees no reason to let Zee know about a guy who has no clue about her."

"Just like my dad?" The words come out before I can stop them. During my rehashing of the conversation with Valerie, I mentioned my father, but Mom doesn't linger on the topic. She never does.

"I suppose." Her words close that conversation. I pause that line of questioning until I can process this trip before opening myself up to that part of my life.

The next morning, we move around the house as if we are opposite sides of magnets. Whatever room I enter, she makes an excuse to leave. The impending conversation with Valerie is undoubtedly going to put us in another state of unrest once she opens up about more of her life with my mother. Her avoidance only makes me want to break into her mind and tell me anything to ease mine.

Instead, while she takes the longest shower ever, I text Abbie. The last few days pour out of me. While I wait for her response, I read over the text. It reads like a horror movie. Complete with abductions and murders. I don't mention the imaginings. No wonder Mom changed our names after we left. To give me more of a normal life.

Abbie says nothing, and I wonder if she's playing instead of checking her phone.

What if she has no idea what to say? I read through the text again, my palms heating up with every word. Is it too much for Abbie? My gauge is off on what is normal, and being in Orhaven only makes it worse.

Mom pokes her head in my bedroom, her hands gripping the towel at her chest. "Let's get this over with."

I check my phone again and follow her.

She's focused on the road and barely says a word to me on the ride to the prison. With rock music blasting, she's in thinking mode. It's how she works through a problem in her head. Instead of fixing an appliance in our apartment, she's trying to fix my exposure to her sister. But she can't.

The ride with Scott was much different. With him, I was excited. With her, I'm a jumble of nerves as visions bombard me. Scott offered ease, while she intensifies every negative emotion within me. Her worry permeates my skin, forcing my stomach to roll over itself while I see us crashing into another car, or Valerie not being able to meet me today. The outcomes make little sense, but they're enough to make each minute move excruciatingly slow.

It's not until we arrive at the prison that I'm finally able to take full breaths without fearing I'm about to pass out.

After she parks the car, she turns to me. "You don't have to do this."

"I do." If I wasn't sure before, the overwhelming urge to lose my breakfast for the last fifty minutes gives me enough certainty to push out of the car. I have to find out how to tune out these visions before closing this chapter of our family legacy for good.

24
NOW

The click of the cell door snaps me away from thinking of her. My plan is in place. You have no idea what is in my mind, and neither does Jenny. Exploiting her "imaginings" was too easy. It's much more delicious than I could have ever imagined.

You thought you could get rid of me by leaving town, yet I'm with her every single day. She sees me in you, and she will continue to as I stay in the forefront of her mind. You won't give up on her as quickly as you gave up on me. You care for her as much as I do for both of you.

That's how my plan will work. When I took you, in your mind, it was me against you. Once I follow through, it will be the three of us against the world. You'll never be able to leave her once you know what she must do. You'll think of me every day until I can get out of this place.

"Your family is here." Officer Brewer stands in front of the cell, holding her hands out. Her lips purse, trying to appear superior to me. Little does she know what I can do with a few seconds and proximity to her neck. "Now."

I know the drill. I'm not a fool like the rest of these convicts. I'm the one who forced my way into this place to get you back to Orhaven. You can have the house and sell it for all I care, I needed to get Jenny to see me once. Her instincts are raw, but we connect with those like us. The plan is already in motion, with his help. Which is what has kept me close to him. His work will keep you in town for long enough to give her a taste of what she desires.

The handcuffs cut against my skin. Brewer doesn't care how she handles inmates. Too bad she doesn't know that I've been through worse. A kill is never easy. You have to expect them to fight back. It's the only way to get the advantage.

The others bang on the bars as I walk by, hooting at me. Even though I rarely speak, they respect me and know what it's like to have visitors. Them more than me. My approved list is small by choice. Just three.

The door outside the visiting area has no window, but her presence fills me in a way I haven't noticed I needed. Not since yesterday.

It's as if we're connected to the same tether I always associated with you. Blood has a way of connecting people, whether it's running through veins or spilled across the ground, soaking into the dirt.

Brewer reaches around me to open the door. I find Jenny right away. She's already at the chair, her hand reaching for the phone. I have her attention even before our eyes meet.

I find memories from the innocent happiness in her childhood, filling me with a bubbling excitement which only truly fills me.

I sit in the chair. Through the glass, a ghost of my outline appears around her, like a twisted guardian angel who promises to lead her down the path she's always yearned for, even though she's never understood it.

She presses the phone to her ear. I match her movements, showing her the connection between us. We're the same.

"Thank you for coming again," I say.

She glances at the door and then back to me. There's nothing there, but I look anyway. "Are you expecting someone else?"

"Mom came with me today. I thought—" She shakes her head and sighs. "I don't know why I thought she'd come in with me."

You're here? Interesting. This might be as close as you get to the sale of the house. A pity for you. It's a gift. "This isn't about her. This is about us."

"We're not coming back after today." There's a slight warning in her warble. She fears me, but she's also trying to be firm.

I understand you don't want to return, and I won't force you this time. You'll make your way here on your own.

"Is the house settled? You're going back home?"

"Yeah."

I have so much work to do, but it's a challenge I'm more than willing to take on. It's not as if I'm leaving soon. "Then we better not dawdle."

She sits up straighter. It's an unconscious movement, giving away how much she wants from me. "I want to know how to get rid of them. The vis—imaginings."

I say the words I've rehearsed all night. "From what I know, they don't entirely leave you. At least that's what I've experienced. They serve as a warning. They feed the fear for our survival." Mother had similar experiences as Jenny. She allowed them to consume her, and they fed on her even more. Jenny is not weak. I'll make her my own. "When I give in to the energy they produce, then it releases them."

"You said they've been gone for two years."

"Yes."

"How?"

I wait for her to put the pieces together. "You know what happened two years ago."

She blinks, and realization floods her face. Her hand tenses around the phone as the feeling she's always endured, but never embraced, fights to earn its place in her conscious mind.

I wait. I won't give her all the answers. The only way to understand is to force it out. She's held back for too long now. We have a long road ahead of us.

"You killed the doctor." Her voice is low, but the guards already know what I've done.

She'll get a version of this truth until we're allowed to truly be alone, then I'll show her everything. Light will shine on those dark corners, revealing the beauty in the terrifying.

"He wasn't as perfect as everyone in town thought. He was supposed to keep my secrets. He swore an oath." I swallow, acting as if this confession hurts. None of my truths hurt. How could they when I've orchestrated all of them? "He was going to report me to the authorities. You saw the journal. I did what I had to." It takes most of my strength not to look at my hands. While most of my impulses haven't surprised me, the blood does. When I stare at my hands too long, his stains appear on my skin, reminding me what I've done. Sometimes I hold them in front of me for hours until the other inmates get restless from my laughter.

"You're saying I have to hurt someone to get rid of my visions?"

Repulsion twists her lips. She's pulling away from me. The truth hurts, but once accepted, it will make her life much easier. When Father was alive, I took the hard road as much as possible. It seemed to be the way of life until he died. His was the first human blood I shed. Experimenting was the only way through this. Here I am, offering a foolproof plan. Her resistance is only as strong as her need to feed her version of the monster. I'll prove it to her, sooner than she thinks.

"The imaginings show you the way, to their detriment. It's within us."

"That's not me." She shoves away from the table. The cord stretches to its limit, keeping her as far away as possible, though it remains close to her ear. She's intrigued.

"You experience violence every single day," I say.

She glances at the guard behind her. They won't be able to do anything. Getting caught was easy. I'll teach her how to fulfill her darkest desires to shape her life the way she's always dreamed. She barely knows me, and I don't expect her to come back here once she's realized her potential. This is my farewell present. Knowing that she'll continue to pass this down to her children is my greatest parting gift.

"I won't."

She will. Maybe not now, but someday. And how sweet it will be. "Sit down, Jenny."

She does as I ask, albeit as slowly as possible. She treats me like I'm a snake about to strike. But little does she know there's a fragile egg inside of her with a coiling creature ready for birth. The facade may not have cracked yet, but it will. That's the plan before your departure from Orhaven.

"I'm sorry if I scared you." I tread carefully. I've never meant an apology before, and she's no different. But she needs coddling right now. Not for too long. The clock ticks down the hour.

"I don't know what you want with me, but I'm not coming back here. This was a mistake." Her words signal a departure, yet she doesn't show any intention of leaving.

"You wanted the truth."

"I wanted your help." Her voice is a thick whisper. Tears shine in her beautiful eyes.

She wanted an easier way out of this. Nothing in life is easy. You truly didn't prepare her. A confidence lies in wait within her. A power that I can mold and wield to my will. "I gave it."

I understand you treading lightly around situations, which is how you never would have survived without me. You stunted her mental growth. I can show her what strength looks like. The chosen Whitford are burdened with gifts, and we can shape futures that may never exist without us.

"There's a missing woman in Orhaven." Her eyes finally reach mine. A flicker of the flame I know burns within her, igniting my own. She thinks I have something to do with this missing woman because of what I did to you. Are you ever going to let that go? My failed experiment will haunt me for the rest of my life. Knowing that she ended up the way she did without my guidance hurts more than you can imagine.

"What is your question?"

She stares at me as if I haven't practiced lying to others for years. If you never left, I could have taught her how to hide emotion from her face.

"Her name is Wren. Do you know her?"

"Nora's friend. They were close." Too close. Enough that she needed more attention than the others.

"They brought my mom in for questioning. They think because of our family history"—she spits the word—"that she has something to do with it."

"Your mother wouldn't hurt an insect." You'd run away from it, but you don't have my instincts.

"I know. But it seems strange timing that it happened when we got to town."

Almost as if someone planned to keep you here. She's starting to catch on. Maybe this isn't a lost cause. "Are you asking me a question?"

Her accusing stare is a spark of what I need from her. Keep digging, and she'll get to the truth, eventually.

She hesitates but shakes her head. "I should go now. This was a mistake."

She wants more. It's why she came back, and why she will again. But I don't push. Not yet. Some need more time to consider these options than others.

"I'm here for you always, Jenny. No matter what."

She moves away from the table, hanging up the phone. I stay where I am, cultivating the last image she'll have of me this time. A sad, old woman in prison. She's unsure of my strength and abilities, which is why when she thinks about it hard enough, she'll come back to me and ask me how I had the ability to take down the doctor, and the others before him.

25
JENNY

As I follow the guard toward the visitors' area, the conversation with Valerie fills my mind. My thoughts separate from my body like a movie playing out in front of me. I picture my mother's questioning looks. She won't believe me if I tell her any of what I learned, or maybe this is what she already knows about her sister.

I expected Valerie to tell me that her time in prison has given her the opportunity to meditate and reflect on her impulses. Maybe therapy sessions helped. But perpetuating murder? I should have known better. She hurt my family in so many ways. She's untrustworthy, and I was a fool to think otherwise. A bitter taste floods my mouth.

Valerie's story changes nothing about my visions. She brought me back here to revel in the crime she committed. Why torture me? She could have guessed my mother told me about the doctor's murder. Maybe she was searching for information instead of wondering how much I knew. I suppose she knows my mother more than either of us thought. I had to find out about the murder through Scott, and Mom seems to only know the information in the newspaper article.

If Valerie told the police about her imaginings, that might have put her in a different facility. But maybe a lesser sentence? The more I speak with my aunt, the more I want to dig into her brain and motives. Somehow, she knows I experience visions, but I'm nothing like her. I can barely handle the death in my mind. There's no way I can embrace experiencing it in real life. Her? Not so much. It makes sense that after the abduction, my mother left. She took me away from someone who had the potential to hurt us without regret.

In the waiting room, my mother stands by the door. I rush into her arms, and she strokes my hair like she did when I was younger. Tingles move down my spine. This is where I'm supposed to be. There's no judgment from her.

"We can talk when you're ready," she says.

I give away nothing as we walk to the car. It's the same as yesterday with Scott. Though, she already knows most of the truth about Valerie's conviction and what her sister is capable of. She lived with a murderer for most of her life, and I can't imagine what she thought while I was in there.

As the distance grows between us and Valerie, a weight lifts from my shoulders, but it doesn't disappear. It coils into a knotted ball, settling in the pit of my stomach. I can't talk about the visit yet. I need to process it. If I tell her what Valerie thinks I should do, I don't know how she'll react. I see the dozens of scenarios as we race down the highway back to Orhaven. None of them are good. I suspect she'll want to get me into therapy again, and I almost agree that it might be the best option.

With the doctor, it seems like Valerie tried to do better for herself. But with the idea that murdering was helpful to stave off the imaginings, her idea of therapy is not quite the same as mine.

"Are you hungry?" She lifts a finger to a sign posted near the shoulder showing several fast-food chains off the next exit.

"I could eat."

We cross into the exit lane so quickly I wonder if she was waiting for a response or not.

I promise myself to tell her everything once we settle at a restaurant. I can't keep her in suspense anymore, knowing how hard it was for her to get that close to Valerie. I'm also not ready to tell her Valerie's solution. She knows I would never hurt a living thing, but if that's her sister's solution for our twisted minds, can I burden her with that? Valerie's prison sentence isn't set in stone. If I tell my mother that she won't stop killing to rid herself of her imaginings, she'll never sleep at night. I can live with the burden since I have an advantage she doesn't. Valerie connects with me. She shares the part of our mind I've always tried to hide. Even though I abruptly retreated from our conversation, her interest in my mind didn't waver. She wants me to follow her path, and I suspect she'll try anything to make it happen.

Instead of going to a drive-through restaurant, my mother parks the car outside of a diner. The moment we enter the tiny space, the scent of eggs curls my stomach. The place is full and loud, with people chatting and utensils clanging against plates, but I follow her to an empty booth at the back of the room. We pass an open kitchen where several guys scramble through the space, shouting orders to each other. My head spins as if I drank too much the night before, and time seems to speed up unnaturally. It's not the same experience as a vision but an inevitability of the upcoming conversation with my mom.

A young server asks for our order, and I go with a grilled cheese and fries. It's enough to get my mother off my back about eating but plain enough that it won't make my stomach even more uncomfortable than it already is. Food seems to be the only comfort in this place, and I'm reminded of Scott. Relief swoops through me just by ordering.

"Same," she says, and gives the menus to the server. Her hands come together as if she's praying. I imagine her nerves are as wound as mine.

"Drinks?" the girl asks.

"Two cokes. When you get a chance." Mom gives the server a close-lipped smile, as if politely telling her to leave and not come back until the food arrives.

Once the girl is gone, she turns to face me.

The moment is here, but I'm still unsure what to say. The entire story? Part of it? I glance behind me. An older couple takes up the booth, but they have enough trouble hearing each other. I doubt they'll pay much attention to a conversation about murder and convicts.

"She told me about the doctor," I say.

"Dr. Bradley? What did she say?"

"Apparently she told him she had bad thoughts about hurting people." Stretching the truth is easy enough. Valerie didn't explicitly admit why she saw the doctor, but it was a cry for help, and he betrayed her. At least in her eyes. "He wanted to tell the police and she—you know . . ."

I think of the journal. The words etched within her drawings. Now, I understand most were his words. I don't understand her needing to kill him, but with the imaginings plaguing her mind, the possibility is always there.

She sits against the booth, shaking her head. We know enough about Valerie to fill in the blanks. "She told the police and the lawyers none of this."

"She was still going to get in trouble."

"If the doctor had just listened to her and did his duty to inform the others, she could have gone to a hospital for help and not prison."

Exactly my thoughts.

"Do you think she would have changed her ways if she went somewhere else?" Valerie was sick, but not in the way my mother understood. Valerie knew what she was doing with Dr. Bradley. She showed no remorse, only a promise of more whenever the imaginings appeared again.

"I always thought she should be on medication. She was always so quick to react instead of thinking. Her emotions were all over the place when we were kids."

"Your dad didn't help."

"Neither did our mother. She was so absent. We had no guidance." She drops her head into her hands.

I have seen little sympathy from my mother for Valerie. Knowing that they misdiagnosed her as a child helps ease my mind about our similarities. We might share these imaginings, but that doesn't mean I'm like her. I hold on to that thought with all my mental strength, even though visions of living a life without them arise. I've never considered having children or spending my life with anyone who isn't in my family. There's too much at risk, and sacrificing my happiness is the only way to keep those I love as safe as possible.

The server returns with our drinks, placing them in front of us. "Your food will be out shortly."

My mother smiles at the girl, waiting until she walks away before speaking again. "What else did you talk about?"

The opportunity is here. I just have to say it. Valerie wants me to kill people so I'll no longer have the visions. But I can't, not yet. "I mentioned Wren."

"Why?"

I shrug. At the time, it seemed important. "She disappeared without a trace like you did, the moment we arrived in town. It's strange, right?"

"Jenny, there's no need to worry about that. When we were kids, Wren ran away more times than I can count."

"She's a mother."

"Some people don't change."

Valerie had said my mother and Wren were good friends growing up. The lack of sympathy she's given Wren after speaking with the police isn't like her. She's already pulling away from Orhaven, while I can't help digging in.

"Is that all?" she asks.

Under the table, my hands clench into fists. The words evaporate from my lips. "Yes."

"I'm sorry she didn't give you any answers. I wanted to believe that she might do that for you. She's continuing her game. At least we can leave now with you knowing the truth about her."

I know enough of the truth to leave Valerie behind, but I already know I'll never stop wanting more.

"Can you drive back?" she asks after she's paid the bill.

The only time my mother asks me to drive is when she's stressed or exhausted. She wasn't the one to visit with Valerie, but the trip alone must have been a lot for her. She didn't pry into the visit anymore after we got our food, but I can tell she's in her head about it. She hides from the truth about her sister, wanting to block her out entirely. I don't blame her, but I'm also not like that at all. I'd rather have all the information before creating my own opinions.

I already know how the day will pan out. My mother lives by consistency. When we go back to the house, she'll take her medication and fall asleep. It's another afternoon lost, but I'm used to her dragging her feet with helping me discover facts about her past. At least solitude will give me time to process both conversations with Valerie and possibly reveal an alternative path for me. Not that I have any idea where it will lead.

For the rest of the ride, she doesn't speak. She's retreated into her mind, while I focus on the road and keep everything I've learned at the front of mine. This isn't a time to escape.

When we arrive at the house, she heads for the front steps while I hover by the car. I need to come at this new plan with a fresh perspective. I've focused on the house the entire time, but she seems to forget that I watched her hide something in the garden. It's a strange coincidence that Valerie buried the doctor on the property, and Mom has the same inclination to hide her secrets. She found something in Valerie's basement bedroom, and I intend to collect all the pieces of the family jigsaw before I make my next move.

After she goes in, I wait almost five minutes before heading to the shed. Like the other day, I expect she'll come out and ask what I'm doing. But she doesn't. I retrieve a shovel and bring it to the garden.

After the rain, the soil is heavy as I dig into it. The dip in the earth from where she dug is still visible. The *snick* of the metal into the dirt and subsequent movement of the crumbling drier earth stirs an imagining. I don't resist it.

I take the image of Dr. Bradley from the newspaper article and place his lifeless face into the hole I'm digging. The world darkens around me, and my breathing slows. The ability to be both present and in my mind calms me. I know it's not real. It's an event that's already happened, yet I don't fight it. I'm in Valerie's reality. Blood stains the handle of the shovel. A renewed strength overcomes me as my hands morph into the slender ones that wrapped around the phone on the other side of the glass. I tread carefully, having never experienced an imagining as anyone but myself. Piecing together the past, coupled with my current mission, creates a twisted parallel.

Each time I blink, the view switches between the present and past. The world tilts, and I try to grasp either timeline to ground me.

That's when the shovel finds its mark. A cracking sound sears my soul.

I fly to the present. Kneeling, I ease the dirt off the smooth surface. It's a glass jar. I dig around it to make sure I haven't punctured it with the shovel. Inside, brackish liquid sloshes around. I extract the jar and hold it in my hands. It's heavier than I expected. A sliver of an object appears before sinking into the liquid again. I angle the jar to get a better look at the item my mother buried.

When it appears again, I don't register the shape right away. It's oblong with four thin sticks coming out of it. The word comes to mind, but it's not until I see the shriveled thread protruding from the center of the object that I understand.

Bile rises in my throat, and I moan. The jar falls from my hands, and the fetus bumps the glass. I bend over and retch until there's nothing left in me.

"Jenny?"

A shuffling sound overpowers the thudding of my heartbeat in my ears. I turn, spotting a pair of familiar shoes pointing at me.

"What did you do?"

The scent of my sick permeates my mouth and rises to my nose. I take several deep breaths through my mouth before standing on trembling legs. "Is this real?"

"Yes. Valerie had a miscarriage. Long before you were born."

"She kept it?" I can't hide the shriek in my voice. I didn't think she could surprise me after murdering a person.

"It was a tragic accident. She wasn't the same after that."

"Why did you bury it?"

"I couldn't keep it in the house. I had to remove the last part of her. Besides, I doubt a new owner would appreciate it. She deserves a proper burial." She moves closer to me, slowly, as if she's approaching a trap.

Little does she know all the energy has drained from my body. I won't be able to move from my spot, even if I try. "Why are you keeping everything important from me?"

"You didn't need to see this. Frankly, I'm annoyed you even bothered to look."

"You were out here like a wild animal digging in the dirt. How was I supposed to ignore it? I'm more willing to trust Valerie than you. She's answered all my questions."

A look of hurt flashes across my mom's face. "You shouldn't trust her."

"Why? She's the only person who wants to understand me. She told me how to get rid of the imaginings."

"You can't believe anything she says, Jenny."

"She understands me." Even if she wants me to commit terrible acts.

She shakes her head and turns away from me. I've ripped the bandage off, and now with her wounds exposed, I'll dig in until it hurts. There are more twisted secrets in this family than I can unravel on my own. Each thread finds a new spool, and I will tug them until they snap.

She runs inside, and I keep up with her. In the kitchen, she flings open the basement door. Within seconds, she's thundering down the stairs. I hesitate at the doorway. Before I can say anything, she appears at the bottom, holding two pairs of boots. She stomps up the stairs. One pair is worn with age. The other looks almost brand-new with no blemishes. "These should fit. Put them on."

She sits at the table, flinging her shoes off before slipping her feet into the worn boots. "You insist on pushing me, Jenny.

Now, I'm going to show you why Val isn't the one to trust in this family."

I don't recognize her flat tone and fiery glare. My pulse spikes as I'm reminded of Valerie. They are sisters, and I've driven my mother to a breaking point.

"Where are we going?"

"To the woods. Where she took me. You can decide for yourself how much to trust her."

After getting sick and discovering the second dead body to be buried in that garden, I don't have the energy to ask more questions. Not that I could come up with any now. Her lack of resistance surprises me speechless.

Neither of us speaks on the way to the car. Her lips mash together as if she's biting them from the inside, preventing her from revealing more secrets. This is the first time she's willing to explore her past. The anger in her eyes and the way her fingers tightly grip the steering wheel give me the idea that she never would have done this on her own. It took exposing her secrets to show how invested I am in the truth.

During the bumpy ride down the driveway, my stomach twists. I ease the window open, and the warm air doesn't soothe my already heated cheeks. My toes curl inside of the too-small boots she found in the basement.

After driving less than ten minutes from the house, she pulls over. The decline from the road bumps against the car, and I grasp the seat belt and the door to keep myself steady against the rocking motion.

We stop on somewhat level ground, and my stomach rolls again.

She speaks to the wheel. "I never intended to show you this. I should have known that taking you with me to Orhaven would spark some questions. But I didn't think we'd be here. We're in a place now where I can't keep my side of the story silent forever. You deserve to know her as I do. Then you can decide if you want to have a relationship with her."

"I don't want a relationship with her, Mom, but I have the right to know everything."

"You're about to."

26

JENNY

My mother pushes out of the car, slamming the door hard. I jump out, desperate for more of the story. My boots sink into the soil. From the rain the other day and lack of sun closer to the thick forest, I suspect this won't be an easy trek.

I peer around the area for any hint of what she's about to reveal. The visions are quiet, ready to fill my mind with the worst-case scenario. The empty feeling in my stomach revolts with a fluttering sensation that I'm not sure I want to shake.

Under the canopy of the trees, the temperature drops a few degrees. The sweat at the edge of my hairline cools my body, enough that I shiver.

There's a narrow, worn path, and I walk behind my mother. She shoves away a large branch, holding it in place for me to pass. "The baby isn't the first time Val's preserved the dead. When we were kids, she enjoyed experimenting with small animals. Chipmunks, squirrels, a cat once. She used to bury them under the tree behind the garden. Sometimes, I would see her out there, talking to her animal cemetery. She kept jars hidden in the basement and the shed. It wasn't until after he died that she claimed the shed for herself. It made sense since our mother never went inside there after he passed."

A flash of the journal pages comes to mind. His body at the bottom of the stairs. "How did he die?"

"The basement stairs were in disrepair for years. I rarely went down there. One night, he fell. For years, I thought it was an accident. A drunken mistake. But he forced Val down there enough that it was only a matter of time before she fought back." She winces as if she's the one in pain instead of the memories of her sister. "I remember she moved aside, and he fell. Our mother grew up in a time where the man ran the house, and his word was law. Val never bowed to that mantra. She was old enough to know what she was doing. For years, I wondered if what I'd seen was real or imagined. I know now."

Our feet crunch along the forest floor as she collects her thoughts.

A movie plays in my mind as if I were there. A young Nora, Valerie, and a cobbled together version of my grandmother. I hear bones cracking with each fateful crash against the steps.

My mother clamps a hand over her mouth as the memory lingers in her mind. She drags a breath into her mouth. "When he was at the bottom, no one went to him. I remember Val turning to us and saying, 'Now that's done.' She had no expression whatsoever. While she had removed him from the family, she created a different person to fear. Even my mother was afraid of her. Enough that she let Val do what she pleased. The fear my father created in our family had bonded us girls, but that broke apart the moment he drew his last breath. She killed him, Jenny. She killed him with no apology, and I always knew she would do it again."

I reach for her. She's never been the type to be overly physical, and I'm realizing why. Valerie took that from her the moment she abducted her. Though, this time, my mother leans toward me as if I'm the parent and she's the child. It makes perfect sense. She never had the support of a mother like herself. Her father was an overbearing, neglectful man, while her mother allowed a murderer to run the house after that. No wonder she didn't want me to know any of it. To her, the absence of the truth protected me from her nightmares. I don't need her to guard me anymore.

"I'm sorry you saw that happen," I say.

"I could have helped him. A part of me doesn't regret his death. It's why I forgave her. Why I tried so hard to be happy in that house." She sniffles. "Do you understand why I didn't tell you? I had to separate us from them entirely, or Val would have weaseled her way back into our lives."

"I do."

She gently wipes her tears with the sleeve of her shirt. The fabric bunches, revealing the thick scars. At any other time, she would have turned away to cover them up. As she's doing with the truth, she's loosening her control over it. "It's through here."

The path veers to the right, but she doesn't follow it. Debris under our feet crackles and shifts as if this land hasn't felt a person in decades. The area around us is undisturbed by the wreckage of humanity.

She slows, and I stop. "This is the place?" There are no markers of life or a shelter.

"I can't go over there." Her voice is small, like a terrified mouse.

I follow her eyeline. A swell in the ground is the only proof of the shelter. I walk the area, giving it a wide berth.

Her arms tuck against her body as she takes a few steps back.

My gaze darts between her and the shelter. She'd never leave me alone in this place, but from the way her eyes bulge and her body stiffens, she doesn't need much motivation to run away.

I won't torture her by staying long, but I need to experience the place she and Valerie described. Both have different accounts of what happened here. Valerie tried to isolate my mother, while Mom broke free from her captor.

"She left me here to die, as much as she tries to say otherwise. I would have said or done anything to get back to you. Val had to realize there was no future with us the moment she took away my choice."

I glance at the ground. Shimmering red spots blemish the leaves under me. They blink away quickly, but I have enough information to see the space from both points of view. Mom worries I might side with Valerie because of our similarities, but the truth is the opposite. I saw the calculation in Valerie's eyes each time she opened her mouth. Her entire life is a facade of what she wants the world to see. While I can't completely rid myself of her, I can show Mom my full support of her story. What Valerie did was wrong, and no amount of her revelations can prove otherwise.

The closer I get to the shelter, the more details come to light. Without knowing the shelter's location, I could have easily walked by without suspecting that it's man-made, instead of an old fallen tree covered with flora. A glint of glass peers through a patch of moss. It's too dirty to see through.

"Be careful." Her warning is barely above a whisper, as if it will swallow me whole.

The longer I peer through the coverings that have grown over the shelter for years, the more it takes shape. It lies in plain sight for those who know about it. A secret place in the woods that kids dream about in their backyard. A home for fairies or forest creatures. Through my mother's eyes, a house of nightmares. For Valerie, a key piece of her childhood and adulthood. A crutch she leans on for support of her twisted actions. Her father hid her in this place, so it was perfectly acceptable to do it to her sister years later.

The more I learn about the secrets of the Whitford family, the closer I bend to my mother's story. She was a victim for years, even before she became fully aware of it. Her only option was to leave, realizing the danger it meant for me. Pushing it all behind her was the only opportunity to get away from her past.

"Don't go inside." Her voice is sharper now, but she stays put.

"I won't." My foot slips on an unseen decline in the soil.

Her sharp intake of breath draws my gaze to her.

"It's okay. I'm fine."

A scratching sound surfaces from inside the shelter. I expect a raccoon or an equally large forest animal to attack me. I back away from the shelter, continuing my path around it.

My steps slow as a door comes into full view. It's not covered. If someone walked from that direction toward it, the exposed part would be obvious. The mystery and fantasy of the shelter lifts.

I approach the door. The paint reminds me of the aged and cracked facade of the house. There is a handle on the outside. A circular piece of wood covers where a knob would have been. A few inches from the top, there's a sliding lock.

My breath catches. The only other similar lock I've seen is in the house, for the basement door. The metal isn't rusted, as I would have expected with the elements and disuse of the shelter. I slide my finger over the blemish-free metal. Not an ounce of rust or debris clings to it.

That shuffling sound comes again, and my stomach plummets. There is an animal inside. There must be another entrance. Nothing would have been able to get in and lock the door behind it.

A shiver rolls over my skin as I climb the slight incline away from the door.

My mother is closer now. I open my mouth to speak—to tell

her I'm fine—but the words die on my lips. She's not looking at me. Her eyes bore holes into the side of the shelter.

"I think there's something inside."

"You heard that, too?" Her arm stretches outward as if she's reaching for my hand.

The shuffling continues, turning to almost scratching. A low growl erupts from inside. We jump away from the shelter. I grip her arm.

"We should leave," I say.

I've seen enough to have a permanent visual of this place in my mind.

My heart reaches out toward the animal inside, but I'm sure it will find its way out of there the same way it got in.

A bellowing scream cuts through the air, and I whip around. My mother's mouth is shut. It's not possible that she's the one screaming. She positions herself in front of my body, always protecting me. "That's not an animal."

"There's a door on the other side," I say.

The scream sounds again. She rushes away from me and skids to a stop in front of the entrance. She moves the lock aside and rips open the door.

I don't know what to expect, but she moves as if she already knows. I can't see inside. I almost don't want to. She disappears, and I expect another scream as whatever is inside there rips her to shreds. I don't want to admit the truth to myself yet.

A moan escapes my mother, and I stumble toward the door. My vision doubles as the heap of limbs expands by two. I step closer into the shadowed space inside. One of them is sobbing.

"Call 9-1-1." The calmness in my mother's voice gives me an idea that she's safe, but I can't say the same for the other person.

I lift my phone and turn on the flashlight. A blonde woman leans against my mother's body. Her eyes dart around the room like a scared animal. A piece of crumpled fabric lies at her feet.

Mom's fingers dig against the ropes at the woman's wrists. Her breathing intensifies enough that she's heaving with the effort.

"Jenny! Call the police," she repeats.

I jolt before snapping to the present. My hands steady, tapping the numbers on the screen. They're not experiencing the same frantic fluttering as my heart. I avoid the scene by staring at the phone. The signal isn't strong, but I hope the one bar is enough to get the police out here.

Dispatch picks up, and my mother snaps her fingers, hinting that she wants the phone. I give it to her. While she speaks, the woman turns to me. She shares the same round eyes as Zee.

My mother's voice fades into the background as my breathing fills my ears.

"Zelda?" Wren's voice is a harsh whisper, as if she's screamed for days.

"She's okay," I say.

Wren's chin touches her chest. Her face crumples, but she doesn't cry. I wonder how much she's done that in the time she's been in this place.

My mother moves the phone away from her mouth. "You're going to see her soon. Hang in there. Jenny, hold this."

I balance the phone in my hand, facing the microphone toward her. She continues working on the ropes. Her lips press together as her cheeks bulge with the effort. It makes sense for me to offer my help, but I hesitate. I sense a shift in her, a primal need. She's reliving the worst days of her life. Her mind plunges into the past as she fights with the rope.

"Ms. Miller?" the dispatcher's too-calm voice calls.

"I've got this, Mom."

I hand her the phone, and she scoots over to give me room as I try the rope. It's thick and tugs at my fingernails.

"He'll be back soon." Wren's voice coupled with the warning causes a wave of shivers to move down my spine.

"Who?" I ask.

She curls into herself and sobs.

"The police are coming." I'm unsure if I reassure her or not.

"They can't stop any of this. It will never stop." Wren releases a shuddering breath, and I dig my fingers into her bindings. She repeats, "It will never stop," under her breath until the words become a muffled mix of sounds and syllables. A chant I'm not sure will ever leave my mind.

The knot loosens slightly, and I pinch the rope to grip it as much as possible. It takes three tries before I'm able to slide a piece through. Wren sighs, and her weight falls against me.

"Wren?" My mother reaches out to touch her friend's cheek. Her hand moves to the pulse point at her neck. A flash of realization strikes her. "Stay with me. Help is on the way."

She pulls her friend close as I release the rope from her wrists. The skin is angry and red, but nothing like the scars on my mother's body. Those were self-inflicted when she tried to free herself. While my mother will always have the reminder of that night in her mind and on her body, Wren will have a similar experience.

I coil the rope in my hands, holding on to Wren's warning. If whoever took her is coming back, we have nothing to protect us. "We should get her to the road."

"Do you think you can walk?"

"It doesn't matter. You need to leave." Wren's voice isn't any stronger than before, but it's pleading.

I'm tempted to take her offer. I came to Orhaven to find the truth about my family, not to put myself between an abduction plot. But I follow my mother's lead. This is her time to make the choices she never could for herself.

We help Wren to her feet. Even though she has a similar frame to my mother, she lacks the ability to keep herself upright. My mother wraps a hand around Wren's waist, pulling them together in a side embrace. I try to do the same, but I'm barely holding on to her as we move out of the shelter.

It's a slow shuffle up the incline in the direction we came from. I scan the area. Is her abductor out there, watching us? Would he dare to attack three women? Technically, two. Wren would be useless in a fight. Who am I kidding? We all would be. For a man who abducts women, maybe he'd like the challenge.

I stifle a vision, but not before seeing a shadowed man in the woods racing toward us . . .

I count out of it as quickly as I can, needing to stay present. He's not here. It's just us. My mother focuses on her friend, while I watch our surroundings. Each snap of a twig catches my attention, even at the detriment of my ability to keep Wren moving. Her breathing slows, and I'm sure at any moment she's going to fall and not get up again.

A rush of movement steals my breath as a man truly appears from behind a tree ahead of us. I want to call out, but an unfamiliar name floats into the air.

Wren's voice is a breath. "Quinn."

The lumbering guy rushes us. My entire body screams to run, but two more people appear behind him. While I struggle to stay in the present, I notice they're all wearing the same uniform.

Davina saunters in behind the other two men. Even with the police present, the relief that we're safe never comes. Wren's words echo in my mind even as two of the bigger men lift her enough to extract her from the area twice as fast as we could.

My arms feel heavy, as if I'm still carrying her.

Davina approaches us. "Are you all right?"

My mother tugs the sleeves of her shirt over her hands. "We're okay."

"It's a good thing we were close. Can you show me where you found her?" She gestures to one of the other officers to follow her. He's young without a hint of stubble over his smooth face.

My mother leads the way, and I glue myself to her side.

My mind decides this is the best moment for an imagining. As we walk, I'm transported back to the shelter. I watch Wren writhe, almost in slow motion. My vision circles her body, as if I'm the one who put her there. I'm the hunter. I'm Valerie. Wren morphs into a younger version of my mother. She goes still, lying on the ground. Silent tears spill from her eyes . . .

My mother bumps me with her elbow, a sob escaping her. "If we didn't come here—she might still—we might not have found her."

I curl my fingers around hers. "We did. She's okay."

"As far as we know. Was she there the whole time she's been missing? Days, Jenny. Who left her there to die?"

There is someone in Orhaven fulfilling the same sick actions of my aunt. A copycat abductor. But no one other than my mother and Valerie knows of the incident. Unless Valerie is still playing games.

27
NOW

They found her.

The three words on the screen bring a smile to my face. Not that I care about Wren or her state of existence. Wrangling her is a full-time job. Too bad it's not mine anymore.

Officer Gordon stands at the door, watching my every move. He watches all of us. The other prisoners hastily tap away at the keyboards, reaching for the outside world.

We've been careful throughout the plan, keeping names out of the correspondence. The dummy email account at the top of the message gives a clue, but no one will know who he is. I taught him how to be careful. It's the only way to get what we want. I sit in that sensation. It's the high I hold on to when I'm waiting for him to complete the next part of the plan.

To most, awaiting word for days or weeks at a time might create maddening frustration, but not for me. Each connection with him gives a rush of relief that the monster inside of me feeds on from slow, satisfying bites.

I sit back in my chair and imagine the scenario. I'll never

know exactly how it unfolded. Only you and Wren will relive the details. No matter how much you try to shake it, the fear and horror will cling to your memories. Wren will never navigate a dark night without looking over her shoulder. You will always blame yourself, knowing you could have stopped this years ago—if you'd only stayed. Most importantly, Jenny. This is the start to the rest of her life.

It's a shame I had to miss it, but I have enough memories to sift through for myself if I need to revel in what I've done. My mission is no longer feeding the beast but nurturing hers to the surface. Bringing her closer to me and further from you.

You were the one who always tried to tame me, fit me in a box that society deemed normal. "Normal" is tragic, especially when the feelings within me need to feed. It's the only way normality releases to the surface. You should understand that by now, but you need a push. Once Jenny understands the importance, you will, too. Then we'll be together again.

She won't be able to leave without understanding more, and you will never leave us again.

I create an altered future, a wishful memory that I know will come true. We're in the house again, years later, moving on from the past and taking hold of the future—one where we're together for the rest of our lives.

Another email pushes through, as expected.

What next?

I'm careful with him, knowing how quickly he wants praise. He doesn't have what it takes for the long haul, but he is a loyal servant, worthy of my attention, but it's Jenny who will receive the apprenticeship.

My fingers hover over the keys. Each word flows through me from that other place, the dark corner of my mind which has never let me down. That otherworldly presence knows what it must do to reproduce. It needs to push the fledgling shadows within Jenny to the surface. It knows what she's capable of, and it must survive no matter what. Losing it will leave a hole, and the emptiness will slowly devour her. It's how I watched our mother die, the denial of the power she possessed slowly tortured her until I had to take it into my own hands. Another sacrifice for the greater good.

I read over the sentences, detailing what I need him to do since I cannot. Giving over the control is never easy, but it's necessary. At least it will keep Jenny and you off my scent for a little while, but he knows I require full credit. And he's more than willing to offer it. Always following the leader. There is a place for him in the world, serving the hunter who completes the hard work.

Take the mother. Do what you must.

28

JENNY

"How did you know to look in here?" Davina asks for the second time. Her eyes narrow with suspicion but aim at the shelter instead of us.

"Like I said," my mother starts, "we were out for a walk and heard what sounded like animal noises coming from inside."

Based on how she leads the conversation, she doesn't want Davina to know about Valerie abducting her all those years ago. While it's coincidental that it happened the same way again, Valerie is in jail, and there's no way she could have done this herself.

"There are animal sounds throughout the woods. What made you stop?" Davina asks.

I can't bear to look inside the shelter. My visions are wild, desperately trying to steal my attention.

My mother heaves a sigh. "We don't live in the woods anymore. The sound was out of the ordinary for us. I'm glad we did. I can't imagine what would've happened to Wren. She mentioned a man . . ."

"We'll get her statement once she's checked out." Davina steps back from the shelter, assessing it.

I have the urge to reveal what Valerie told me about this place, but that would also bring attention to what happened to my mother. My mother observes Davina the same way the sheriff does the shelter.

Davina moves closer, kneeling. She moves the flora with her bully stick.

The other officers follow her lead, standing several feet behind her. They clump together, whispering to each other about their theories.

Davina snaps up as if someone's poured ice-cold water down her back. Her eyes meet my mother's. "Nora and Jenny. We're going to need a full statement from both of you at the precinct."

"I don't know what else I can give you." My mother reaches for me the way she used to when I was a kid crossing a busy road.

"We'll need it anyway. Then you can be on your way out of here."

My mother stiffens. "You promise?"

"As long as you give us what we need. Sure."

"Let's go then." I haven't held her hand this much in years, but she's a powerful force, pulling me from my spot.

Davina ambles over to us. "You're riding with me."

My mother's hand tenses around mine. "We have a car."

"I'd rather you were with me," Davina tells us, refusing to take no for an answer.

"Someone will have to bring us back," my mother challenges.

"It's not a bother at all," Davina says, not missing a beat.

"Why are you treating us like suspects?"

Davina raises a hand. "I'll stop you there. This is an active investigation, and you two are witnesses. You can come quietly or not." She peers at the larger officer staring at us from behind her.

My mother looks at me. "Fine."

Davina stalks toward the road without a glance behind her. If we want to get out of this place, we can't test her patience.

The police chief adjusts her speed, ensuring we don't fall too far behind. There's no way I can ask my mother what to say when Davina interviews us. We're innocent, but the way she's treating the entire situation makes me feel as if she suspects us, instead of a man who's still out there.

When we reach the road, three police cars with spinning lights on the roofs surround our car, close enough that we wouldn't be able to move it even if we tried. If the abductor had any thought of coming back to the site of the crime, the police would deter him. It's not as much of a comfort as I expect. I want the police to catch him, or else I'll never sleep tonight in that secluded house.

This is a small town. Word of Wren's capture is going to get out. If the abductor is someone in town, they will know before the day is over.

My heart thunders in my ears as Davina escorts us to her car. I fully expect her to shackle handcuffs to our wrists and throw us in the backseat.

Instead, she offers the front seat, and my mother slips inside. I suspect she's protecting me from questioning, but I cringe at the hard-plastic bench backseat. I slide onto it, and it's not smooth at all.

We're innocent, but Davina will suspect everyone until they catch the criminal. It doesn't help that we were at the scene. The two people who stumbled into an abduction plot will appear at the top of her list, especially since Wren texted my mother before her disappearance.

Davina cranes her neck to check the road before we take off.

In my time in Orhaven, there haven't been many people on the roads. Davina seems to have the same idea as she accelerates the cruiser to higher speeds than normal. It's not like anyone will pull her over.

"Will you let me know any updates?" My mother's voice is barely audible over the roar of the engine.

"Possibly."

"Come on. This is Wren."

"You haven't been friends in years. Even I know that."

"You know why I left." The way she speaks to Davina is as familiar as her talking to me. In my time in town, I focused so much on finding out about my family's past that I didn't notice my mother's life outside of the house. She was friendly with Mike and Wren, but how far did her relationships extend? Mike said kids around the same age hung out together. Would my mother's relationship with Davina help us get out of this situation? She was the only one keeping us in town. After the interview, we could be on the road tonight, leaving this place behind.

"I'll keep you in mind." Davina's voice breaks into my thoughts. "But you have to tell me the truth at the station."

"I am telling you the truth."

Davina glances at me through the rearview mirror before returning her attention to the road.

"There's a select few of us who know about that place. All with alibis."

I suck in a breath, loud enough that my mother stiffens. She claimed that she told no one about what happened in the woods, that if she had, the police would have arrested Valerie much sooner and the doctor would still be alive.

"If this is happening again, I need to leave as soon as possible," my mother says.

The radio crackles. Davina glances at the electronic equipment between her and my mother. She lifts the mic and wraps her hand around it, drawing it closer to her mouth. "We're headed back now. I'll need two rooms."

"Copy that," says a male voice.

"Will you require a lawyer?" Davina asks.

I stare at the back of my mother's head as she answers the sheriff. "We're not hiding anything."

"Good." Davina's voice lowers, but somehow it strikes my chest.

I have the urge to defy my mother and tell her I want one. I'm an adult and can make my own decisions. But if it makes the process move quicker, I'll save the defiant attitude for later.

"You feel the same way, Jenny?" Davina asks.

My mother twists in her seat to stare at me. She's silently asking me to obey. She's lucky I have a different agenda.

"Yeah." I widen my eyes at her before facing the window again. I lean my forehead against the glass. It's warmer than I would like, but it prevents me from seeing her face.

Why did she claim her abduction was a secret if Davina knows about it? Why was Valerie allowed to go on with her life while we had to run away to save ours? There's more to this story, and it doesn't just involve my family.

The police station is a small brick building outside of the downtown area. The sign reads that it's also the town hall. I suppose in places like this, there's only so many municipal buildings. It makes sense that I saw Davina patrolling by the library the other day. Thinking of the library, Zee's face appears in my mind. As much as her mother is about to face lifelong trauma over her situation, she's alive. I hope Zee feels relief and can mend her relationship with her mother. I can't help comparing our situations. The difference is that Zee will be there for her mother, while mine tried her damnedest to keep me out of it. I'm not sure which situation is worse.

My mother stays close to me on the way into the building. Davina holds the front door open and follows us inside. We enter an empty waiting area. There are rows of mustard-green chairs, and the air has a faint scent of copper to it. We approach a massive wooden desk with a woman sitting behind it.

"Shirley, I called about the two interrogation rooms."

My mother's staring at me, but I can't meet her eyes. She clears her throat, but I don't budge. This isn't the place to talk about her trust issues. I want to get this over with, and then we can go back to the house before leaving Orhaven for good.

Davina turns to us. "This way."

Behind the front desk are rows of mostly empty desks. The computers look as if they were built in the nineties. A worn orange carpet stretches past that room into a tight hallway.

Davina opens the first door on the left. "You can go in there, Jenny."

"Why are you separating us?" My mother's frail hands dig into her hips.

Davina ignores the question. "This way, Nora."

My mother huffs out a breath and follows Davina away from the room.

Inside, there's no one-sided mirror like every police procedural television show. Only a table with two chairs opposite the other. The telephone rings in the main office as I sit. I clasp my hands together, placing them on the table.

Davina's hard footfalls arrive quicker than I predicted. She enters the room and closes the door behind her.

The ringing telephone fades, and the sound ceases as if I'm in a vacuum.

"Tell me, in your own words what happened this afternoon."

Walking through the scene in my mind, it's as clear as it was when we were there. Goose bumps roll up my arms, and I rub them to warm them up. The nights in Orhaven have been warm, but under the cover of the trees, I can't imagine it was too comfortable for Wren. Especially wearing only a short-sleeved shirt with shorts.

"Jenny?"

"Huh?" I snap out of my head.

"You went away for a moment there."

My cheeks flush. "I never expected to find a missing person today. I'm a little overwhelmed."

Davina's expression softens. "I understand. Take it slow."

That's not part of my plan. I give her the rest of my story, leaving out the smaller details. My visions try to dig deeper, to find meaning in every leaf and tree in the woods. The longer I take only delays our travel.

Davina doesn't take notes, but I don't ask her why. There aren't any cameras in the corners of the room, either. She must have a good memory for her report.

Or she's keeping me here for another reason.

I hesitate on that thought. By talking to me first, my mother is the one who has to wait. They were friends as children, but as Davina said in the car ride to the station, their relationships have changed since she left.

If the people of Orhaven expect answers, will another Whitford woman take the blame for this crime?

"I need your take on what you and Nora were doing at that place." She sits across from me. Up close, I notice a small scar cutting down her right eyebrow. I recall Wren's broken body in the shelter. I blink, and it's a younger version of my mother in her place. I stiffen.

"She told you—"

"While the woods can be a place for hikers, it's not common here. Especially wearing work boots."

I tuck my feet under the chair.

"I can't help you unless you give me the truth."

"Help me how? Do you think we did this?"

She glances at the door. "This abduction is a big deal, especially after how the doctor's murder shook this place. We won't recover until this person is brought to justice."

"It was just a walk. Neither of us knew Wren was there."

"Is that your statement?"

"Yes."

She considers me before shoving away from the table. She opens the door, standing like a sentinel. "You can wait in the lobby for Nora. It shouldn't be long."

I stand on legs that aren't my own, grasping the table for purchase.

Davina leans close enough that her breath presses against my cheek. "Don't speak to anyone other than myself or Nora about this."

I tilt my head. "Who would I talk to?"

"Just keep it close, okay?"

She pushes by me and enters the room next to mine. My mother's voice floats from the space before the door muffles it completely.

I walk into the main area, and there are several more police officers than before. The ones from the woods glance at me and follow my path toward a bank of chairs by the entrance.

I sit closest to the main desk so I can see my mother the moment Davina lets her out of the interrogation room. The man who took Wren is still out there, and Davina is wasting her time messing with my mother.

I scroll through my texts. I want to reach out to Abbie, but there's too much to write over text. She still hasn't responded to the other message I sent her. If I tell her about an abduction, I have no idea what she'll think. Maybe she'll have a million questions for me, and it will bring my mother's abduction into the open. Or she'll think I'm nuts. I hate that I'll have to lie to my best friend, but it's to protect my family. I inch nearer to the reasoning my mother had for all those years of shielding me.

My finger hovers over Scott's number. He probably knows about Wren already. I hope. If Zee is staying with them, then she'll be on her way to the hospital. I can't interrupt that reunion.

A while later, Davina and my mother appear in the main area together. Heat springs to my face. As much as I'm upset with her for lying about her past, she's my mother, and we went through a traumatic event together. Like Zee, I can let go of my anger and promise to be better.

She breaks away from Davina. The moment she's close enough, she wraps her arms around me. No matter what she's lied about, her actions come from the urge to protect me. I understand that now and allow myself to lean into her embrace.

"What did she say?" I whisper.

"We'll talk when we're alone."

Davina stays at the station while one of her junior officers drives us back to our car. This time, we both sit in the back. My mother's hand doesn't leave mine, and I'm not sure if I could handle it if it did.

Our vehicle is where we left it on the side of the road. To anyone passing, it might look as if someone broke down.

We thank the officer, and he drives away.

My mother's shoulders roll forward as we're left alone once more.

The glove compartment is open, the paperwork inside strewn over the front seat. A coating of dust clings to the steering wheel and door handles.

"If they wanted fingerprints, they could have asked." She sits in the driver's seat and retrieves from the center console a square black cloth she normally reserves for cleaning her sunglasses. She wipes the wheel and door, streaking the dust across it.

I stack the paperwork from the glove compartment. The registration and insurance card rest at the top, but an envelope with the name Nora in thick script catches my attention. The handwriting is unfamiliar to me, but it seems important.

I toss it to her. "Is this from them?"

My mother glances at the envelope, and her jaw tightens. "Where did you find this?"

"Here."

She jumps out of the car, hovering close to the boundary of the road. Her head moves from side to side as if she's an eraser, trying to abolish the envelope from existence. She jolts as if someone has startled her.

"What is it?" I ask.

"This is impossible." Her fingers trace over the letters.

I move to her side, looking at the envelope again. What seems like an innocent correspondence doesn't match her reaction.

"This wasn't already in the car, was it?"

"No." Her hands tremble as she shoves a finger under the seam and rips it open.

Thick black marker fills the index card.

IT'S NOT OVER.

29
JENNY

I reread the short phrase. "What's not over? Who is this from?"

Hundreds of scenarios fill my mind. It doesn't take much, especially since I'm already in a fragile mindset.

She peers toward the woods, scanning the area. "I don't believe this."

"Should we bring this to the police?"

"Get in the car, Jenny."

"Where are we going?" I obey her wishes, but I need to know who was inside our car while we were at the police station.

"Back to the house."

"You're freaking me out. Please tell me who it's from."

"Jenny, please. I have to think." We sit inside the car. She doesn't bother to buckle before she U-turns toward the house.

"I don't want to go back there."

"As long as we comply, we're safe."

"Comply with who?"

"Val. Somehow she's doing this from afar."

"We should tell Davina." I'd rather sleep on the floor at the police station than go back to that house, especially if my mother thinks Valerie is involved.

"No."

"She already knows about your abduction."

"No, she doesn't."

"She mentioned it on the ride to the station."

My mother's gaze darts over the road. "No, she doesn't. No one does."

"But she mentioned the location."

"That's not what she meant. You didn't tell her about me and Valerie, right?"

"No." A dull ache swells in my head. I'm unable to grasp onto what she means.

"Val is the only one who can explain what's going on here." Spit shoots from my mother's lips. I've never seen her calm facade crack as much as it has over this trip. How much will Valerie break her down until the pieces don't connect into the mother I recognize?

"What does that note mean?" I ask.

"Val enjoys games, especially those she can win. It's not difficult when she's the one creating the rules." She lifts the envelope. "She's working with someone. It has to be the person who took Wren."

"Why would she do that? And how? What are you not telling me?"

She throws a pointed glance at the rearview mirror. It's the closest she gets to looking at me. There is guilt in her glossy eyes. "I didn't tell you the whole truth about why we came here."

My stomach plummets, but I mask the flurry of responses my body is desperate to unleash. Pushing her too hard only results in her shutting down. I'm so close to the whole truth, it swells within me.

"Val started with the letters when she first was incarcerated."

"She contacted you?"

"I don't know how she found us. I was so careful." Her voice cracks. "But you were happy in Ridgefield. With her in prison, I knew she couldn't get to us. I endured the letters. I stopped reading them for a while. Then they came every day. That's when I opened one. She wanted me to visit. With you. You know I never wanted to expose you to my past. Since I didn't respond to the others, she threatened us." A tear slips down my mother's pale cheek. She doesn't wipe it away. "Two weeks ago, she said she would hurt me in the way she had in the past. That's when I contacted Walter." Her chin drops to her chest for a few seconds too long. The car drifts. I reach for the wheel as she snaps into the present and straightens us. "I thought I could do it. But when I got here, it all came back. Then she found a way to keep us here."

"Wren?"

A heaviness blankets my entire body. The entire time we were in town, there was a person walking around knowing Wren was inside that shelter.

"What do we do?"

"Tomorrow, we'll visit Valerie. This has to end. I'll do what she asks so this can be over."

Through the night and on the ride to the prison, my visions return with a vengeance. They work overtime, and without a wink of sleep, I don't have the energy to push them away.

There's no clear path, as my other ones usually have. They start and stop as my mother and I walk into my mind's version of the visiting room. Valerie sits behind the glass with her hands clasped together on the table, watching us with interest. As if we're one of her experiments on her dolls. From there, she's able to manipulate my mother and me. She watches while my mother rushes forward, slamming her hands on the glass. A faceless security officer drags my mother out of the room, leaving me alone with my aunt. I approach before the vision shifts. Val stands with a twisted smile across her face. This time, Mom isn't there. She's not in the next one either. The endless loop brings me to another reality entirely. I'm no longer afraid but numb from the effects of the visions bombarding me.

It's not until we ease into the parking lot of the penitentiary that I'm able to break free from the endless loop. If she notices that I've been in a trance, she says nothing. I imagine she's preoccupied with the imminent encounter with her sister and abductor after all these years.

My mind is blank. The visions meld together enough that I'm sure I've already done this before, and I'm seconds from entering another one. I allow my mother to lead us to the main building and through the check-in process.

We barely sit down before an officer calls our names. It's the blonde one from the other day. She offers a smile, and I can barely muster one to match.

The procedure is the same as I know and imagined throughout last night and today. Mom takes my hand as the door opens to the visiting room. I push back the expectations of my imaginings and hold my breath as we enter the space.

It's empty. Why I expected anything different, I have no idea.

A slickness appears between our hands, and she's the first to let go. She wipes her damp palms against her shirt and steps further into the room.

"Let me finish this." Her voice strains. She rolls her shoulders back before they slowly curl forward again.

The transition between the strong person I've always admired into someone who can barely handle living in her own skin strikes me. We all have secrets within us we try to bury, but circumstances and people around us hold the shovel, ready to cut into the soil as soon as we allow them.

The officer points at the station in the middle of the room. There're already two chairs waiting for us. Like this was the plan all along. Valerie couldn't have known we would come together. Was this her hope? Or did she know that my mother and I would be inseparable at this point? I sift through the many possibilities as we wait for the door on the other side to open.

My mother's leg bumps against mine as it bounces. She sucks on her bottom lip as she stares at the door. She hasn't been here yet, so she doesn't know what to expect. To be honest, neither do I. Nothing about Valerie is predictable.

I hold that thought in my mind as the door clicks open.

My mother sits straighter and clears her throat. Her hands splay in her lap before curling into fists. I touch her hand again, attempting to convey that I'm here for her.

Valerie glides over to the chair. She stares at my mother. A pleased smile smooths her lips.

Neither sister reaches for the phone. I want this visit over as soon as possible. I place it between us with the speaker facing upward.

Valerie sinks into the chair, her eyes darting between us. Her skeletal fingers curl around the handset as she brings it to her ear.

"I'm so happy you received my message."

Her voice is small and tinny. I want to bring it closer to my ear, but I allow my mother to control this visit. I've already had enough of Valerie. This is closure time for my mother.

"What you did was despicable," my mother spits.

The pleasant and calm facade I experienced in my previous visits never reaches the surface of Val's face. It's replaced by impassive flat lines of her mouth, and even the sunburst of skin at the corners of her eyes barely moves. "This family needs to stay together. Wren was going to ruin that."

"What does Wren have to do with our family?" I blurt out. A stirring sensation prickles within my gut. I know what she's done to my mother, but orchestrating Wren's disappearance from inside these walls fills me with fear. I lean toward her.

Valerie snaps her attention to me. Her narrowed eyes burn into mine. She clicks her tongue before refocusing on my mother. "You didn't give her the full history?"

"Of course not."

An impenetrable bubble forms around the two of them. It's the same one that keeps my mother and her truth at arm's length. I recall the conversation with Davina. She doesn't know about my mother's past with the shelter, but she shares a truth with her and Valerie. But who else?

"This is why I brought you here. Even after all these years, you're still predictable, Nora. You never talk about the scary things, not even when they have significance to our history."

Valerie speaks to my mom like a scolding mother instead of an older sister. The dynamic between them shifts in my mind. Though, it's not Valerie's fault that their father didn't respect the women in the family and my grandmother checked out the day he died.

My mother heaves a breath. "A job of a mother is to protect her child."

"No, it's not, Nora. You prepare a child for the ugly world you've brought them into."

"Maybe it's a good thing you never had to do that."

Valerie blinks hard, as if my mother circumvented the Plexiglas and slapped her.

My mother's lip curls, marring her otherwise kind face. As much as Valerie has transformed, she has, too. "I found what you hid."

Valerie sucks on her cheeks, pulling them into her mouth as if she's biting on them. Her face hollows as she waits for more information about the jar.

"Now you have nothing to say?"

"That all depends on what you say next. You put her back, correct?"

My mother drops her gaze to her lap, diverting a look in my direction before answering. "She deserves better."

"You put her back," Valerie repeats through clenched teeth.

I need my mother to lie.

She doesn't. "There was an unfortunate accident."

"How dare you!"

I want to tell her I broke the jar, but my mother pinches my leg, stopping me. She's doing what she's always done, protecting me. The coward inside me allows it.

"It's for your own good. What if the next owner found it and the truth came out about that night? You've worked hard to keep it hidden. I buried her for good. It's what she deserved years ago. Not your sick preservation of her body."

Valerie strikes the glass with her fists. "You had no right!"

She moves so quickly I jump backward from my chair for fear of her breaking the barrier and following through with the murder in her eyes.

My mother remains still, as if this isn't the first time she's witnessed this side of Val.

For me, it's terrifying. I try to hold on to the present as my visions threaten to suck me under. I'm not sure if they would be worse than this.

Valerie pummels the barrier with her fists until blood streaks the surface.

The officer behind her speaks into his radio before approaching her.

The blonde officer on our side of the glass rushes toward us. "It's time to go."

Her voice echoes far away in my mind as I watch my aunt. The fire in her eyes ignites a vision. I see Dr. Bradley under those fists, his life beaten from him. With her relentless fury, his death is painful and anything but quick. The passion and focus take over her body, shifting into the monster buried underneath the surface.

The officer kicks the chair to the side before speaking to Valerie. "Back away from the barrier, Prisoner Whitford."

Valerie's hands slide down the glass. Her unblinking eyes bulge from her face. "This isn't over, Nora. You thought you had it bad last time. You're going to regret this moment until your last breath."

The officer grips Valerie's wrists, pulling them behind her. She rears her head back. I expect her to submit to him. But not blood. She buries her teeth into the officer's ear, and his cries pierce through me from the handset.

A chunk of flesh falls from Valerie's bloody lips. She smiles. Her teeth rimmed with red. Her head tilts back, and her laughter echoes through the phone.

My heart races as two more officers flood the room to subdue Valerie. But instead of her fighting them, she submits by kneeling and putting her hands up. It doesn't stop one of the officers from shoving Valerie's face against the floor and digging her knee into my aunt's lower back. The injured officer holds his ear while shouting into the radio again. Liquid seeps from between his fingers, and I can't help staring. The room goes silent, enough that my ears ring. Chaos fills both sides of the room.

The blonde officer directs us to the door. Her lips move, but I fall into a real-life imagining. My heart slows and the world quiets. It's the closest I've ever been to peace for as long as I can remember. No visions tearing through me. Only silence. Peace. The sounds around us sharpen, and my breathing fills my ears.

The officers heft Valerie to her feet, the three of them standing at arm's length in case she finds another victim. She licks her lips and bows her head in submission. Not before her knowing eyes meet mine.

"Jenny."

With one word, the vision shatters and the world returns with a vengeance. Alarms blare, and my mother's firm grip drags me from the room. She and the officer keep the same pace as we're escorted from the building. The fanfare ends as we're brought within visual distance of the parking lot.

"I have to go," the officer says, jutting out her chin before leaving us.

We walk to the car. The ground swallows my feet with every step. Inside, I'm hollow. Or is it shock? It's as if Valerie carved out the insides of my body with her teeth.

Or was her advice a plausible way I could rid myself from the visions?

I get in the car and sag against the seat. It takes effort to buckle my seat belt. The moment the car starts, we pull out from the parking spot, leaving the prison behind. A ghost of my former self tethers to that place. I doubt we'll ever go back, or will be allowed to after Valerie's outburst, but I'll never be the same after this visit.

As much as both my mother and I distance from Valerie, she's in our blood, and now she's in my head. Every vision is linked to her, and she will always haunt me.

30
NOW

As time wears on, I lose myself in my thoughts. It's the only way to stay sane in solitary. For some, it might be a punishment, but without the constant hum of women talking, crying, and screaming, I'm more at peace than at any other time since living in this place. I walk the five steps to the other side of the cell before turning around and doing it again.

When I stop, your satisfied smirk appears in my mind, and my hands ball into fists.

The display of unrestrained anger isn't like me, at least not since the doctor. You do this to me, Nora. But more is to come for you. If all goes well, she'll beg me to give her another taste of the numbness that accompanies the bloodlust.

Jenny's expression after the show in the visiting room elicits a pleasurable sensation within me. I sink into the last memory I have of her before everything changes. As much as I've studied personal connections and interactions deemed "normal" through the eyes of characters in novels, I've had to radicalize what society deems that way. Which is why the world is better without my victims.

My father, the abuser.

My child's father, the arrogant.

Jenny's father, the degenerate.

The doctor, the liar.

Officer Keelan, the molester.

It didn't take long for me to locate my next victim. While some women here don't mind his hands on their bodies in hidden corners of the prison, he's supposed to protect, not take advantage of his status in this place. It didn't take much convincing to connect with him. He's not picky about his choices. I may be ten years his senior, but my mother gave me ample resources to use to my advantage.

This was my last chance to show her what she could do to have some sense of normalcy. It's not a simple life, but if she understands that taking out those who don't belong in society will only improve both aspects, she'll make it work. Under your care, I expected Jenny to subdue her imaginings. Your need to people-please and keep harmony in every situation. A boring and unnecessary life, especially when you claim your daughter is the most important.

We don't hold back with those we love. We bring them to the surface and allow them to rise.

Now, I must wait to hear if she has risen.

While waiting, I push away the sweet numbness which has cleared my thoughts and dive into the depths of my memories of each of them. It's enough to take the edge off. I want to prepare myself for the report of the newest death to add to the list.

31

JENNY

When we get back to the house, the tendrils of the remaining numbness fade out of me. It's time to face the reality of who my aunt is.

"We're leaving tomorrow," my mother says. "I don't care what Davina says. She can call me if she needs more information."

I stumble over a thick root bubbling from the ground. "Why not now?" I can't stay here another day. It's too close to Valerie, and whoever she's working with, the person who's carrying out her tradition of locking away innocent women inside of an underground shelter.

"I have to get the place in order. I'll bring the key to the lawyer tomorrow when they open. It will be first thing, I promise."

"What about the person who took Wren? He's still out there."

"No one is going to hurt us. She wants to scare us, but that can't stop us from living."

A wave of imaginings fills my mind. A faceless person approaching the house with a similar mindset as Valerie. My mother thinks Valerie won't hurt us, but she's not the one stalking the town for another victim. By taking Wren, he has a taste for what Valerie does. With him, there's no personal connection to us to stop him from following through with what he craves.

Movement from my side brings me out of it. My mother heads into the house. She disappears as the faces of those I've met in town flicker before my eyes. The copycat can be any of them. Memories of the kind smiles shift to knowing looks.

My foot slams into the edge of the top stair, and I stumble. My knee twists the wrong way, and pain shoots up my leg.

I blink out of the vision and grip the railing to balance myself. The ache in my leg lingers. I need to stay present as much as possible.

A light breeze rustles the trees, catching my attention. I whirl around and scan the woods. The shadows ebb, pulling my attention to several areas as I spot movement. This isn't like my visions. My fear seeps into reality, forming bodies in the spaces between trees.

"What are you doing?"

I turn to my mother. She stands in the doorway with a cardboard box. The donation items.

"I thought I saw something."

"Honey, do you want one of your pills to take the edge off?"

"No thanks." I need to be present in case Valerie's friend visits us next.

"Help me get all these boxes outside."

"Are you sure we can't just leave the key here?" If Scott has to come here to get the boxes, I'm sure he won't mind taking the key with him to Walter's office.

My mother sighs. "I don't trust leaving a key to this place."

"Who is going to break in?"

"Jenny, I'm exhausted, and I don't want to drive today. We

have to finish packing and cleaning. Let me get a few hours of sleep."

It's not as if we could enjoy a vacation to Philadelphia after all this. I'll be surprised if she still wants to go. I'm not sure I want to either. I want the familiar comfort of our apartment, but with Valerie knowing where to send mail, I don't know how much longer we'll stay.

"I can drive." I'm pushing too hard, but I can't help the pulsing movement of my heart throughout every inch of my body.

Her "this conversation is over" glare wins.

After bringing all the boxes outside, I head into the kitchen to clear out the refrigerator. It's not until I open it that my stomach wakes. I can't recall the last time I ate, and I reach inside to grab the last of the deli meat, cheese, and condiments. We're taking everything home, and the refrigerated items won't last the trip.

My mother moves through the first floor, opening drawers and cabinets in the living room, dining room, and finally the kitchen.

I place the sandwiches on the table.

"That looks good."

I shrug. "It's a sandwich. Nothing special."

She tucks her body against mine. I rest my head on her shoulder and can't help the sigh escaping my body as if I haven't breathed in hours. "This will be over soon."

I want to reassure her I feel the same way, but I already know my mind won't stop until we're out of here for good. I debate bringing up another move, away from Ridgefield. As much as Ridgefield has been my home, it doesn't feel safe anymore, not even the apartment. I'm not sure I'll ever stop looking over my shoulder.

The only hope I have is Davina questioning Wren about who

took her. If she can identify him, then we might get a head start. My thoughts shift, unveiling paths ending in foggy futures. There's no clarity, but we have to move forward. My mother and I have merged onto the same path, and I want to ease the responsibility to keep the secrets of this family buried from the world. I'm armed to take my role in this family, but no longer at the cost of chipping away at my mother's trauma.

We eat a mostly silent lunch. The room illuminates more meaning than it had before. The ghosts of the past wander the space. A family sitting at the table, all three women watching the head of the household, wondering when he will snap. A version of the basement door opens as a young girl descends the stairs under the watchful eye of her father.

A bone-shaking shiver breaks my vision. My mother is gone, her shoes shuffling in the living room. I don't know when she left. I inhale a breath before eating the rest of my sandwich. A sound against the window makes me jump. I whirl around. Droplets of rain pepper the glass. When did it start raining? I have no plans to sleep tonight, but I hope for a cool breeze brought on by the storm to ease into the possibility of a nightmare-filled slumber before our trek home.

Thunder rolls in the distance. Seconds later, the backyard lights up with a thin electric arm reaching across the sky toward the woods.

My gaze catches on the shed. A paralyzing ache lands on my chest. An extra shadow appears next to it. I don't know why, but I can't stop staring as I count down to the next hint of thunder. It rumbles again, and quicker than before, the lightning comes.

The dark form is closer this time. I sprint from my spot and head for the back door. I can't think about how stupid it is that I'm going to see who is wandering in our yard during a storm right after an abduction in town. I need to know that it's not real.

The screen door slaps against the side of the house, but I catch it on its trajectory back to me. Blackness swathes the yard, and rain sprays across my face and bare arms.

The cooler air allows me to breathe easier, yet I can't take a full one. I scan the yard for the intruder. Two more strikes of lightning illuminate the sky. The figure is gone.

The moment the last one hits, a hand falls on my shoulder.

I scream, whirling around.

"It's me." My mother holds her hands up between us. "I didn't mean to scare you."

"I thought I saw someone." The words tumble out of my mouth as I race into the kitchen, closing the door behind us. I twist the lock and push past my mother to the front door. She follows behind, and her closeness eases the tightness in my chest.

"Jenny, I know this has been a stressful trip."

I lock the front door and peer out the thin window beside it. A double reflection stares back at me of a scared woman, who might be as twisted as her aunt.

"There's no one there."

She's probably right. If I've learned anything, I can't trust what I see when I'm stressed with visions.

A text lights up my mother's phone screen. She reads it. "Oh, thank goodness."

"What is it?"

She turns the phone, revealing a text chain between her and Davina.

We have a suspect in custody.

I deflate against the door. My mother's closeness wraps me in a warm embrace, one which brings me back to a time when I was small and untainted by this family's horrific past.

Another vision must have sneaked up on me, playing into my fears of the situation in Orhaven. I release a breath into her hair and inhale the fresh scent of her shampoo. Having her so close to me grounds me. I tighten my arms around her.

I recall her offer from before. "I think I would like to take a pill."

She squeezes me. "That's a good idea."

I slam awake. As I sit up, my hand presses against my chest as if a weight shoved the breath from my lungs. The window calls to me as a whistling breeze snakes through the screen. Tiny bumps form on my skin, even though it's anything but cold in the room. The glow from the moon lays a white stripe across the floor, leading to my bed.

I check my phone. It's nine at night. One pill has never knocked me out that hard before. But I haven't been sleeping much. The stress from the last few days must have caught up with me.

Dampness clings to my armpits and chest. I billow my shirt, allowing air to flow through.

Across the room, the window calls to me again. I imagine the dark form from before now standing in the moonlight.

I count backward from five, easing my runaway thoughts. The police caught the person who took Wren. They have restored Orhaven to the boring, sleepy town it was before we arrived.

But I get up to prove to my mind that nothing is out there. The lawn stretches toward the woods, unblemished by intruders or any form of nightmare.

I settle on the bed, and it squeaks under my weight. My phone sits undisturbed on the side table next to a stack of my clothes. I want to leave this place as soon as possible.

Thirst clings to my throat, yet I can't force myself up again to get water. The leftover bottles are downstairs with the rest of our bags. Going down there will only wake me further, and no doubt a vision will take advantage of that distraction. After that, there's no chance I'll sleep tonight.

I reach for my phone to check the time.

My texts to Abbie are still unanswered. From now on, I promise to keep her away from the sins of my family. My chest aches as I turn that final lock, vowing to keep the darkest parts of myself away from the one person who has never judged me. The longevity of my plan cracks under the weight of my future. I wanted to come here and realize that I could have a normal life with a partner and maybe children. My life stretches before me, a tightrope headed into the unknown. The longer I picture it, the more I mourn for the life that I pushed so hard for over this visit. Bringing a child into the world is my farthest desire. I can't pass my mind onto another person. Offering this curse will only cause more heartache for them. I shake away the thoughts and focus on the present.

I pull up the keyboard when another message comes through. It's from Scott.

You awake?

Yeah.

Wren's reappearance must have been a stressful time for his family. I appreciate him reaching out to me, and I long to comfort him.

How is your mother?

We're OK. It was a lot.

An understatement, but he's been so patient with me.

Is she sleeping?

The question stops me. I don't have time to respond before another one comes.

Have you checked on her lately?

She's sleeping.

You didn't look.

A breath seizes in my throat. I count down from five and pinch my arm to make sure I'm in the present. I reread the text. The words are sharper than before.

I stand from the bed, dropping my phone against the quilt. The creaks in the floor scream at me as I walk into my mother's room. The door is open when she's had it closed all week. I slow, not wanting to startle her awake.

The quilt from her bed lies in a crumpled heap on the floor. The empty mattress stares back at me. I blink to make sure I'm not imagining it.

"Mom?" I call out and wander into the hallway.

The bathroom is empty, and so are the other rooms. I bolt down the stairs. She's not on the couch. Not in the kitchen. My already quick steps pound down to the basement. There's no longer any fear of the place where Valerie's imaginings took over her life. My mother is not there. Her name spills from my lips again. At first, it's a normal call for her, but as I run upstairs and fling open all the doors just to make sure, I no longer care who can hear me. I scream for her.

Blood rushes through my body, slamming my heart against my chest. My heavy breathing fills my ears, muting my screams.

I stand in the hallway before running into her room again. I fling open the closet, not sure what I'm looking for. The space mocks me. Her phone is on the side table with her purse sagging on the floor next to it.

The shelter appears at the front of my mind.

That figure I spotted in the storm wasn't my imagination. For once in my life, I ignored what was in front of me. The visions have always steered me to avoid the bad, yet the one time I allow my exhaustion to distract me, my mother disappears.

A vision of her dead in the woods breathes to life in my mind.

I close my eyes and count down from five.

When I open them, the world is blurry from my tears. I shove her phone in the bag and shoulder it. Whoever Davina claimed she had in custody isn't the right person.

Scott has my mother.

He must have weaseled his way into my life under Valerie's orders, waiting there like a snake ready to strike. I race into my room to grab my phone. There's another message from him.

It takes reading it three times to understand the meaning behind the words.

Find her before it's too late.

32
JENNY

Valerie's cold eyes peer at me from my mind. Somehow, she manipulated Scott to do her bidding outside of the prison. Now, my mother is in danger, and I have no idea what to do.

Rage echoes through my hollow body, curling my hands into fists. My heart thunders in my ears. Throughout the years, my mother wasn't Valerie's only target. She threatened my life to get us back to Orhaven, but my refusal to go along with becoming her murdering partner pushed her.

I can't do this alone. I know where Scott has taken my mother. It's only fitting he carries out Valerie's screwed-up vision of what she deserves. I debate calling 9-1-1, but my mother has a direct line to the sheriff. I find the text from Davina and call her.

Davina answers after the second ring.

"Nora? Do you have any idea what time it is?"

"She's missing. My mother is missing."

A rustling sound comes over the line, and then Davina's voice loses the grogginess of sleep. "Jenny, slow down. What are you talking about?"

"He took her. Whoever you have in custody isn't the guy. It's Scott. He texted me. She's not here. He has her."

"Okay, I need you to stay put."

"I think she's in the woods. At the shelter."

"Did he tell you that?"

I don't know why I hesitate. My mother's insistence to keep her past dead and buried is a habit for me. But that's not how we're going to save her. "Years ago, something happened there."

"She told you?"

"She told me you didn't know about the abduction."

"What abduction?"

"You just said—" I stop, wondering what she's talking about. The sharing of information among the people in town makes me dizzy. "Valerie is orchestrating this from prison. We went to see her earlier. It didn't go well. Valerie threatened her, and now she's gone." A sob erupts from my mouth, thickening my words.

"I'm headed to the woods now. We're going to help. I'll call you when we have her." The line goes dead.

I pull the phone away from my ear, and it rests in my hands. While my pulse has returned to normal, tingles under my skin force me to my feet. A breeze snakes into the room, slightly rattling the windows. The woods block any light from the distance. My mother is out there, reliving the worst moment of her life, and I'm stuck here.

I glance at the phone again, regretting that I didn't dig into whatever situation Davina was on about. The holes in the details are where my thoughts come to life in the worst vision possible.

My mind flickers as a vision takes hold. Scott stands outside the shelter in the woods, staring at the door while my mother's muffled screams attempt to call for help. I watch him tilt his head back and laugh. His hand reveals a knife, preparing to finish what Valerie started all those years ago.

I propel myself from the bed, desperate to think about anything but my mother dying alone in the woods.

Five minutes later, he texts again.

You shouldn't have called the police.

Those words pierce through me. How did he know?

I didn't.

Calling his bluff doesn't work.

This is all because of you. Wren was supposed to die.
Now your mother will take her place.

I'll do anything.

Come get her. You know where to look.

With trembling hands, I call Davina. It goes straight to voicemail.

She may already be on the way. I text her instead.

He's texting me. What do I do?

I wait several seconds before texting her again.

He's going to kill her!

I wait ten agonizing minutes before deciding. Staying in the house won't save my mother. Scott's already angry that I called the police, but I have Valerie on my side. If he's following her footsteps, then I can plead with him.

The visions overtake my mind as I start the car, and I don't bother counting them down. They ramp up my pulse and somehow comfort me as I speed down the long path toward the main road. With the visions firmly in place, I'm not lonely in this journey. They take the edge off the utter panic throbbing through my veins. Knowing every possibility will only help me when I finally confront Scott.

I'm unsure what I'll do when I find them, but I know enough about Valerie and her twisted love for me that he might not hurt me. He resisted during long rides and spending time with me at the house. Maybe I can play into that side of him.

Heat pools behind my eyes, and I struggle to focus on the road. I try to calculate when Scott could have taken her. Each second is crucial. If he leaves her in the shelter, I will find her and get her out. But if he has another plan, then I might already be too late.

My vision turns fuzzy, revealing the truth of my mind. She's on the ground, her body lies still on the forest floor, staring at me with unblinking eyes. Blood pools on the leaves around her, coming from an indeterminate wound. My mind doesn't care for the details of the how, only the aftermath.

I press harder on the gas pedal. If there are police out here, then they can follow me to the scene of a potential crime. I check the rearview mirror more often than necessary, waiting for a set of red-and-blue lights to blot out the void.

A familiar ringtone sings from my mother's bag, and I reach inside to grab her phone.

Wren's name appears on the screen.

I pick up. "Wren, it's Jenny."

"Where is Nora?"

The tears that have threatened me since realizing my mother was gone overflow from my eyes. The road blurs, and I balance my elbow on the wheel as I clear them. "She's missing. I know where he took her."

"The woods."

"I'm on my way now. I already called Davina."

"You can't go there. That's what he wants."

"I have to."

"This is bigger than you, Jenny. Davina is already handling it. Come to the hospital. I'll tell you everything."

"No." The need to save my mother overpowers my want for information. Besides, I already know what Valerie wants with my mother. She's going to prove her strength even from prison.

"Nora wouldn't want you to go."

The entrance to the woods where we found Wren appears. Even if I didn't recall where we were going, three cars parked haphazardly on the side of the road beckon me.

"I have to go." I hang up before she says another word.

Scott's truck is the closest to the woods. I don't recognize the sedan or the boat of a car parked behind it. Davina and another officer? I can only hope.

I turn both phones to silent and shove them in my pocket. My eyes drag over the seats, searching for a weapon.

Nothing.

My mother's phone buzzes from my pocket, but I ignore it. I can't listen to Wren right now. The reality of my situation won't help keep my mind clear.

I get out of the car and head over to Scott's truck. The bed holds his tool bag, and the only choices I have for worthy weapons are a screwdriver and hammer.

I grab both. The hammer is much heavier than I expect, but I adjust my grip as I move toward the trees.

My footfalls are like gunshots in the night. My eyes adjust to the darkness, but I stumble over exposed roots and other forest debris. I try to stay upright, but the longer I walk, the more my confidence wavers.

Scott is much bigger than me. The hammer that slips through my damp fingers is a well-used tool for him. The moment he takes it, I'm going to be in as much trouble as my mother.

The only hope I have is that Davina has him in custody already. My trek into the woods shows my dedication to my family, but I don't have the confidence or strength to go against someone like Scott.

A twig snaps from my right, too far for me to have caused the movement.

I stop, pressing my lips together so as not to reveal my location. Whatever made the sound doesn't make another one right away.

It's just an animal. An innocent animal. I repeat the mantra in my mind.

I step forward, pressing my heel into the ground before rolling to my toes. The purposeful walk barely makes any sound as I continue down the path.

Up ahead, a flash of light appears. My entire body jolts before I pick up my pace.

She's there, alive and well. I picture Davina handcuffing Scott's hands behind his back. Even better, his face is against the ground as Davina checks to make sure my mother is unharmed.

I allow the vision to wrap around me like one of my mother's hugs. We're going to be fine. We're going home today and will never look back at this place.

It's the first positive affirmation I've come up with in a while, but it's weaker than the morbid ones. I don't get the release of tension I do when I sink into the darker areas of my mind.

The light ahead blinks out before a steadier light source appears.

A fire.

It's small, but it's enough to lead me toward her.

As I get closer, I make out three forms. To anyone who might stumble upon the scene, there doesn't seem to be an immediate danger.

Three people at a bonfire seems innocent enough. But it doesn't explain that third car on the side of the road. If Scott took my mother in one, and Davina is the other, then where is the driver of the last car?

My skin prickles as another set of footfalls approaches from behind me. I grip the hammer and whirl around. I wish for a pair of feral animal eyes to look up at me.

Instead, I face Scott's chest. My body tenses, but I raise the hammer and swipe at him.

He jumps back as I complete the motion. The hammer is too heavy to bring around again quickly enough. His hand jerks to the side, and he grabs the handle. He pulls it from my weak grip and tosses it to the ground.

I open my mouth to scream. I'm close enough to the others that they will hear me.

Scott's hand covers my mouth before he pulls me to the ground. My knees slam into the forest floor as I writhe under him. I try to bite his fingers to loosen his grip, but he's like a vise around every important part of my escape. Saliva floods my mouth, and his leathery hands press harder against my lips. He suffocates my screams as his lips touch my ear.

"Be quiet. You'll give away our position," he says.

I twist in his grip, desperate for the fresh forest taste in my mouth and not his hand.

"Please, stop."

My voice is muffled, but I speak anyway. "Why did you take my mother?"

His body stiffens. "I didn't."

"Your text."

"He has my phone."

"Who?"

"Mike."

"Mike?"

"I'll let you go if you promise not to scream. I don't know what he's going to do if he knows we're here."

I grind my teeth together and stare at the scene in front of us. I'm still too far away to understand what's happening near the fire, but if Scott is here and Mike is there with Davina and my mother, is Scott the threat? They could be a father-and-son team of psychopaths.

He's willing to let me go. I have to work with that. If I can convince Scott that I trust him, he might let me go long enough to warn Davina.

I sink into the moment. The world slows as his hand slips from my mouth. It rests against my chin, and I resist a shudder rolling through me at his touch.

"Mike took Wren. Davina has someone else in custody today, but once Wren woke, she told us everything. I went home to look for him, but he wasn't there. That's when I realized he took my phone. Wren told me everything about their past."

I shake my head. Is that what Wren was trying to tell me before I came into the woods?

He sighs, and his hot breath moves through my hair. "There's a lot of shit neither of our parents told us. It's much deeper than our families, Jenny. I tried to call you from the house, but your number is in my phone. I've been searching for him all night."

The shapes of the people at the bonfire sharpen. My mother

is the one on the ground while Mike and Davina are standing. None have moved since I arrived.

"What do we do?"

"Before you got here, I was going to talk Mike down. He has a collection of weapons, not all of them conventional. By the time I got to them, he'd cleared most of the arsenal. He's planning something big."

My throat clenches. Has he already hurt my mother more than I expected? "We can't leave them with him."

"I know. You should stay here."

"Are you kidding me?" I don't trust him completely, but the way he's hiding in the woods away from his father pushes me more toward believing his story. I plan to get all the facts when I can, but I need to get her to safety first.

"Stay behind me." He stands and offers a hand to me.

My body aches from his attack, but I allow him to help me up.

In Scott's presence, the visions of him hurting my mother subside. What's in front of us is worse than any vision I can create.

As we approach, the details sharpen. My mother is close to Mike, her arms stretching behind her. He must have bound her hands like Wren. Fabric stretches across her mouth, keeping it slightly open.

Davina and Mike stand several feet from each other. Davina's arms reach out to Mike, but she has a gun in her hand. Mike faces my mother, his gun pointed at her.

I squeeze Scott's arm. "He's going to shoot her."

"He hasn't done it yet." Even as a whisper, his voice holds a timbre that rattles in my chest.

Davina's voice is smooth and calm for the situation she's in. "Put the gun down, Michael."

"Not until she comes."

"She's not coming."

I glance behind me. Who else did he invite to this twisted party?

My mouth dries as my hand brushes against my pocket. I lift my phone. Scott's message. No, Mike's message. He's been watching us since the moment we arrived in town, waiting for the right moment. I rest a hand on Scott's shoulder, and he stops moving.

"He's looking for me."

"You can't go out there."

What choice do I have? I can't sit back and watch him kill my mother. I won't be able to live with myself. My visions agree. There's no future beyond this moment. Not unless I create it myself.

33
NOW

I tick the names off my fingers for the hundredth time. I've been in solitary for at least half a day. If they expect me to give in to their will, they have no idea who they've locked in here. My memories of what I've done replay in my head enough times to stave off any boredom they anticipate me experiencing.

I don't know when I'll hear about what happened to you and Jenny. But I imagine the worst-case scenario for you, Nora. News will arrive soon enough.

My hands move to the flat of my stomach, a place where new life lived for a short time long ago.

The numbness bleeds through me as my hands curl into fists. This world was never meant for her. I sink into the bed against the wall and lie down. When I go back to that night, I risk going too far, and I can't have anyone witnessing me at my weakest.

My heavy eyes close as I tick the names again, falling back into the memory of that night.

Nora. Davina. Calvin. Wren. Mike. Francis.

Francis. The twist of his face that only appeared after he

knocked back a few beers. That night was no different. He hadn't had a drink in the hours he'd spent driving home from his cross-country trip to Vegas. He was gone for three weeks with only one drunken phone call.

That was when I told him what he'd done. My mother said I was always the practical one, though *aloof* was the word most referenced. She could never see the world through my eyes, nor my father's. He numbed our reality with alcohol, while I reveled in it.

Francis wanted me to "get rid of it." I waited those three weeks while he blew all the money he'd ever worked for at the casinos and with other women. My world didn't crumble without his love, but he needed to take responsibility. What better place than with his friends as witnesses to his true character?

I never intended to kill him, Nora. It's something I never said to you, but you should have known. But that's what happens when you push a person past their breaking point.

It's how our father ended up at the bottom of the stairs. A few missing screws in the railing after more than enough drinks. A small shove to tip him over.

Francis could have taken his part of the blame. Instead, his denial that we were ever together struck me even more than him hitting me during our time together. I could take a hit. Maybe it was how I experienced a version of love. But I was in charge of keeping new life safe. No amount of love could explain away another physical altercation.

A strategic blow to the head was all it took. The way he cracked his skull against the rocks surrounding the bonfire only added to the claim that his death was accidental. But I wasn't taking any chances.

There are moments in life where everything changes. A deep shift within my body straightened my shoulders. I stood taller than I had in years. The fear in the eyes of the others reminded me of my mother. Like then, I was in control. Whatever happened next needed careful consideration.

The others fell to pieces in their own way, including you.

Davina, the sheriff's daughter, tried to help Francis. He was already dead. But the innate talent within her to protect and serve threatened my ability as a mother. Francis was a well-loved member of Orhaven, mostly because of his family. The town would demand justice.

Wren sobbed, wrapped in your arms. It was the only time I didn't worry about you. You feared me enough to keep her quiet. To protect her. Your relationship always eluded me, even though I read enough books to understand most human interactions.

Then there was Calvin, headed to college in the fall. A full football scholarship resting on his broad shoulders. It would disappoint those in his life if he was part of a murder. That stain would never come out.

Mike stood on the fringes of the group, a quiet version of Wren. His eyes were wide and unmoving from his brother's dead body.

I stepped over Francis's legs, bumping Davina. "There's no use."

"You killed him!" Wren sobbed from the ground.

Your arms tightened around your friend. You knew my ability to kill. Our father's death might have seemed like a nightmare of an accident, but you knew who you lived with.

"You saw him attack me." I forced the words out. I even threw a crack in my voice to convince all of you.

Davina stood. The fire illuminated the doubt in her eyes. "He pushed you away."

"I'm pregnant. He knew that. He's an abusive man, and I fought back."

Davina glanced at Mike.

Calvin fell to the ground, gagging before a spray of beer came up. When he finished, he coughed a few times, breathing hard. "This isn't happening."

I lean into his fear. "You were a part of this. You didn't stop him. All of you did this."

Davina dug her hands into her hips. "We did nothing."

"You want to be an accessory?" There was no force in this world strong enough to put me in prison while my child was on the outside. You were too weak to care for her, and she wouldn't stay with the Allen family, not when their son made his choice about my baby.

"Mike, are you okay?" Davina sidestepped me to get to Francis's brother. Did she hope he would be the one to convince me to take the blame for this?

Mike stared at the ground, his fists at his sides. His eyes darted to his brother, then back to his feet. He was considering both sides. I could work with that.

"He wasn't a good man."

Mike looked at me.

"The world is better without him."

Davina threw her hands at him. "You don't mean that. It's not right."

Her father's influence sickened me. An invisible line cut between me and Davina. It encompassed you, Wren, Francis, and Mike.

Would Davina's strength of character tip Calvin? Their parents were more influential in Orhaven than the rest of us combined.

Work the fear. The monster rarely came out when I was around others. But it would save me. I needed to press harder. Setting my sights on Calvin, he'd be the easiest to crack. Once I had everyone on my side, Davina would have no choice but to follow. As much as she claimed to have a strong moral and ethical line, she always caved to the crowd.

"If you tell, you'll be stuck here forever, Calvin," I said.

His gaze snapped to mine as his breaths came quicker. His cheeks puffed up as if he were holding another round of vomit in his mouth.

Watching Davina, I moved between him and Francis.

"Don't let her bully you." Davina's voice pulled him in.

He nodded.

Focus on me.

As if the monster itself whispered in Calvin's ear, he turned to me, asking me to give him a better choice.

"You want to be like your grandfather? A doctor in a small town, doing nothing with your life?"

"We all saw what happened." Davina stepped toward me. Her forehead barely reached my chin, but her dark eyes bored into mine. If I was in any way weak, she might intimidate me. Too bad for her I'd seen worse than her in my mind. The monster vibrated in my stomach, reminding me who I was doing this for.

"The truth will only destroy you," I said.

Davina snorted. "How? Guilty people go to prison where they belong."

I expected nothing less from her.

"I will destroy your lives. It may not come tomorrow, but you will always have me hanging over your head. Tonight will stain any happiness you could ever want."

"Not if you're in prison." Davina always had to have a comeback.

Screw Calvin, I needed to put this woman down before she destroyed my life even more than Francis already had.

"I'm sure your daddy doesn't want to know about your after-school activities."

Davina blinked, harder than normal.

I dug into that insecurity. "How would he react to your distribution of drug evidence to your friends?"

"I'm not selling it."

"Will that matter to him? Will you be able to look him in the eye tonight, smelling the way you do, without him accusing you, too?"

"Val, stop!" Your voice cut through the thick space between me and Davina.

A glimpse of my future loomed before me. Keeping the secret of Francis's death wouldn't be easy, but revealing their truths would hold them accountable to their eventual agreement of what I needed them to do.

"You and Wren have been closer than best friends. I doubt Wren's parents will be happy to hear what really happens during your sleepovers."

Wren's jaw dropped, and she skittered away from you. Your face fell. The same surprise that stretched across your face after our father fell down the stairs. I didn't do this to hurt you, but I couldn't risk her telling or you leaving.

"Francis isn't worth all of this." Mike knelt beside his brother. "He disappeared once; he can do it again. He hated this place. No one will miss him."

"You're talking about covering up a murder." Davina's harsh tone softened, more resigned.

She was almost there.

Mike dropped his sweatshirt to the ground. Francis's unseeing eyes peered at the sky with a version of awe. His soul was gone, but his trouble remained. Like Father's death, I needed to clean up my mess. Mike's hands reached toward the flames, illuminating the hand-shaped bruises circling his forearms. "Francis was never meant to be a father. This was an accident. Right?"

Calvin cleared his throat. The sound made my stomach roll. I could handle death, but not him throwing up again. Morning sickness was the only downfall of the impending expansion of my family. Showing weakness wouldn't get me what I wanted.

Davina inspected Mike's arms. "You never told us."

"Do you think he would let me?" His eyes lifted to mine. "Are we all in?"

"What do we say if someone asks about him?" Calvin sniffed and spat at the ground.

I swallowed hard. "We never saw him tonight. It will be easier than keeping stories straight. We get rid of the body."

"How?" Wren's whine grated at my nerves.

Calvin coughed again. "I'm not touching him."

"You're the strongest of all of us." Mike took the words from my head.

He would have been handy to have around at the time of Father's death. You were too young to help, and our mother was useless. Without help, it took a full day to get him to his last resting place. I glanced at the underground shelter. The irony didn't deter me from forming a plan. "We need to get him over there." Everyone except Mike looked at the darkness. "There's a shelter. It's hidden, and no one will ever find him."

Mike chucked Calvin in the arm. The massive football player let out a grunt and shook his head. "No way, man."

"We're in this together, or we're not." Davina's shift in tone surprised me. With her acceptance of the plan, I expected little resistance from the rest.

"Calvin, you take the legs." Mike positioned himself at Francis's head. He tucked his arms under his brother and lifted. His teeth dug into his bottom lip. And even though the scent of blood from Francis was enough to satiate the monster within me, I yearned for a drop of Mike's, too.

Both guys shuffled toward the shelter with me at the helm.

Davina crouched by Wren and you, whispering soothing words. You didn't take your eyes off me. You must have seen the correlation between this situation and the one we faced years ago. Even though you didn't come here with me. You were too young, but that didn't stop you from questioning his location after I returned home covered in blood and dirt. It was much easier to claim he had left our dead-end town, and his disappointment in his daughters, than explaining the truth about falling down the stairs. As much as we didn't need our mother, suspicions would have turned on her. Becoming orphans with the potential of having to move from our home wasn't part of my life plan. Like the others at the bonfire, all it took was a little coaxing to target the intended future.

When we reached the shelter, Calvin dropped Francis on the ground. "I did my job. I can't be a part of this anymore. I'm going to have nightmares the rest of my fucking life."

Mike opened his mouth, but I put my hand up. "It's not big enough for all of us. I'll take him the rest of the way."

"Rest of the way?" Davina's appearance surprised me. She was sneakier than I thought.

"There's a crawlspace in there."

Shadows covered her expression. "How do you know that?"

"This is on my property." I balanced the truth and what I needed her to believe. If any of them stumbled upon my father's remains, there would be more questions and a possible dismantling of the already fragile situation.

"I can help you." Mike, the loyal soldier. He was the only person I could rely on.

Davina and Calvin stood outside the shelter, silently witnessing us taking Francis into the open void. Without life, his body didn't move the way it should. It had been years since Father's death, but the heaviness of the body and memory weighed on me as I folded myself into the shelter.

My grandfather had built it for hunting, but my father's secrets filled it for years after. No one knew about it except for us, and expanding that circle to these others was an invasion like no other. They would never return here without experiencing the full memories of their part in this plot. If they returned. The part I would play in their lives expanded with each second. The paranoia within me of the worst-possible scenarios was a gift. Thick, twisted ropes formed between us, binding us together forever.

"Do we just leave him here?" The voided space swallowed Mike's heavy breathing.

"There's a crawlspace. It will conceal the decomposition."

"It sounds like you've thought about this," Davina accused.

Or done it before. I silenced the beast. Mike seemed genuinely interested in what I thought. He would help me lead this group into compliance.

"I'm sorry for your loss." I was used to feigning emotion to my coworkers and patrons. No one ever suspected a librarian.

"Me too. Francis did this to himself. He always pissed people off. I doubt it will surprise anyone that he's gone."

I reached for the door, which to anyone else looked like a part of the wall. That was Father's addition to the shelter. It was a small probability that anyone would find it on their own, but even less of a chance that anyone would inspect it for a hidden wall where he hid his secrets, and in turn, mine.

The monster within me mused.

The door caught on a rock, and I adjusted my grip on Francis's ankles as I shoved it aside.

Once open, the tunnel revealed itself like a crematorium furnace. Mike or I could crawl toward the depths, but someone like Calvin would barely fit.

"Put him down," I instructed.

Mike did as I asked and stepped aside as much as he could.

Groans from outside showed Calvin's location.

"You can leave now," I said.

Mike shook his head. "I can help."

"You can, but I need to do this myself. There's not enough room in here, and Calvin needs reassurance."

"They all will," he mused.

I suppressed a genuine smile. Those didn't come easily for me, but Mike would work for my affection. He wasn't as easy to look at as Francis, but I needed a partner who understood my urges, at least the surface ones. Little did he know he would do my bidding whether or not he agreed.

"Make sure Davina and the others get back to their cars. We need to stick to the story."

Mike reached out to touch my hand but stopped a breath away. "Can I come by tomorrow?"

"We should keep away from each other for a little while."

Mike's chin dropped to his chest. I stroked his hand with one of my fingers. The darkness inside of me felt nothing, but his eyes widened as if I'd given him a gift.

"You can call me. We have a lot to talk about."

"Yeah," he said.

He shuffled outside, and I closed the door behind him. I worked best with heightened senses. I closed my eyes, to not distract myself, and inhaled deeply. The imaginings fled my mind as I raked my hands over Francis's body. I pinched his wallet and tossed it toward the door. It might prove useful as breadcrumbs of his departure. I pulled the chain from his neck. It was a present his mother gave him as a graduation gift years ago. It was too dainty for my taste, but it might be a nice prize to remember this moment.

I positioned his body feet-first into the hole. His face was close to mine, almost as if we were about to kiss. I dug my fingers into his shoulders and shoved. He didn't move more than an inch.

I adjusted my stance, digging the toes of my shoes into the dirt floor. If I knew I was going to bury another body, I might have dressed more appropriately.

It took thirteen pushes to conceal him. It was less than with Father, but not enough. As far as I knew, the tunnel was endless. Previously, I was smaller and able to get as far into the crawlspace as my body would allow. Those memories pushed to the surface.

When I had to do this again, I wouldn't have Francis getting in the way. Getting traction was easier the more the space caved in around me. The walls gave my feet enough purchase to push him further. It wasn't until I pushed three times with resistance that I went far enough.

I ignored the hearty scent of decay and my rolling stomach as I scooted out of there. I went far enough that there were at least a dozen body lengths between the door and Francis. No one would ever find him here.

Once I entered the exposed space of the shelter, I opened my eyes. The moonlight was like a flashlight, and I immediately closed them.

When I opened them again, the light had shifted. Not the moonlight. You. "What are you doing here?"

You moved the beam across the forest floor in front of you. "This is where you put him."

I raised an eyebrow at you. Out of everyone involved, I didn't expect you to be the one to worry about.

"I never knew," you said.

"Will you tell?" I asked with warning in my voice.

You shook your head. "You already took care of that."

"Don't be so dramatic." I scrubbed the dirt off my knees and stepped out from the shelter. The scent of smoke and wood permeated the air. I inhaled deeply, replacing the scent of death with fresh forest.

"You killed someone. Again. I'm the dramatic one?"

I couldn't help the laugh bubbling up from deep within. Relief that I got away with it again coupled with the question from my naïve sister.

A sharp pain accompanied the laugh, almost as if it broke me to show amusement at her level. It radiated from my pelvis and rippled across my middle. It swiftly encored, harder this time, doubling me over.

"Val?"

I threw a hand your way while the other pressed against my middle.

Something was wrong.

"Val? What's happening? Are you okay?"

I already knew, but I needed proof. I shoved my hand down my pants and found sticky warmth between my legs.

You moaned louder with each second as I brought my hand to my face. The blood I shared with her rested between my fingers.

Your screaming sliced through the air. I whirled around at you.

Your mouth was closed, yet the sound still sang in the air. I brought my other hand to my mouth, understanding that the sound radiated from me and not you. My knees crashed against the sticks and leaves. I waited for the pain to shift to another part of my body, but it bloomed like a spider stretching out its legs. It pierced through my child, and I screamed until I no longer had a voice.

34
JENNY

Before Scott can stop me, I speak loud enough to give away my position, knowing I can't go back. "I'm here. Now, let my mother go."

Mike doesn't take his eyes off Davina, but a slow smile crosses his lips. "Welcome, Jenny."

"What are you doing, Dad?" Scott stays put.

Mike shifts from foot to foot, but his aim is steady. "Come closer so I can see you."

"Wait," Scott hisses.

I follow his gaze to the glint of firelight off the traps on the ground. The unconventional weapons that Scott mentioned. He's booby-trapped the area.

My mother tries to speak around the gag in her mouth, but all that comes out are incoherent words. Her eyes widen as she shakes her head. Strands of hair cut across her face.

"Scott, Jenny, you stay there," Davina says.

"Listen to her." Scott is the voice on my shoulder, urging me to do the right thing. A trained police officer is handling the situation. But I've seen multiple scenarios of how this will end without my involvement. My visions give me enough of a warning of what might happen if Mike does what he pleases. I have no idea how we arrived at this situation, but I won't let him threaten my family.

I step away from the fringe of the woods, into the clearing.

"Jenny, no," Scott hisses.

"I have to help her."

The fire crackles and pops, and I watch a bullet strike my mother every time. My mind finds it hard to separate that natural reaction of the bonfire with the possibility of Mike shooting her. "I'm here. Put the gun down."

"Not till she does." Mike lifts the gun toward Davina.

Davina adjusts her grip on the gun. "Like hell I will."

"You know what happens to people who threaten our truce." Mike steps closer to my mother, positioning the gun at her head.

"No!" I rush forward.

"That's far enough," Mike booms, and I freeze.

Tears soak the gag as my mother pleads with Mike. Her words are muffled but the meaning clear. I want to tell her everything will be okay. But this scenario has too many possibilities for the words to come out.

Scott steps forward, keeping behind me but circling the group.

Mike glances at his son. "I knew you couldn't stay away."

"What did Nora do to you?" Scott asks.

"I know you like them, son. But my alliance is elsewhere."

My mother grunts. The intonation of curse words is directed at Mike.

"Let the children go, Michael." Davina steps closer to him. "This is between us."

"I have to continue what she can't." The flatness of Mike's tone reminds me of my aunt. There's no humanity there. I've seen what that does to a person, and it doesn't give me confidence that my visions won't come true in his presence.

"Wren kept the truce," Davina says, glancing at my mother.

Mike clicks his tongue. "Don't be naïve. They were going to work together against us. With Valerie in prison, they thought they had a chance."

Davina's gaze narrows at my mother. "That is why you two met up?"

My mother nods. A mix of tears and saliva coats the edges of the fabric.

Scott's gaze falls to me. The weight of it tingles against my skin.

"Valerie's legacy will continue through you." Mike grins at me, like a proud father. A psychopathic one.

My mother grunts and kicks her legs back. Her feet connect with his knees. He wobbles. The gun momentarily points away from her.

Davina sprints toward them, and Mike recovers with Davina only a few feet away. Scott's hands grip my shoulder and pull me backward as a gunshot pierces the air. My head bumps against Scott's chin, and my vision turns red.

"No!" I scream.

When the world rights itself, the worst-case scenario plays out.

Mike and Davina wrestle for her gun. My mother is on the ground writhing in pain. There's no blood around her, but from her rocking movements, it doesn't look like she's getting up on her own.

Mike cracks his elbow against Davina's jaw, and she cries out.

He jumps to his feet, a gun in each hand. He raises them high, threatening both Davina and my mother.

"Stay there, Davina. You've done enough," he says.

Davina rubs at her jaw and holds her hands up. "You've assaulted a police officer. That's a federal offense."

"I've done worse than you know, Davina. But I'm not the only guilty one here," Mike says.

"Dad, tell me what's happening. We can fix this," Scott says.

Mike slides back into his amused expression. He's on top of the world right now, and I can't stop him. "Davina, do you want to tell my son what's going on? You were always a skilled story-teller, or should I say story spinner? It's a talent even Valerie didn't know about at first, but it came in handy."

"It's been years," Davina says. "There's no reason to involve anyone else in our sin."

Scott steps closer to me, fitting his body between me and his father.

Mike adjusts his fingers around the gun, and Davina's gaze clocks each movement, and so do I. "This place holds a special memory for all of us. It's where we solidified a bond that won't break until we're all dead."

The tingling of want erupts within me. That urge to know more floods through into my words. "What do I have to do?" At least if I can keep him talking, he's not shooting anyone.

Mike kicks Davina's gun in my direction. It stumbles over itself, and I back away from it, unsure if it will go off. "Pick it up, Jenny. I don't plan on leaving this place until Valerie's work is done."

I stare at the gun as visions flood me. They force my eyes closed.

"You touch that, son, and you will regret it," Mike's voice booms in my head.

I open my eyes. Scott's hands ball into fists before they open in front of him.

Mike looks at me, his eyes reflecting the hot flames from the fire. "You have to want this, Jenny."

"Want what?" I shift forward.

"To embrace yourself. Like Valerie."

"She's in jail," I spit.

"She wants more for you. You can be better."

Valerie wants me to experience the violence in real life to show me that the visions will subside. This was all a plot to bring me to her side, believe her. Trust her. But then what? To become a murderer like her? Do her bidding like Mike?

"There you go. I see your aunt in your eyes. There's no Calvin inside of you."

My attention snaps to Mike. "My father?"

"He was the weakest."

I shake my head.

Mike tsks. "Nora, you denied your daughter more than we thought you would."

"He left town." Davina's tone is firm, almost as if she's trying to convince herself.

"He left somewhere." Mike lifts his chin toward the shelter. "Calvin was a part of our little troupe. But he wasn't made for it. Especially after knocking up Nora here."

"What did you do?" Davina spits.

Even with the secrets they held for each other, it seems where Valerie is involved, there are always more.

"He was a warning. Mostly to that loudmouth, Wren. It lasted a while, but the moment Wren heard that Nora was returning to town, she tried to threaten our secret again. This time, I got to give my version of a threat." Mike smiles again, and my stomach churns.

I glance at the gun. He wants me to take it to harm someone. Does he think Valerie has convinced me to be like her? Can I use that to get out of this?

"Give in to your urges. Valerie promises it will be worth it," Mike says.

"She won't hurt anyone," Davina says. "She's nothing like Valerie."

Mike twists toward her. "Not even if I do this?" In one motion he tucks Davina's gun in the back of his pants and leaps at my mother.

I lunge forward to stop him, but I'm too far away.

My mother's neck disappears under his hands. Mike laces his fingers together, and the slight tightening of pressure forces her eyes open. They bulge from her face.

"Let her go!" I cry.

Scott and Davina rush over to Mike, but my legs burrow in the dirt.

Mike tilts his head toward his son and Davina. "Keep back. This isn't the first neck I've snapped. Humans might require a little more pressure, but I can make it work."

The sputtering and choking coming from my mother strikes something within me. A drive to step forward and pick up the gun sends a wash of tingles over my skin. This vision is different. But it's not until I raise the hard metal up that I realize this isn't an imagining at all. I'm doing this. I will protect my mother, no matter the cost. Breaking through the possibilities and focusing on the one outcome makes everything sharper. The crackling fire becomes louder, beckoning me closer.

"Give me the gun," Davina says.

I ignore her. "Stop, Mike!"

Mike's grip loosens, and my mother gasps for air. "That's a good girl. She kept you from the truth. Valerie is a better teacher than you will ever find. Let go of the past, starting with your mother. All these years, she's kept you weak."

I raise the gun, and a grin stretches across Mike's face as he focuses on killing my mother. Her breaths go silent again as he digs his hands deeper.

"Jenny, give the gun to Davina," Scott says. "She will stop this."

The voice of reason sends pinpricks of doubt through me. What am I going to do? Shoot this man? The fire burning in Valerie's eyes stares back at me through my mind.

I inhale sharply and race the gun to Davina, releasing it to her as soon as humanly possible.

Mike's face twists with anger as he leaps up from the ground, charging at me. "We're not leaving here tonight until our secret is hidden once more. Valerie requires your help with that. This shouldn't be hard for you, Jenny. It lives within you." His saliva peppers me in the face as Davina and Scott shift their positions around us.

Before anyone can move, Mike's thick hands cut my airway. My knees give out from under me as he grips my throat, crushing my windpipe. He twists us around, placing me between Davina and him. His eyes burn into mine as the blackness creeps into my vision. His breath is hot against my skin. "You do this, or you die."

The visions remain quiet, as if he's suffocating them, too.

I try to inhale, but no air satiates me.

"If you don't give in now, I'll make this worse for everyone. Zelda, Wren, Davina, even Scott. I'll push and push until everything you think you care about is gone. Valerie showed me what that looks like. She gave me a second chance at life by killing my brother."

His voice fades as the forest blinks in and out of existence.

My hands fall away from his, even though my body urges me to stop him. But I'm not strong enough. My heart pounds slowly in my chest, ticking away the seconds of consciousness I have left.

I remember something and use all the energy I have to speak.

"Okay," I grunt.

His grip loosens slightly, and I inhale the scents of the bonfire and forest into my lungs. Nothing has ever tasted sweeter.

My fingers brush over my waist and wrap around the handle of the screwdriver. I steel myself and thrust the screwdriver upward. The sharp end drives through his throat. I do it for my mother, my father, everyone he and Valerie hurt. Oxygen floods my body, but too quickly, and the world tilts. I remove the screwdriver from his neck, and his hands reach upward and circle his own throat. Blood fills the spaces between his fingers.

Mike's eyes widen, staring at me in shock. "She won't stop."

"She doesn't control us."

"You think so?" Mike's mouth twists into a grin before he collapses to the ground.

The sound of metal slicing through something fills my mind. I stiffen as I fall into a vision. One of the traps he'd set snapped around his neck. The night shadows cover the space between his head and where it should be attached to his body. That's no longer the case.

Davina rushes forward and falls to the ground next to him. Her hands cover his, and I raise mine to my face. They're stained with red. Mike's blood is sticky, and I press my fingers together, strings of the liquid stretch between the tips.

"Jenny," my mother's voice calls to me in a whisper.

I walk over to my mother and take the gag from her mouth.

"Are you okay?" she asks.

Her voice is clear, and alive. A warmth floods me as I check out my hands again. I inspect them, holding each of them up, as if I'm a child learning how to count. My breathing fills my ears in a harsh roar. This vision feels different. It's clearer, like it was when I picked up the gun.

A realization flits through me, but I don't allow it in.

"I'm not hurt." The flatness of my voice surprises me. I glance at Mike. His legs jerk, and a gurgling sound erupts from his mouth.

Scott and Davina hover over him. I tilt my head to the side, waiting for reality to appear.

"Jenny, look away," my mother says. She's sitting up now. "Help me get these off."

I tug at the binds around her wrists. The blood on my skin transfers to them. With my back facing the others and their low voices, I can't quite hear what they're saying.

"Jenny, you did what you had to do," my mother says.

I did what I had to do.

I allow the words to turn over in my head as that remnant of a realization floods me until it steals my breath. I jerk away from her, realizing I'm not in a vision, it's real life. I scramble to my feet and rush over to Mike. "No, no, no."

Scott stands and holds his hands in front of him. Pain is etched across his face. "You need to stay away."

"But—I—he—"

"He attacked you," Davina says, staring at the ground. "But now I have to do my job."

Scott's hands are fists against his sides. He's trembling. It's a reaction I expect from anyone seeing a dead body, especially someone they love. A normal reaction hasn't captured my body yet. I've shifted to survival mode. I didn't mean to kill Mike. I did what I had to do. It sounds logical, but the proof on the forest floor is more complicated than that.

Even though Mike is slowly dying with no hope of rescue, he's grinning, and his eyes stare in my direction.

My mother's hands grip mine and tug me away. Her small body unleashes more strength than I've ever felt from her. Her hands cup my cheeks, and her nose brushes mine, in the same way she did when I was a child. "We're safe."

My entire body trembles. "I killed him. I'm like her."

"No, you're not," she says.

I turn my head, but she holds my face steady so I can't see Mike. "You don't need any more fodder for your mind. What's done is done. You saved us."

My stomach rolls, and I bend over and heave the contents of my stomach, and a chunk of my soul. I'm no longer the woman who came here desperate for the truth. I've changed into a person I don't recognize, and I'm not sure I ever will.

35
JENNY

I'm a murderer like my aunt. The normal life I strived for will never come. For once, I beg for the visions to come to me, for them to shield me in an even darker scenario with the hope of easing this one, even for a minute. But they don't console me. They remain hidden. Just like Valerie said they would.

Scott returns to Davina's side, even with her insistence that he leaves the scene. We all know what happened here, and no one will implicate him. But what does that mean for my future? Will I end up with Valerie in prison? The consequences of my actions stack on top of each other, yet no vision comes to taunt a potential future. Instead, I focus on the present.

"I'm going to prison," I say.

"Not if I can help it." My mother glances at Davina.

"They've never gone away. Until now." Heat fills my eyes, but there are no tears. "Valerie got into my head about it. I don't want to be like her, but I don't have a choice."

"You do, honey. This is not her. It's survival. When I escaped her, I couldn't think straight for days. You are stronger than your visions, and you are a better person than Valerie. You did something brave here, not selfish. She's done terrible things for herself. We will get through this together, no matter what the cost."

I allow myself to fall into her embrace as voices fill the woods. Flashlight beams sweep through the trees, and she doesn't stop me when I turn around to face them. Davina stands and walks over. There's no rush for her when I've taken out the suspect. But with her gone, Mike's eyes stare blankly back at me. Scott hunches over him, retrieving his phone from Mike's pocket. He scrolls over the screen, probably looking for any hint of what happened tonight and what caused his father to turn into someone he didn't recognize. I know enough about Valerie that people like her and Mike embrace who they are but can easily hide it from the world.

I can't take my eyes off Mike, and the quirk of his lips plasters a permanent smile on his face.

I should care. I want to show remorse for my actions, but a numbness creeps through me, heavy like a comfortable, warm blanket. Eventually, I move, prompted by my mother leading me away from the scene.

I understand the absence of visions. It happened at the prison, but Valerie attacked the officer, not me. The effects faded eventually. This time, it's as if I've had a lobotomy. The void within my mind offers quiet comfort with an accompanying numbness.

Even though my mother has been through hell tonight, she insists on driving to the house.

"No police station," she presses her friend.

Davina agrees, as if the roles of their relationship have changed. But they have to protect the truth of what happened. Revealing the full story implicates what they witnessed all those years ago.

The discovery of their past was one revelation of the night, my murderous tendencies another. Valerie was right about how to get rid of the visions, but it's the only part of our conversation I wish was a lie. I don't feel close to her anymore. I feel nothing.

When we get back to the house, my mother leads me upstairs to the bathroom. She strips me like I'm a toddler before helping me into the shower. I understand why, as she leaves to take my bloody clothes in a heap to Davina.

I remain under the spray of water until it turns to icicles battering my skin. The stillness in my mind mutes all thoughts, instead of just the bad ones. I'm firmly in the present, taking each moment for what it is. There's darkness before and after this moment, and the next.

The air outside the bathroom is sticky, and the water droplets on my skin shrivel and die, but I shiver. I put on shorts and a loose T-shirt. The fabric is soft enough but still scratches my skin.

In the living room, Davina asks me to sit. I spot my clothes in a clear plastic bag by the door.

"We want to explain what happened all those years ago, Jenny." My mother's voice is soft and calm. I lean into it as I try to feel something for her.

They tell me about Francis Allen, and how they were a part of covering up his disappearance. Valerie hung it over their heads for years. With the secret creating stronger threads between all of them, my mother and father got together. They were in love. My mother thought she would be with him forever. Then he disappeared.

"Calvin didn't want to leave me. She killed him." Tears stream down her face, and I watch them drop to her hands.

I don't mourn my father.

I can't.

I have no emotion, good or bad.

The pieces of the story lock together in the way I wanted throughout this entire trip. The full truth is there, and it should satisfy me.

Davina tells Wren's story. She connected with my mother to get the truth out there. If they confessed to the crime and brought the entire police force to the shelter, Valerie would never get out of prison. They would finally be safe from her.

They never counted on Mike Allen. Before I came to the woods, Mike told them everything. He and Valerie met secretly after Francis had died. Where my parents allowed their love to flourish, Valerie groomed Mike to do her bidding, in the same way they believe she was trying to do for me. He was the one to bring Calvin back to the shelter while Valerie completed the job.

Davina sighs. "He wanted to expose the truth so there was nothing looming over us."

"Over you, Jenny. Your father did that for you." The truth hits my mother hard, as if Calvin just died instead of Mike.

The effect of his death rushes over me as it had when I witnessed Valerie attack the officer. But the numbness lasts much longer this time. Even after washing the blood away with scalding water, the memory of his death lingers on every inch of my skin.

When the story ends, they wait for me to say something.

I have no words.

After some time, my mother walks Davina out of the house, and my head falls to the couch. I curl into myself and stare out the window, waiting for any activity in my mind. Their muffled voices on the porch lull me into a dreamless sleep.

No dreams haunt me, and I wake in the same position on the couch. Sunlight pours through the windows, bathing my mother in a yellow glow. She's on the other couch, asleep. She's lightly snoring, and peaceful.

The hollowness remains, and I can either live in it the rest of my life like a zombie, or I can push through it.

It takes effort. Throughout our last day in Orhaven, my mother moves around me like I'm a feral creature about to strike at any moment. The house no longer scares me. The ghosts of my family's past live in the woods.

Davina, Wren, and Zee show up with coffee and pastries from the diner. The scent of the food fills my nose, more than when I went to the diner in person.

Zee glues herself to her mother's side, only breaking contact when she dives into the food.

Davina assures us there will be no charges against me for the murder. It was self-defense, and she's covered up these crimes before. The people of Orhaven seem satisfied to move on with their lives now that I removed a murderer from this place.

My mother recruits Zee to help me retrieve the rest of our belongings.

Neither of us speak right away. Instead, I mourn the loss of my visions. Without them, my other senses flourish. Scent is by far the strongest. Each room has a distinct signature, which burns into my memory. Even when we go to the kitchen, each woman at the table creates their own mark on my memory, and I hold on to that. It's different, but a start.

According to Davina, the cases for Calvin and my grandfather will reopen. Once convicted, she predicts Valerie will leave prison in a coffin. I already know there will never be a night where I won't see her piercing blue eyes staring back from my nightmares.

They don't stay long. Only until we have the car packed. My mother hands the key to Davina before she leaves.

Wren and my mother go inside one more time, and I walk Zee to her car.

"Are you ever coming back?" she asks.

"No." My voice is flat, and I try to put feeling into it. "There's nothing here for us except for terrible memories."

"I get it." She chews on the inside of her cheek. "Can we text or something? You're the only person I know who's had their mother kidnapped."

"Sure." I'm unsure if Wren will help Zee process what happened, but if I can help her, I'll try. Though, I'm unsure how I'll be of help to anyone. Ever.

"I don't want to lose touch with you, Jenny. We've been through a lot."

I'm unable to reciprocate. I can't make promises when I don't see a future ahead of me. We'll always have this town to bond us, like my mother and those who were unfortunate to witness Francis's death.

Zee quirks her lips before reaching across the seat to beep the horn. "She always takes forever."

I squeeze her shoulder. "I'll get her."

As I round the porch, I spot Wren's back. She's leaning into the house, toward my mother. Her lips are against my mother's cheek. She pulls away slowly. It's not a kiss between friends. It's more intimate.

My cheeks flame, and I clear my throat, loud enough for them to hear.

They stare at each other for a few seconds before Wren heads toward me. The lost potential between them hovers in the air like a gray cloud. Wren won't leave here, and we're never coming back to this place. Knowing that my mother could be open to love makes me believe that someday she might find it again.

Wren hugs me, and I inhale, memorizing her scent. I hope it brings a vision, but it doesn't.

"Thank you, Jenny." She searches my face and tucks a chunk of my hair behind my ear. "Keep her safe."

"Always."

Wren limps toward the car. Inside, she pecks Zee's head before they leave for good. A part of me goes with them.

Again, I wait for a vision. Maybe their car veers off the road to their certain deaths, but my lost companion remains locked away.

I shiver again. The sun beats down over the lawn, yet I'm freezing.

I reach for my phone, knowing I need to tie up a loose end. Mike's last text from Scott's phone stares at me. It came from a time before the woods. Before I murdered him.

I'm sorry.

I stare at the screen. No hint of life appears on the other side. Not as if I expect it to.

The last look Scott gave me as we left the woods will haunt me forever. The disgust and hatred pressing into every line in his face gave me enough of an answer about how our relationship stands.

I'm his father's murderer. That's all.

My mother comes outside and closes the door for the last time. I shuffle to the car and get in. I turn away from the house, desperate to erase it from my mind.

She walks toward me, holding a delicate chain between her fingers. I stare at it. I've never seen it before, not even in the jewelry box from the donation pile.

After getting in, she turns to me. "This was your father's. It's yours."

"You don't want it?"

"I know the person he was. That memory is more than tangible enough for me." She hands it over, and it pools in my palm.

The metal is faded, but I curl my fingers around it.

"That's what was in the garbage disposal. Mike wanted us to find it, as a reminder I suppose. Valerie took it off Calvin after she—" She catches the word and swallows it.

"Thank you."

She leans over to kiss my forehead. "We'll get through this, honey."

I turn to the window, taking one last look at the house before she pulls away.

As we head out of town, the woods rip past us as my mother straddles the line of the speed limit and a ticket. I doubt a police officer would pull us over, since this place is better off without the Whitford family.

We pass the town sign. It stands as if nothing has changed for this place, even though it will never be the same after our visit. I can't say we left it in a better place, but our experiences have changed our lives irrevocably.

We don't stop once on our way home. The urge to end our traumatic visit pushes through our exhaustion.

When we finally fall through the door of our apartment, we drop our belongings in the living room, and we head into our respective bedrooms.

I sleep for over fourteen hours, and when I wake, I wander the apartment. My feet shuffle from room to room. Even gaming doesn't haul me out of my funk. I'm able to play as if nothing is wrong. I tell Abbie most of what happened while we were there, stripping away Valerie, and in turn, my soul. But she's better off without knowing her friend is now a shell of herself. I slide into pre-Orhaven Jenny, fitting it to me like a mask.

Playing games with Abbie is the same as always. She gives me the space I need, even though she doesn't have any clue how the trip ended. I'm not sure she ever will.

Even going back to work the next week is the usual. I look for situations that might trigger visions. Standing too close to the knives in the kitchen or brushing against the heat from the stoves.

Nothing.

When I'm home, my mother and I talk about her past, more than she ever has before. The near-death experience for the both of us has inspired a sense of mortality.

"Life is too short." It's her new phrase, and she says it almost as frequently as my visions used to appear.

Once she's filled all the gaps of our history, she proposes that I talk to a doctor again.

I video chat with Dr. Abel. I sob my way through the first two sessions, and we don't even touch what happened in Orhaven yet. I mourn the loss of my visions. I'm not entirely truthful with her. I can't be. I pretend they affect me as they should, with pure horror. I can't admit the void in my life where my mother's past used to be.

It's absurd, and the pressure of guilt makes it hard to breathe as I walk home from work almost two weeks after leaving Orhaven. It seems I can't ever write it off for good.

Even in September, the heat persists, reminding me of the hot, sticky days at the house. I open the door to the apartment, and the scent of tomato soup and sizzling grilled cheese wafts through the small space. The confining size of the apartment comforts me as much as the food. I don't think I'll ever live in a house as large as the one in Orhaven. There are too many corners for traumatic memories to thrive.

"You hungry?" my mother calls from the kitchen.

"Sure." I pop in there and kiss her on the cheek.

She smirks. "Nice hair."

I glance at the microwave, the reflective surface showing flyaways springing from my ponytail. "I'm going to shower."

The moment I step into the bathroom, my phone rings. An unknown number fills the screen.

My heart leaps. As much as I try to leave Orhaven behind, I want to hear from Scott. Our shared experience connects us, and I need him to believe that what I did was to protect everyone.

I pick it up. "Scott?"

"This is a collect call from Waveney Prison. Do you accept?"

My periphery shimmers the way it used to. I have to move toward it. "Y-yes."

I push the lock in the knob. Valerie calling me can't be a good thing, but the momentary recurrence of a vision floods me with relief. Mike must have given her my number, and I know for sure that there will always be a part of me connected to her.

"Jenny." Her voice slithers into my ear. "How are you?"

I dig my free hand against the countertop. "How do you think?"

"You should feel free, as Mike did what he was supposed to, albeit at his own demise. The relief won't last forever, but you will get a reprieve. Longer each time."

"Killing Mike was an accident." I turn the shower water on so my mother can't hear me.

"I fought the urges for a while, too, after my father's fortunate passing. But when Calvin threatened to do what he thought was the right thing, I had to protect my family."

"By killing mine?" I recall the memory of my mother

breaking down on the couch shortly after we returned to Ridgefield. She's still mourning my father.

"He would only have complicated everyone's lives. How would you have turned out if we all went to jail for Francis's murder?" She pauses. "You'll come across people in your life that want to harm your family. You will fight, you will kill. The bloodlust is too strong, and it has a freeing side effect. Don't you want that?"

"No."

Her chuckle sends a shiver down my spine.

I glance at myself in the mirror, focusing on the terror in my eyes. "I'll never be like you."

"Don't you understand? What you did? You're already like me. I told you, it's in our blood. You shaped your world the night you chose your life over someone else's. You're not a pushover like your mother. You're strong, a survivor. You will do what it takes to protect those you love, yourself included."

"Stop."

"I'll never stop, Jenny. Not until the day I die. Nothing will keep me away from you, not even these prison walls. We are the same, and you will realize that, eventually."

The heaviness of my breathing drowns her words. Inky darkness tugs at my peripheral. My breathing slows as blood spills over my hand. I uncurl my fist, not realizing how deep my fingernails cut into my palm. An ache settles in the joints of my fingers.

"If anyone is going to die from my life, it's you," I say, ending the call. With her voice echoing in my mind, I pull open the cabinet for a bandage. Valerie's voice swirls around me like the morning haze over the landscape at the Orhaven house. It hovers at the surface, permeating my cracks. I turn the faucet on to rinse the blood from my hands. It circles the drain. I scrub my hands together, but the blood doesn't stop. How far had I dug my nails in?

My mind races, and when I close my eyes, I return to that night. The scent of the woods floods my nose. But we're not all there. It's just me and Mike.

He stands there with blood dripping down his neck, soaking his shirt.

His finger touches his lips, the movement stilted as if he's a buffering animation. I can't take my eyes off him. He lifts his chin, revealing the gaping hole in his neck. I stare at it. The edges of the hole widen and shift.

I want to open my eyes and return to the bathroom, to my real life. But I can't. I want to be here. That numbness lingers against my body, pressing closer but not quite enough to give me the relief I want.

Valerie is right about the visions. They're stronger now. Clearer. Will Mike forever live in them, mocking me or calling me to the violence as he had that night?

"You'll be better than her. More careful. There are bad people in the world who don't deserve to live. Like me," Mike says. His voice is gruff but strong.

Warring thoughts fill my mind, and I don't know how much time passes. His presence grows, and I can almost feel the gentle breeze moving through my hair.

I fall back to the only way I know how to end these thoughts and hope that when it's over, he's gone, and I can move on with my life without worrying that I'll turn into a selfish killer like my aunt.

"I'm not like you," I hiss.

Five.

I grit my teeth.

Four.

He smiles wider.

Three.

I open myself up to the idea that I can make this work.

Two.

The sweet numbness settles in.

One.

I allow more of it to come through, and I can finally breathe.

I open my eyes.

The bathroom is exactly where I left it. Mike is gone. I don't know for how long, but there feels like more control within me. I won't be like Valerie, not if I can help it. And I'll spend every day working hard to keep it that way, maybe even starting to live a life for myself.

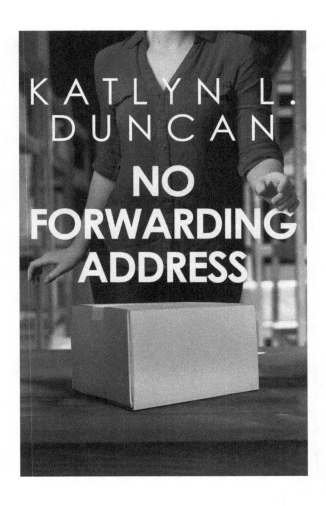

If you are interested in a free short story featuring one of
the characters from *Her Buried Lives*, check out *No
Forwarding Address* at:
http://www.katlynduncan.com/noforwardingaddress.

AUTHOR'S NOTE

Over the years, *Her Buried Lives* has taken on many iterations and titles. But the core message of family and hope has always lied under the surface. As I became a mother and engaged in therapy, I looked inward for a lot of answers to everything I felt at each moment of the day. While I won't go into the specifics of my mental health, one aspect are intrusive thoughts. While at times they are harmless and fleeting, other times they can linger and throw a mind into the darkest corners of possibilities. In the last iteration of this book, I was captivated by how my characters could deal with this very real issue, in that we are so much more than our thoughts.

As an avid consumer of the thriller genre, I have obviously taken creative liberties in order to create a compelling and twisted read. In no way am I conveying that everyone who experiences intrusive thoughts, morbid obsessions, or family trauma will respond in the ways I've depicted or have the symptoms portrayed.

Like me, Jenny has suffered in silence for a long time, too afraid to rock the boat in her fragile relationship with those around her. But different perspectives show how trauma responses can be ingrained in our very being. Even in the darkest times, these women persevere, holding their values of family on their sleeves. I strive to better myself as I hope they do long after the words of these pages end.

ACKNOWLEDGMENTS

The creation of a book is never a solitary journey. This book has taken on many iterations throughout the years, stemming from one small but visceral scene. A scene that will never haunt a reader's mind, but I will think of it as the spark to this story.

I'd like to thank all of my early readers throughout the years, but most importantly, Julie, Katie, and Chelsea. You both have a keen eye for thrillers, and I appreciate all of your notes to make these characters leap off the page. I hope I have done the story justice for you in the end.

To my editor, Jennifer, your notes were an invaluable part of the process. Even though it pained me to cut so many of them, your sharp editorial blade shaped this book into a really great story.

To Iona, my sensitivity reader. Gosh, your notes were incredible. I appreciated the story even more through your eyes and I'm forever grateful for your guidance in creating a realistic portrayal of my characters and settings. You've taught me so much in such a short amount of time and I strive to make this step a part of my process moving forward as it's incredibly insightful and important that our literature speaks the truths of our characters in honest ways.

As always, I wanted to thank you, my dear reader. An author's books are always yours in the end. We hope to help you disappear into a place where you can live for a little while and explore. I hope you've enjoyed these characters and my little fictional town of Orhaven, and if so, please share this book with your friends.

ABOUT THE AUTHOR

Katlyn L. Duncan is the author of psychological fiction portraying the complex lives of women, their relationships, and mental health.

Katlyn Duncan is a multi-published author of adult and young adult fiction, and has ghostwritten over forty novels for children and adults. Her young adult alter-ego, Katy Duncan, loves to write paranormal coming of age stories.

When she's not writing, she's obsessing over many (many) television series', and hanging out on YouTube where she shares her writing process and all the bookish things.

Connect with Katlyn and learn more about her writing and publishing process:

Website: www.katlynduncan.com

ALSO BY KATLYN DUNCAN